W9-CHS-605

THE THEORY OF
OPPOSITES

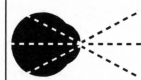

The Theory of Opposites

Allison Winn Scotch

THORNDIKE PRESS

A part of Gale, Cengage Learning

GALE
CENGAGE Learning·

Farmington Hills, Mich • San Francisco • New York • Waterville, Maine
Meriden, Conn • Mason, Ohio • Chicago

GALE
CENGAGE Learning·

LIBRARY OF CONGRESS CATALOGING-IN-PUBLICATION DATA

Scotch, Allison Winn.
    The theory of opposites / by Allison Winn Scotch. — Large Print edition.
        pages cm. — (Thorndike Press Large Print Core)
    ISBN 978-1-4104-6718-8 (hardcover) — ISBN 1-4104-6718-X (hardcover)
    1. Life change events—Fiction. 2. Large type books. I. Title.
PS3619.C64T44 2014
813'.6—dc23   2013047187

Published in 2014 by arrangement with Weed Literary Agency LLC

Printed in the United States of America
1 2 3 4 5 6 7 18 17 16 15 14

For anyone who has written
her own map.

And for Michelle, Laura, Elisabeth,
Katherine and Annika,
who have helped me write mine.

Luke: "I can't believe it."
Yoda: "That is why you fail."

1

If you were to believe my father — and many people do — you would believe that there is no such thing as coincidence. That life is a series of intentional moments that lead us from one to the next, each one ping-ponging us from one destiny to another, all of which carry us on the wave of life up until the inevitable: death.

In a nutshell, my dad is the guy who has more or less eliminated the idea of free will and has instead doomed us all to fate, to that old and ever-present irritating adage: everything happens for a reason. (Air quotes.)

My father is a bit of a legend, or at least he was until he lost the Nobel for his mathematical studies to Punjab Sharma, his protégé who now heads up a rival lab at UCLA. The ceremony made the front page of the *New York Times,* not because of Punjab's accomplishments but because approximately ten seconds after the award announcement, my father bum-rushed the podium, ripped his blazer and tie from around his neck and threw them at the judging table, shouting, *You wouldn't know a fucking genius if he were actually spawned inside your own brain!"* And then, just as security brought him down, literally down — they belly-flopped him to the ground — he managed to grab a flute of champagne and hurl it at Dr. Barton Meriwether's head, slicing open the esteemed doctor's left eyebrow.

When my mother came to pick him up (she had long stopped attending award events, claiming they were nothing more than "geekish men who were constantly comparing figurative dick size," which was actually a pretty spot-on assessment), she dryly asked, "I suppose you'll tell me this was all supposed to happen. That you destroying years of goodwill and ruining your reputation in one fell swoop was all predetermined."

My father chewed the inside of his lip, stared out of the Town Car window and pouted.

So if you were to believe my father, you'd likely chalk up my day — the day that started everything — as fate. There are, after all, no coincidences in this world, and he built his career proving it. You'd believe that getting my wallet stolen from my bag on the subway last night was meant to be. And that not noticing said theft until I was racing out the door this morning was also part of the master plan. That when I finally did notice, I was distracted because one of my agency's biggest clients was descending upon my office in less than an hour, and as the agency's lead creative executive, I still hadn't sorted out how to make adult diapers sexy. And because I was so wrapped up in my own headspace, I didn't think to cancel my credit cards or panic over the petty crime. Rather, I instead ran into the bathroom where Shawn was still showering because he (this was also not a coincidence) had woken late, and I yelled to him that I was taking forty bucks and his Metrocard. And that when I went to grab those forty bucks, I also found last night's receipt from that hip new wine bar on 16th street — *Grape!* — even though Shawn told me he was playing a game of pick-up with his other Internet–rockstar friends last night. And that just as I was doing a double-take at the receipt and simultaneously stuffing the cash into my pocket (no wallet), my phone buzzed with a friend request from one

Theodore Brackton, my boyfriend out of college, whom I had google-stalked only the night before. And in a brief but fiery moment of panic, I thought that he could have perhaps sensed this: that I was out there wondering, googling, ogling from the secure distance that only an anonymous IP address can provide. But before I could even really contemplate the fact that Theodore Brackton might have been stalking me back — not to mention give any sort of weighty thought to the receipt and the wine bar and my long-lost credit cards, my phone beeps with a text from my boss, Hannah.

Text from: Hannah Burnett
To: Willa Chandler-Golden

STOMACH FLU ALL NIGHT. CAN'T MOVE; SKIPPING ADULT DIPES. KNOCK THEIR PANTS OFF. (LITERALLY.)

I groan and yell to Shawn to cancel my credit cards.

Then I shove the receipt into my cash-filled pocket and rush to the door, forgetting that my housekeeper had used Murphy's Oil on the hardwood, though I have repeatedly asked her not to. The heel in my new shoes gives way, and I feel myself fighting the tug of gravity — an arm splays, my hamstring clenches — but I can't stop the fall. I land roundly on my ass, and that is when — despite the positive EPT test that I took four mornings ago — I feel the rush of my period.

Yes, my father would tell you that none of this is coincidence — that it was all simply meant to be, that no matter what I did that morning or what Shawn did the night before, that I would wind up on the greasy floor with a pulled hamstring and another month of failed conception. He would cite the world's axis and the gravitational pull and human psyche and various algorithms that I long stopped listening to. (Nor did I read his bestseller: *Is It Really Your Choice? Why Your Entire Life May Be Out of Your Control.*) My father would say that this is all part of a larger plan, and that if I wanted to be wise, I'd lean in and listen. Millions of readers already have. (Has he mentioned that *IIRYC? WYELMBOOYC* was a *Times* bestseller for forty-two weeks in a row? No? He hasn't?)

I push myself up and adjust my skirt.

And that is when the wiser part of me would remind him that he didn't win the Nobel after all.

But I wasn't all that wise just yet. That comes later.

So more likely, I would probably just be on my way.

2

"I saw your dad on Piers Morgan last night," Alan Alverson says to me in the elevator.

"Hmmm," I say and pretend to read an urgent email, though we both know that there's no service in the elevator.

"He really might be the current genius of our time."

I look pointedly at Alan, who insists that we call him *Alain,* as if he were French, and not born and raised in Livingston, New Jersey.

"Did he convince you of this before or after Piers brought up his current restraining order?"

"Well, it does seem like he was robbed of the prize."

Alan has a very specific, very annoying way of over-enunciating. A nerve in my temple pinches, though I'm unsure if it's due to his defense of my father or his exacting way of clicking his Ts and curling his Rs.

The elevator dings, and we step off before I can argue. I was never quite sure how to accept this over-the-top, unknowing praise of my father; our relationship was a complicated mix of reverence and uncertainty, of yearning and emptiness. To his readers, to Piers Morgan viewers, he was a god. To me, he was mortal (most of the time, but not always — sometimes, on his best days and my haziest, he was a god to me too).

"Good luck with Dependables," Alan mutters before making a perpendicular turn toward his cube.

I reach into my pocket for a Breath Saver and remember the receipt. And the cash. And the wallet. And Theodore's friend request. And my period.

"Shit," I say to no one in particular, but Isabelle, my assistant, overhears and offers a look of sympathy. She hands me a latte.

"Adult Diapers will be here in fifteen. PowerPoint is cued up. Croissants, muffins and fruit are on the conference table."

"Izzy, you're . . . what?" I step back and assess her.

"I'm . . . 120 pounds?" She hesitates. "Are you allowed to ask me that?"

"No, how old are you?"

"Oh, twenty-four."

"And you live downtown."

She nods.

"And you're single?"

"If this is about a blind date, no offense, Willa, I've seen most of Shawn's friends on Facebook, and I'm not interested."

"You're friends with him on Facebook?"

"I have 2300 friends." She shrugs. "I mean, Shawn's hot. Like . . . I don't know." She takes in my skirt that's still awry, my silk shirt that should probably have been ironed. "Yeah, like, he's gorgeous. What does he do again?"

"He's a coder."

"Right! Like Mark Zuckerberg? Shawn is way cuter than Mark Zuckerberg, but MZ did invent Facebook, so I'd probably give him a pass. But anyway, Shawn's friends are like Mark Zuckerberg but they didn't invent Facebook. So no blind dates. Thanks though."

"Okaaay. Um, Shawn's pretty great," I say, not entirely sure if her statement is the worst or best back-handed compliment ever. "Okay, well, have you ever been to that new wine bar, the one on 16th Street? I think *Time Out* just had it on its cover." (In fact, the only reason I've even heard of it is because I flipped through *Time Out* last week in my gynecologist's office.)

"Oh? *Grape!?* Sure. Months ago."

"I thought it opened last week."

"Private invite."

"Of course."

I hesitate and look at her, closely, intimately. She shifts in her biker boots. She is young, she is beautiful, she probably has never had to worry about fate and coincidence and life's disappointments and her husband's wine bar receipt when he was supposed to be at his weekly pick-up game with other young and genius Internet icons. (At least four of them were named to *Wired*'s Hot 40 Under 40! Though three of them were wiry and bald, but no matter.) Izzy won't worry, not yet, about her womb drying like a prune, about her vaginal mucus fluidity, about her peak temperature during ovulation, about sex growing stale because it feels like the only point is for procreation. (*Sex is the perfect example of my theory,* my dad would say. *If you hadn't copulated at that exact moment, on that night, at the second of climax, you would have had an entirely different child!* He would say this with triumph, as if every parent everywhere hasn't already considered this. That if the wife hadn't mounted the husband who was mostly asleep while watching some cooking

18

show that skewed toward the female demographic but that her husband secretly loved, and insisted that *this was the peak moment* of conception, their bouncing baby boy could have been a less-bouncy baby girl. Or twins. Or a miscarriage. Or another month of a missing second line. Who's to say? Well, my dad is actually, if you asked him.)

"Izzy, in your opinion, what would a married 36-year-old man be doing at *Grape!*?"

"Drinking?" She looks at the clock behind me. "Twelve minutes until adult diapers arrive."

"Drinking. Right, of course. They probably went for a post-game drink last night."

"I guess he could also be picking up women," she says casually, clicking on Gilt .com, paying no mind to the destruction of her words, not fully understanding the implication of what she's imparting. "Ugh, I mean, those guys are the worst. I'd never hook up with one. Though — don't tell anyone this — my friend Candice *totally* made out with some Goldman guy last week. After they slept together, he mentioned his wife."

"Well . . . thank you," I say. "This has been very helpful."

I sip my latte and head toward my office.

"Oh, actually, now that I think of it, Willa,

19

I did get an email from the promoters. Was yesterday Tuesday? Every Tuesday is ladies' night. They kind of like me to go, so if you want to join me next week, I'm in!"

I linger in the doorway of my office. Of course she would get an email. Of course last night was ladies' night. Of course Shawn wasn't there for a post-game drink with his buddies. There are no coincidences. I hate it when my father is right.

Text from: Willa Chandler-Golden
To: Vanessa Pines

SOS. Been in mtg w/Dependables for hrs. Quick: sexy synonym 4 accidental urination?

Text from: Vanessa Pines
To: Willa Chandler-Golden

Angelic tinkling?

Text from: Willa Chandler-Golden
To: Vanessa Pines

2 spiritual. Think: Harrison Ford in diapers. What's the 1st word?

Text from: Vanessa Pines
To: Willa Chandler-Golden

Ew.

Text from: Willa Chandler-Golden
To: Vanessa Pines

Helpful. How r u a bestselling wrtr?

Text from: Vanessa Pines
To: Willa Chandler-Golden

Luck

Text from: Willa Chandler-Golden
To: Vanessa Pines

No such thing.

Text from: Vanessa Pines
To: Willa Chandler-Golden

Bullshit.

Text from: Willa Chandler-Golden
To: Vanessa Pines

Someone just proposed "inadvertent wetness." Kill me.

Text from: Vanessa Pines
To: Willa Chandler-Golden

U need a new job. Where's Hannah?

Text from: Willa Chandler-Golden
To: Vanessa Pines

Out sick. Same idiot just said accidental
moistness.

Text from: Vanessa Pines
To: Willa Chandler-Golden

Some1's getting fired. And Hannah's not
sick. She needs rehab.

For the first time in at least two weeks,
Shawn is waiting for me when I slink home
after an epic seven-hour meeting with Adult
Diapers, in which I made the grim discovery, much to their executives' displeasure,
that there really is no way to make grown-up
Pampers sexy.
    "Hi! I'm glad you're home," I say.
    Shawn gulps a deep sip of his beer and
nudges his chin upward as a greeting.
    "Hey," he says. "Oh my God, am I beat."
    When we first moved in together, we
would meet every night at the deli on the

corner or the Chinese joint down the street or some version of dinner under ten bucks within a one-block vicinity. We'd hem and haw over what to order until we would finally come to an agreement over something that we could split 50/50. We did this every weeknight without fail, and we would sit on the same side of the booth or tucked into a tiny side table, and we were shiny and new and a tiny bit smug at our couple-dom — and people around us would smile, our euphoria at having found each other apparently contagious. Lucy, the cashier at the Chinese restaurant, would throw in an egg roll for free because as she said, "You be so happy. Me be so happy."

Eventually, things (like euphoria) settled down into a low simmer, and five nights a week at a restaurant down the block became untenable. Shawn's career exploded; natural complacency set in; we stopped trying to impress each other with twenty-minute make-out sessions to earn free egg rolls; sex became dull when everything revolved around my ovulation cycle. Now, we have reached the apex: I come home from work, and he nudges his chin up, his fist tight around his beer, and says, "Hey."

It's the natural evolution of things, my dad would say. *"You can't go around screwing like banshees all the time* (figuratively speaking, but literally, too), *and our brains account for this,*" he'd add. So that Shawn and I meet only two times a week for dinner now isn't of much concern. Or it wasn't, not until *Grape!*

I'm so caught up in this notion *(banshees! let's at least try to be like banshees!),* that now, with him half-asleep on the couch, I say:

"Let's run down to Hop Lee — see if we can be cutesy enough to get Lucy to throw in some egg rolls."

"I'm so spent. I honestly can't motivate off the couch, much less out of the apartment," Shawn says. "Can't we just order?"

"Okay." The air seeps out of me like a deflated balloon. Like this wasn't a big deal, like him running down to Hop Lee and kissing me until we got free food wouldn't have been a grand gesture.

And maybe he senses my discontent or maybe he hears me exhaling my disappointment, but he says: "Oh, screw it!," and thunks his beer down on the coffee table, leaps over the couch and wraps an arm around my back, dipping me like Astaire would Rogers.

"Can we go to Hop Lee?" I ask, my head still tilted toward him, his hand still pressed against the small of my back.

He pecks my neck and flips me upright. "That was my maximum energy expenditure for the evening. But I didn't want you to think I couldn't make the effort."

"Duly noted." I smile and bite my lip, delighted at his playfulness, like maybe he read my mind. "Good day?"

He plops right back on the sofa.

"Not terrible, actually. Got the job with Tech2Go. They matched my fee from the Microsoft job. How did it go with the pooper pants?"

"Shitty."

"Ha!" He angles his face back toward me so I can see his genuine laugh. He doesn't do that as often as he used to — sink into his laughter. He's always tired or working or hunched over one of his various laptops or devices that demand more than I do. *You have forty-seven new messages and you have to answer them all immediately or this phone will blow up like a grenade in your hand! Don't worry; your wife will be there in the morning!*

"You're cute when you laugh, you know."

"Laughter is the best medicine," he replies, reaching for the remote and scrolling through the channels.

I dig through a kitchen drawer for the Hop

Lee menu. "Oh, do you have cash? Because you canceled my credit cards, right?"

"I called. No new charges — it probably wasn't stolen. You must have lost it."

I search his tone for something close to judgment: Shawn *has* never lost his credit cards, never *would* lose his credit cards. He's too stream-lined, too meticulous for that. He was the child of MIT professors. He was raised with order, with linear thought, with to-do lists that ensure safe passage from one cushion (Choate) to the next (Harvard). He'd never leave his bag half-zipped or zone out to his iPod on the subway, which I've been known to do from time to time, but only because '80s metal rock is my guilty pleasure, and I'm too embarrassed to listen to it anywhere but in the company of strangers. No, Shawn was secure, predictable, and for these reasons, he would never, ever lose his credit cards.

I watch him on the couch, already sucked back into some *National Geographic* documentary on African tribesmen. And then I remember: *Grape!* Perhaps he's less anal, less risk-averse than I thought. He and his friends, kings of the coding world, out blowing their IPO-funded wads of bills on lithe women wearing tank tops a size too small. It didn't *seem* like Shawn, but then again, there was the receipt.

I stare at the ceiling, so fervently wishing we could just go down to Hop Lee and earn those egg rolls. Finally, a little too sharply, I announce:

"I didn't lose my wallet. Someone took it."

"Willa, you've been known to lose it."

He's not wrong: I have lost my wallet three times since we've been together.

Before I can leap to my own defense, Shawn's phone comes alive with the seemingly ever-present buzzzzzzz of a text (if a site crashed in the woods and a coder couldn't text about it, would the site have actually crashed in the woods?) and he falls silent, reading, then typing.

Hello, hello, were we not just having a conversation? Why is your phone more important than egg rolls?

"Amanda wants to know if we can take Nicky this weekend."

"But we . . . um . . . okay . . ."

He is already typing her back.

"Shawn!" I say, more firmly than I mean to, or maybe exactly as firmly as I mean. His flying fingers abort, and he snaps to.

I say, more kindly: "We haven't had a weekend to ourselves in a month. I mean, I don't want to be the bad guy here, but . . ."

"Will, we're all she has. And you love Nicky."

"I do love Nicky," I agree. But I think: *but not as much as I used to. Pubescent twelve isn't nearly as great as adorable seven.* And then I hate myself for even giving voice to conditional love and what it might say about both me and my own prospects as a mother.

". . . *Mister Card. Is. Calling. Mister. Card. Is calling.*"

"Who's Mister Card?" Shawn asks.

"MasterCard," I say. My face points down but my spirits buoy upward — *I knew it was stolen! I knew I didn't lose it!*

I grab the receiver.

"This is the fraud early warning department. Is this Willa Golden?"

Golden is actually Shawn's name. When we married three years ago, I was desperate to shed the moniker — Chandler — that had followed me around like a shadow, my dad's shadow, for so long. And though I knew Shawn was my destiny, knew he was my "meant to be," I'd never quite adjusted to the switch. Golden. I wanted so desperately to slide into it without a hiccup, but the truth is that I still hesitated when someone called out "Mrs. Golden!" in a restaurant, still looked twice at my driver's license to ensure the proof. Shawn was mine. I was his. Willa Golden. Like the "Chandler" part was maybe just the in-between phase of my life.

"Yes," I say to the MasterCard agent. "This is Willa Golden."

"We have some suspicious activity on your card, and we'd like to go over the charges with you."

I look at Shawn and pump my fist *(my card was stolen! I knew it!),* and he looks at me and shrugs.

I turn back toward the phone.

Yes, I think, *I was right. I win.*

And then the moment passes, and I remember how much I love Shawn, that *Grape!* can't be what I think it is, and my dad wouldn't call this a win. No, in fact, he might even chalk this up as a loss.

Later, Shawn and I settle into our Thursday night routine: our Chinese food and the highest-rated network reality show, *Dare You!,* in which contestants are goaded on by the opposition and the host, a chisel-jawed blond named Slack Jones who has gone on to fame and notoriety thanks to the decade-long gig. If you land all the dares, you win $100,000. (There is a small portion of the population who devote their lives to preparing to be contestants. Google it. You'll find the forums. It's strange, but I suppose not the strangest obsession out there.)

Though I'd never admit it aloud, I watch the show to assess what can go wrong due to the forces of gravity and nature or engine speed or torque or rope slack while simultaneously assessing what can go awry due to human nature: can the contestants control their fear enough to abate their shaking fingers as they clutch a wire while belaying across a skyline? Can they calm their tempers enough to get through a task in which their frustratingly inept partners are responsible for pulling their own weight up a volcano? Can they tiptoe quietly enough not to disturb mountain lions; can they repress their gag reflex when forced to drink a smoothie made of urine?

The push-pull between what's in their control and what isn't is what makes *Dare You!* so fascinating to me, though inarguably most people watch it just to see a lot of stupid people do a lot of stupid shit.

"Listen," Shawn says, when they break for a commercial. He wrestles an egg roll from the box on the coffee table and bites off the top, the greasy crumbs landing on his chest. "I know that Nicky is going through his awkward phase right now, and I know that

30

you want some us-time . . ."

"Don't you want some us-time? I thought you liked our weekend routine."

"That came out wrong. You know what I mean."

I'm not actually sure I do know what you mean, I think. Grape! *That might possibly be the dumbest name for a club in the history of ever!*

"Anyway, I'll make it up to you, okay? I'll plan something lavish and romantic and sexy, and you won't be able to keep your hands off me." He smiles, and I smile back, mostly because I want to believe him. It was just one receipt, one small thing, one tiny fabrication as to his whereabouts. *Grape!* It was probably nothing. (My dad would remind me here that nothing is ever nothing. Everything is something, and all roads lead to here, blah, blah, blah.) I pretend not to remember that Shawn hasn't planned anything romantic or sexy in at least a year (I blame the Microsoft job — hey, Bill Gates, how do *you* make your wife happy?) and, frankly, not too often before that either. Which is just as well because I'm not overly comfortable with grand displays of affection. We like Chinese food. We like *Dare You!* We like our couch on Thursday nights. I wouldn't mind making out for free egg rolls, but Shawn doesn't have to whisk me off to Bali (or whatever) to prove his devotion. Though not hanging out at nightclubs and lying about it would probably be a good start.

He reaches over and squeezes my calf, and then Slack Jones pops up on the screen to introduce tonight's first task, which involves couples being lowered into a pit of vipers. If they manage to hold themselves perfectly still, the viper will leave them be. If they don't, well . . . there's a medical tent on the premises. (And it's true that last year one contestant did die when he lost his wrestling match with a grizzly bear, but the network was very adamant — and thus avoided litigation — that the contestant had signed away any medical liability.)

"Haven't they done this one before?" Shawn asks. He has stuffed the rest of the egg roll in his mouth, his cheeks bursting as he speaks. He grins unapologetically. He did this once on our second date — his chipmunk impression — and it made me laugh so hard that wine dribbled down my chin. Izzy is right: Shawn is the coding-world anomaly: his green eyes and his chestnut stubble and his jaw that rivals Slack Jones's make him too handsome to loiter behind a screen all day.

"That was with rattlesnakes," I answer, absorbing the cut of his jaw and the clarity of his eyes. He was handsomer than I was pretty. I never totally understood why he chose me, other than that was simply what was meant to be. Vanessa told me that I needed to see a therapist for my self-esteem, but I was content just to be. Just to know that he had, in fact, chosen me, and that's what the universe intended. She even texted me the contact info of her favorite shrink, but it lingered in my inbox for two weeks before my phone automatically deleted it.

I suck up a lo mein noodle, and before I can even think to stop because just two minutes earlier, I swore that it didn't matter, I say: "How was the pick-up game last night?"

"Good," he says, his eyes back on the TV. "Shit, that woman in the red is totally going to lose it."

"Who won?"

"What do you mean? The show just started."

"No, who won the game? The pick-up game."

"Oh." He flickers back to me for a moment, and then back to the show where indeed, the woman in red is trembling with such fortitude that production may need to call a seismologist. "We didn't really keep score. Just shot around. You know. A few guys were sick, so we mostly just blew off steam."

"Hmmm."

I want to say more, I want to catch him in the net of knowledge with which I'm armed. I want to flaunt the receipt in front of him and shout — a-ha! But . . . I don't. Because that will open up so much, and sometimes, no matter what my dad prophesizes, it is easier to just not know. The knowing is too hard.

"Holy shit!" Shawn squeals. The woman in red has started shrieking, unable to control her fear, and it's impossible to say which happens first: the vipers sense her weakness and attack, or her weakness betrays her and she was screwed before she even started.

"That is awesome!" Shawn yells, slapping me five.

I smack his palm with fake euphoria, wondering what's more terrifying: the false reality airing in front of us, or the actual reality that might be unspooling in my lap.

3

Shawn falls asleep on the couch, his hand still clutching his phone, which occasionally shudders with the arrival of a text or an email or some other breaking alert from the Internet world that never sleeps. I watch him for a moment — breathing in, breathing out. It isn't just that he's good-looking. That's the easy part. That's the part that girls like Izzy notice. It's also that he's magnetic, in the way that superstars are. Enough that his handsomeness almost doesn't matter. Vanessa calls it "the trifecta" — hotness, smarts and the elusive x-factor — even though she doesn't like him as much as I wished a best friend would. It's the way he looks at you, the way he's so steely, so solid.

His phone buzzes again, and he stirs, and for a moment I'm embarrassed that I'm watching him this way, that my neediness is so ripe, that I am admiring the wave in his hair and the way that his lanky body assumes the length of the couch.

I move toward him and shake his shoulder.

"Shawn, come to bed. It's late."

He grunts and turns his face toward the pillows, still deeply in slumber.

"Shawn, come on. It's time for bed."

He flutters his eyes open and they spin into focus.

"Is today the day? Are we trying?" He reaches for his phone to check his calendar.

He thinks I am waking him for baby sex, I realize. *Have I become the wife who only wakes him for baby sex?*

"No. Just . . . come to bed."

"Five minutes," he says, though he is already falling back into his dream.

I wait another beat, hoping he'll return to me, but he's gone. I shut down the lights in the living room and tell myself that this alone time isn't so bad. That sleeping in the bed on my own every once in a while isn't the worst thing in the world. Just before I enter the bedroom, I pause at the doorframe and turn back toward Shawn, hoping this feeling's not the start of a greater divide.

Shawn and I have been trying for a baby for seven months now. When we married, we came up with a plan — or mostly Shawn did, but I listened and approved: we literally wrote it down in diagram form because, at heart, we are both diagrammers, we both appreciate order. We agreed that we needed two to three years to settle in, to establish who we were as a couple, and then we'd have a kid, and then we'd probably have another, and maybe along the way, we'd adopt a dog, erect a house with a white picket fence, and live happily ever after.

Or something like that.

It made sense, though, at least how Shawn had mapped it out: that he could land some big contract jobs, bank money so that we didn't have to worry, and that when the time came, I could quit my job (if that's what I wanted, of course, he added), and stay home with the kids or maybe volunteer or work in the library or . . . something. I nodded my head and said yes to all of the proposed itinerary. I liked kids well enough, and though I'd never been consumed with the desire for motherhood (a trait passed on by my own overly-rational, cool-headed parents), I figured that at least half the point of getting married was to start a family. And Shawn was already a perfect uncle to Nicky; he certainly could make up for any deficits in my own parenting.

So now we were right on plan, right on schedule. Only my womb wasn't cooperating. Seven months of nothing. Seven months of anticipation, of hope, of periods. I told Vanessa I was considering Clomid, and she regaled me with horror stories of women who promptly grew hair on their face. "Like, almost a full beard," she said, though I was 99 percent sure that she was making it up because Vanessa is unencumbered and single by choice for now and mostly well-intentioned but also slightly selfish in the way that a best friend can accept. I told my mom, who sighed, and because we have all been brainwashed by my father, she said the words that I'd already been thinking: "Maybe this just isn't meant to be right now."

But then, after seven months, there was that faint pink line four days ago. And something shifted in me, like I could already sense the baby, feel its little bean body sprouting inside of me. And then, just this morning — *was it only this morning?* — my period came, and I realized how stupid I was for getting ahead of myself, for getting ahead of life and fate and all of the idiotic inexplicable things that fill up the space between the two.

Shit. I hate it so very much when my dad is right.

Alone time. Maybe there is more of that

in our future than we anticipated.

I close the bedroom door and reach for my laptop. It whirs to life, and I rearrange the pillows on the bed and settle in between them, then quickly run through my list of bookmarks.

I click on Facebook, my pulse tangibly quickening, like clicking on something as mundane as Facebook is illicit, like I should know better. Maybe, actually, I should.

Atop my homepage, Theodore Brackton's friend request glows like a firework, a nuclear bomb. Because even though Shawn is my fate, I do wonder, every once in a while (and recently, it seems more often than that), if fate couldn't have been different. If I hadn't somehow misread the stars, or if they'd aligned differently, if everything couldn't be different.

I hover my mouse for a moment.

Accept.

Deny.

Ignore.

I hear Shawn stir in the living room. He must have flipped off the TV because the background noise slips into nothingness.

"Shawn?"

No answer.

I consider trying to rouse him again. Bring him to bed. But Facebook beckons, and besides, there's also now my doubt, the seed of mistrust planted. I consider Izzy's innocent musing — *I guess he could also be picking up women! I'd probably give Mark Zuckerberg a pass!* — and I wonder, apropos of nothing, if Mark Zuckerberg's wife is on Facebook, and if so, if she'd mind if I emailed her and asked her what she would do in my situation. *WWMZWD?*

I stare out the window at the street lamps.

It's true that Shawn had always been faithful, had never given me any reason to worry. And it's also true that I should probably have just been more forthright, just *asked* him why he was at *Grape!,* instead of poking around with my vague questions while he was already sucked into the vacuum of *Dare You!* But ours wasn't a marriage of confrontation. Ours was a marriage of convenience. (Which makes it sound very Russian bride-y, but I don't mean it that way.) What I mean to say is that Shawn is my Point North; he's the thing I don't question because I was raised by a man who taught me that questions lead nowhere, that answers are murky and misleading and whatever is going to happen is going to happen anyway. So why bother asking? I didn't ask too much of Shawn because he was mine. That was my answer. The fact that maybe I wondered if I didn't deserve him, with his handsomeness and his wild success and his *Wired 40 Under 40!* was almost beside the point. Vanessa would note (and has noted) that this is entirely the point (of a visit to a therapist), but therapy, to me, was like answers: a distraction from the journey. The path was already chosen. Why think too hard about it?

Shawn and I met on Match.com six years ago, before he blew up in the Internet world, back when he and I were just Shawn and Willa. He sent me a note with the intro: *what are two normal people like us doing here?,* and it made me laugh, so I ignored my instincts that Internet dating was for weirdos and cyber-freaks, and I wrote him back and said: *Just tempting fate.* Which I thought was super-clever given my dad's theories that fate is what happens to us, not something we have any influence to tempt. I pressed "send," and then wondered why on earth I was mixing my dad into my dating life. Shawn missed the reference (or didn't google me right away) and replied within the hour.

I scanned Shawn's profile, and I could see why he thought we'd be a good match. We were both middle children; we both liked reading classic novels; we both listed "people who argue just to argue," as a turn-off; and we both listed, "someone who is in charge and confident" as a turn-on. When asked what country he most compared himself to (Match.com urges you to complete their two-page questionnaire "to give potential interests better insight to what makes you *you,*" and no one dares run the risk that his or her future spouse misses out on *you* because you stupidly opted to skip the questionnaire . . . so everyone fills it out), he cited Switzerland. And I thought: *omg! I'm totally Switzerland too!*

And he was. And I was. And together, we were Switzerland on turbo, Switzerland on crack. Which works very well for a marriage, actually, until it stops working because one spouse finds a receipt from *Grape!,* and can't help but wonder if the other spouse is actually, perhaps, North Korea. Or . . . something.

Accept.

Deny.

Ignore.

My finger twitches over Theodore's friend request, and I tamp down my instinct to click on any of my options. (*"Instinct is nothing more than a human's misguided attempt to think that he has some semblance of control."* — New York Times bestseller *Is It*

Really Your Choice? Why Your Entire Life May Be Out of Your Control, p. 33) Maybe it doesn't matter which I choose — I'd lived my life telling myself as much. And yet still, the prospects loomed:

Accept.

Deny.

Ignore.

When did Facebook become the analogy for the rest of our lives?

I startle awake at 4:12 a.m. The lights still on, the laptop still perched on my stomach. Shawn still asleep on the couch, I assume. We never used to do this — sleep one without the other — and as I reach to flip off the bedside lamp, I wonder when our habits started shifting.

He's tired, I think. *Working all the time. He was named to Wired's 40 Under 40 for God's sake!* I can't expect him to be present in all ways in all places at all times. I bet Mark Zuckerberg sometimes falls asleep at his office too.

My light flips off with a loud click, and I squeeze my eyes shut, hoping sleep will come, hoping that my anxiety won't win the battle over my fatigue. But before I can even hope to drift into slumber, my phone beeps twice.

Beep beep.
Beep beep.

I slide my index finger over my home page to discover a text from my boss Hannah. A photo actually. Or at least I think it's her. It's a close-up of her breasts, of two fat, overflowing, sweaty cantaloupes with a crevasse between them. They could be anyone's breasts, quite honestly, or anyone who is well-endowed enough, but the necklace charm — the four-leaf clover she never removes — identifies the bosom.

For a moment, I worry that this is some sort of penance she is making me pay for the disastrous Dependables meeting. I consider typing something back, something that says: "Adult Diapers can never be sexy! Adult diapers are about assurance and stability, not flash and come-hitherness!"

I gaze up at the blackness of my ceiling and suddenly realize that my marriage might be a bit like a box of Dependables.

But before I even type my snappy response to Hannah, I lose my nerve. Overt confrontation was never really my thing. Maybe she doesn't know how poorly the meeting went. Maybe she's just on a bender, and it's better to let sleeping dogs lie.

So instead I type: *Don't think this was meant for me?*

And say a silent prayer that in fact, it wasn't. Maybe there are such things as accidents. My dad speaks to the big, overarching push-pulls of life: that all is as it should be. But does that mean that my boss can't mistakenly sext me? And if so, where do these happy accidents begin and end? With a missed connection on Facebook? With a false positive on a pregnancy test?

I roll my fingers over my laptop and it breathes to life.

Google: EPT false positive
Google Search results:
Livestrong: how to take a pregnancy test
Amazon.com: 20% off all EPT tests!
The Wendy Williams Show: I Didn't Know I Was Pregnant!
BabyCenter.com: 3 False positives/Ept faint line??????

Bingo.

From *@iluvbooboo:* Here's the deal: I peed every day since day five after sex and each time it showed a line. But maybe that was just a pee line? How am I supposed to tell the difference between a baby line and a pee line?????? Can anyone help?????????

45

From: *@mamabear:* The same thing happened to me! EPT sucks! I want to kill EPT. They get my fucking hopes up every time, and then I always get my Aunt Flo. Aunt Flo, I hate you as much as EPT!!!!

From: *@dreaminofbaby:* Ladies, let's start a petition against EPT. EPT: do you actually stand for Essentially a Piece of Trash. From: *@iluvbooboo* I am IN!!!!!!!!! Where do I sign?

From: NurseEllen: dear *@iluvbooboo:* false positives are very rare. I suggest you consult your doctor for a blood test. Or maybe this is all part of God's plan for you.

From: *@iluvbooboo:* Nurse Ellen, respectfully, both you and God's plan can go fuck yourself.

I try to log on to add my encouragement to @iluvbooboo. Something simple like:*You go girl!* Or: *Who are you to say what God has planned?* Or: *So only people who are lucky enough to have a plan with God get a kid?*
I try several user names — WillaGolden; WillaChandler; Willa ChandlerGolden — but can't remember the right one. *Sorry,*

this user does not exist! Which is just as well anyway because right when I give up, Hannah texts me back.

Oops. Srry. Not for u.

There, I think. *Accidents happen. Maybe my dad isn't always right.*

My father didn't become totally obsessive about his theories on fate and inevitability until his twin brother died. By all accounts — and surveying my grandmother's worn, sepia-toned photos in which he looks like a perfectly normal, perfectly perfect little boy, this information seems verifiable — he didn't truly fall into the deep end of never-ending rationality until the accident. In my dad's defense, William's death was an honest-to-God act of total randomness, a confluence of events that came together as a perfect storm — both literally and figuratively. A road trip through Florida, a last-minute hurricane, a downed palm tree smack through the roof of their crappy highway hotel. The tree trunk landed on the right bed — William's — completely shattering his chest cavity and killed him instantly. My father — in the left bed — jolted awake and saw that the distances between life and death, between coming out totally unscathed and having your heart crushed

47

inward, was simply nothing more than the decision to pass out on the mattress closest to the door.

My dad spent days, weeks, months asking himself, *"What if? What if it had been a different motel? What if it had been a road trip through Tampa, not Miami? What if we'd stopped for chicken noodle soup and not driven all the way through?"*

But none of this brought William back. None of this changed anything.

So my dad pressed on with his Ph.D., and he quit trying to come up with reasons why and what and how he could have done things differently, and instead, he set about proving why, in fact, nothing could have been done differently at all. Over the years, he burrowed further and further into this hole.

My mom likes to tell me the story of when I was born: that when I came out kicking and bloody and purple, the doctor held me up and cheered, "It's a girl!" And my mom shouted, "Impossible! She was supposed to be a boy!" She began weeping in the way that only seriously hormonal, post-birth women can — after all, she'd already painted the nursery and bought only navy onesies and beanies.

But my dad? No, this wasn't surprising to

him. By then, he was well into his third paper for the *Journal of Science,* well on his way to the next coming of Einstein. Instead, he looked at me and shrugged and said, "Well, we're still naming her William. That's life. Even if I wanted to, I couldn't change it now."

My mother pointed out that now was exactly when they *could* change it, that the birth certificate hadn't been signed, that announcements hadn't been printed or mailed. But my father insisted, and since my mother was her own worn-down version of Switzerland, the version that comes after years of loving a man who you have realized may be completely off his rocker but also might be the most brilliant man alive, she acquiesced. They compromised on Willa when I entered kindergarten because everyone assumed I was just a boy who liked to dress up in girls' clothing. And I might have been little, but I can still remember the joy I felt at receiving my new moniker: that after so many years as William, it was a relief to try to be something new.

4

"I need something super-awesome to impress Nicky with this weekend," I say to Vanessa the next morning, the early June air thick with humidity, clogging our pores, matting wisps of hair firmly against our temples.

"A prostitute?"

"He's twelve."

"So next year."

"Right. Put a pin in that."

"At thirteen, he becomes a man!" Vanessa throws her arms up in the air in mock-rejoice, and a cabbie yells out his window, "Great ass!"

She blows him a kiss, and we turn a sharp right into Central Park, Vanessa's elbows pumping furiously to authenticate actual exercise.

"You know, we're not actually 'power-walking,' " I say. " 'Power-walking' implies real speed, an attempt to increase your heart rate."

"I *am* attempting," she says. "Besides, can't you just be happy that I got out of bed to walk you to work?"

"You say that every Friday."

When Shawn and I married, Vanessa made me swear that I wouldn't become one of those women who lost herself entirely to her new husband. Whose sentences always started with "we," whose plans always had to be confirmed with the other half. (Though admittedly, with our mapped-out life plan — children and a white picket fence and that cushy volunteer job at the library — we became pretty much this exactly.) It wasn't that she wasn't happy for me — she was, but still, she made me promise. I assured her that she and I would never drift apart, even while considering that one can never be sure of anything that the future may hold — the future just . . . was. And so dutifully, we walked through the city each Friday morning: me, on my way to work; her, searching for inspiration for her writing from whatever pulsed around us.

"So I got the job," she says, as we wind down past John Lennon's Imagine Circle, through the thicket of tourists with their cameras slung around their necks, already bottlenecking the walkway in the early hours of the day.

"Job?" I ask.

"The *Dare You!* companion guide, remember? *Daring Yourself to a Better Life: How These Simple Steps Will Put You on the Road to Happiness.*" She's stymied by a Japanese man who doesn't seem to know if he should move left or right. "Listen, I mean, I know it's not for a Pulitzer or anything, but it's a huge paycheck with a pretty sweet bonus."

I remember now. I'd loved the book's concept in theory — daring yourself to live outside the lines and change your life from within — though probably less so in practice. Also, I didn't really believe in any of it. But still.

"I think it's awesome," I say. "Who needs a Pulitzer?"

"Your dad?" she says, and we both smile.

We hit the park traverse and stop in tandem for a horse and carriage plodding by us.

"Theo friended me two days ago," I say, knowing that I have to tell her sometime.

"And you wait to tell me until now?" She ties her sweatshirt around her waist and rewraps her ponytail.

"I've been distracted. For one, Adult

Diapers tanked. Hannah's going to be a mess today."

"Because of her coke habit."

"No. Well, that too. She inadvertently sexted me at 4 a.m."

Vanessa emits a deep-down belly laugh. "God, what a disaster she is."

"But she's still going to be a mess because the meeting was as horrendous as a meeting can go. Jesus, did the universe screw me this week."

"The universe didn't screw you, Willa. Hannah did. You can't expect for life to go smoothly when you spend your nights inhaling the better half of a kilo of cocaine."

"Well, I mean, maybe she doesn't have control over . . ."

Vanessa halts abruptly and flashes a hand. "Stop. Just stop. Before you even start in with that crap from your dad. *No one has a choice. We all lead the lives we were meant to live.* Oh, bullshit, Willa. Just bullshit. Hannah has a choice to stop doing coke. She just doesn't choose it."

If you didn't know Vanessa, you might think that these mantras are part of her new self-help gig, like she's next in line to be the next guru for better living. But Vanessa's been this strident for as long as I've known her. *Own your choice. Live your life. Be brave.*

Be bold. She had the entire Nike campaign — *Just Do It!* — tacked to her college dorm wall when we first met. And besides, why argue with her now when I'm not even sure what I'd argue in return? Vanessa is sure about her truths, but I don't know what to believe. I don't know about free will and fate and destiny and my father's *New York Times* bestseller, which was hailed as "the greatest self-help book since *The Secret!*," even though I grew up swaddled in this mumbo-jumbo, swaddled tightly enough to sometimes feel suffocated, like if I didn't break free, I could be smothered alive. But a lot of it made sense to me all the same. And besides, isn't it easier not to upset the apple cart?

But if I said that aloud, Vanessa would tell me that *there I go again,* not *owning my choice.*

"Well, anyway," I say, matching her step through the park. "Today is going to be damage-control, and Nicky's coming tonight, and I'm still not pregnant, and so I forgot to mention Theo."

"I'm sorry about the still-not-pregnant thing," she says, meaning it.

"Ugh," I moan and actually shake my fists at the sky. "Fuck you, universe!" A mom pushing a Bugaboo scowls at me and makes a sharp perpendicular turn away from us.

Vanessa shakes her head and grins, and I drop my chin to my chest.

"Actually, the truth is . . . I'm not even devastated by the whole not-pregnant thing. I know that I should be, but . . ." I watch the mom stride down the path, then loop under a bridge and disappear out of view. "But . . . maybe not everyone is meant to be a mother." *Maybe @nurseellen is right,* I think.

"According to you, everyone is meant to be whatever he or she's meant to be," Vanessa says. It does sound ridiculous when she puts it that way.

"Touché," I say. My shoelace has come untied. I crouch to fix it. "Also, I think Shawn might be cheating on me. But that's probably insane. It's probably nothing. Just, you know, an overreaction on my part." I don't meet her eyes until I find that I have to.

She holds my eyes for a beat, then offers me her hand, pulling me up.

"Sweetie, you never overreact. It's not in your gene pool."

I exhale and lose myself for a minute, staring at the expanse of buildings in front of me, their steel, their power, their unquestioning architecture. *Life should be like that,*

55

I think, fully aware that my dad spent a lifetime proving this theory: one brick on top of the next, each with its place, each with its purpose. Eventually, you reach the highest floor, and you can stare down with the understanding how you got there.

There I go again, agreeing with my father. I find myself doing that sometimes, even when I wish that I knew better.

Hannah looks uncomfortably warm when I arrive in her office. She's wearing a navy turtleneck better suited for February, and her cheeks are too pink, like the underbelly of a pig. For a second, I imagine her as bacon. Her hair is matted to her temples with a sheen of perhaps both sweat and some sort of day-old gel or mousse, if anyone still uses mousse anymore.

Hannah's gaze rolls off me and moves to the files on her desk.

"Let's not talk about the text," she states flatly.

"Consider it never spoken about again."

I fumble with my hands and try to think of something to say to make this any less awkward than it already is. But before I can, she starts:

"So when I told you to knock the pants off Dependables, you knew that I meant,

56

like, do a *good* job, not a totally shitty one, right?"

"Pun intended?"

Her already puffy eyes narrow to slits.

"Sorry, sorry. Bad timing. Shawn made the joke last night." I pull back the chair in front of her desk and sit. And that's when I notice the empty boxes stacked in the corner.

"Are you moving offices?"

"If you call it that."

She reaches for a poster that she's torn down in haste and unceremoniously dumped on the floor. The masking tape loops now stick on the wall, limply hanging at half-mast. "Do you see this, Willa? Do you see this? Do you know what it says?"

She shakes the poster, with its image of New Hampshire's Mt. Washington, in my direction. And though the poster is crumbled and fraying now, and moving to and fro and actually totally unreadable, I know that I should nod my head and say yes. Besides, I *do* know what it says, what it reads: the image has been taped to her office wall since my first day here. She shakes her poster more virulently.

"Live free or die, Willa! Live free or die!"

She stands suddenly and throws the poster to the ground, kicking it for emphasis.

57

"I'm sorry, Hannah, I'm not following." I think she may be suffering from a psychotic break? (*There is no such thing as a breakdown in psychosis. Our psyches have been developed to withstand nearly any sort of physical or emotional strife. Do not let anyone else tell you otherwise! Any classification of 'psychotic break' is simply a diagnosis not to be able to confront reality! But reality is exactly what we must confront!*" — New York Times bestseller, *Is It Really Your Choice? Why Your Entire Life May Be Out of Your Control,* p. 58.)

"No, of course you're not following. I told you to knock their pants off, and you so thoroughly did the opposite that they dropped us," she shouts.

"Dropped us?" I offer meekly.

"You lost the account, Willa. William. Willa William Willabee. And I hold you solely responsible!" She has retrieved the poster from the corner to which she ceremoniously kicked it and has now started shredding it into teeny, tiny pieces, tossing them around her desk like confetti.

"I, well, I'm not sure that's fair . . . I mean, you weren't even. . . ."

"Oh it's fair! They said you were texting through half the goddamn meeting!" she shrieks.

A quiet falls on the cubicles outside. I can

hear it — I can sense them all turning to stare — just as she balls up the remainder of the poster and aims it at my head. She misses, and it bounces off the glass partition behind me.

"And even if it's not fair, too bad for you. Because I just got canned. And so that means that you are getting canned too!"

She exhales and flops into her chair, like she has literally just performed an exorcism.

"Wait." It dawns on me. "I'm fired?"

"Alan was given my job this morning."

"Alan Alverson?"

"Live free or die, Willabee. Live free or fucking die."

"I don't . . ." I snap my mouth shut because I don't have any idea what she's talking about, much less how to respond.

She rolls her head upward and meets my gaze square on.

"No," she says slowly. "You *don't.* You never do."

The TV is blaring when I unlatch the apartment door, which is odd because Shawn is at an all-day coding conference. I abandon my half-filled cardboard box on the floor. It turns out that the accumulated contents of five years of dedicated work don't amount to all that much: a few insignificant industry

59

awards (my campaign for a dandruff sham-
poo was nominated for an Obie but lost to
Herbal Essences), a framed photograph of
me with David Hasselhoff (he was the
spokesman for an engine oil we repped),
some documents that I'll probably never
look at again.

I reach into the box and grab a fistful of
papers. Just to be totally sure that, in fact, I
truly do *not* look at them again, I cram them
into wads and throw them in the garbage,
slamming the lid shut with force. But it's
one of those automatic lids that eases its
way closed, so it just sort of lingers in the
air, then slowly begins its descent. I watch it
make its pitiful fall when the noise from the
living room brings me back.

Why is the TV on so goddamn loud?

I head to the couch and run my hands
under the pillows, in search of the remote,
and then I realize: *Shit. Shawn may be here.
And he may not be alone. (!!!!)* My mind
spins in all the various ways that my life is
about to become undone: that the universe
giveth me Shawn and also taketh him away.
I duck under the side of the sofa, because
that's what they do in the movies, and I
don't know what the hell else to do. I
squeeze my eyes tightly shut and wish that
I'd called that therapist.

60

Shawn may be here and he may not be alone! Grape! It doesn't matter that I'm his Switzerland! He might be defecting.

A toilet flushes, and I press myself further into the couch, like that can render me invisible. I squeeze my eyes shut. There are footsteps *(one set or two?),* and then the bounce of the cushion as someone settles back in on the sofa.

Suddenly, from above me, I hear a voice that is most definitely not Shawn's say, "Hey."

"Holy shit!" I scream and jump to my feet.

Nicky starts cackling, curling himself into a ball and flat out howling.

"Oh my God, Jesus! You should have seen your face."

My chest cavity feels like it might detonate.

"God, Nicky, you startled me. What are you doing here? Don't you have school today?"

He shrugs, like that's an explanation for whether or not he has school today.

"Does your mom know you're here?"

"She knows I'm coming here tonight." He locates the remote and turns it up a click, as if actively attempting to blow out my eardrum.

"Turn it down!" I shout.

61

"What?" he shouts back.

His eyes return to the screen. He's watching a documentary on venomous spiders, and at this exact moment, a hairy, slithery tarantula gets its close-up. Nicky's mom had warned us that he was going through "a dark period." That he was increasingly becoming consumed with death, not least his father's and why it happened and what it meant in the grand scheme of things. But Amanda didn't have any explanations for that, for Kyle's fate, just as none of the other 3000 families had explanations. How do you explain to a child that his dad went to work one morning, a morning like any other, and then nineteen terrorists decided that it was the right time to fly a plane into his building, and that's what ended his life, even when his wife had just discovered that she was pregnant, and really, Kyle's life in many ways had just begun?

You can explain the facts and include all of the right words, the right adjectives, the right level of vitriol and disgust, but still, after all of that, there is no explanation, no answer to his question of "Why?"

My dad would say, of course, that there is no correct answer to "why" because there is no rational answer to begin with. "Such is life," he would say, as if he invented this phrase, which he didn't, even though millions of his readers have been brainwashed to think that he had.

I take the remote from Nicky and lower the volume two beats. The tarantula has taken down its victim now: a field mouse that is at least twice its size. Nicky is rapt, wide-eyed and slack-jawed, watching the feast. I sit beside him, and he breaks from his gaze and offers me an impish grin.

"This is pretty effed up, isn't it?"

"Yeah." I sigh. The mouse is gone now — deader than dead, felled by a threat it never saw coming.

"Yeah," I say again. Then I add: "This really is pretty effed up."

EXCERPT:
New York Times bestseller, *Is It Really Your Choice? Why Your Entire Life May Be Out of Your Control,* p. 73.

In 1975, my colleagues at the University of Australia, Brisbane, conducted a study on 400 rats. They constructed a series of mazes (the maze being a metaphor for our lives, dear reader), and along the way of each maze, placed a series of traps, of temptations, of obstacles. At the end of the maze sat a pungent piece of cheese — the scientists settled on Roquefort, and thus, this experience was deemed the Roquefort Files, a tongue-in-cheek shout-out to the lead scientist's favorite show, *The Rockford Files*. (A wonderful play on words that I only wish I had coined myself!)

They gave approximately one-third of the rats a tiny nibble of the cheese before placing them in the starting gate, so these animals understood (and sensed, both literally and intellectually) what they were hunting for. (You surely see the metaphor here too, dear reader, correct? That they were introduced to their end game, just as humans often set their own end game, their own personal aspirations. Which, if you've read this far into the book, you know I believe are completely out of our control.) The remainder of the rats either got a sniff of the cheese or . . . got nothing. (Welcome to life, fair rodents!)

My colleagues' goal was to determine whether or not when offered a variety of temptations or alternate routes to the cheese, the rats who understood the reward and the task at hand would be less swayed to stop along the way in the maze, if they would work diligently toward the goal, even when traps were sprung, when marbles were rolled in their direction, when loud noises should startle them in the opposite direction. And whether or not these rats would have a higher success rate than the rats who weren't yet sure of what they were working for or had only had a literal sniff of the grand prize.

Here is what they found, dear readers: they unleashed the rats and discovered that there was not one single correlation between the animals who understood the goal — and thus it can be assumed who also aspired for the goal, because, let's be honest, there are few things that a rat craves more than cheese — and their rate of success compared to the rats who were left to wander the maze listlessly, dodging obstacles out of self-protection rather than out of aspiration. Rats from all three sets of groups got lost, got turned around, and quite a few ended up contained in the ultimate trap of the snapped-shut cage. Similarly, approximately one-third of the rats made their way to the Roquefort, most often by luck, and certainly, simply because they just kept moving forward. A few ran fast enough to elude the traps; a few others went slowly enough that the traps sprung before their arrival. There wasn't much rhyme or reason to any of the successes at all. Just rats running through a maze, following the walls to their next destination, their choices and instincts rendered pointless.

Dear readers, I don't think I need to point out the metaphor here, now do I?

The cheese always stands alone.

5

Shawn isn't home by 7:30, so I send Nicky out to get a pizza on the corner, and when he asks if he can duck into the deli for Skittles, I think, "What the hell, I'm not his mom," and hand him three extra dollars. I'd tell him to pick me up a cheap bottle of wine, but I don't want to know if he has a fake ID. At twelve in New York City, you can't be sure.

At twelve in New York City, I was the last thing from sure. My older sister, Raina, was the confident one (she's now a partner at Big Law with a perfect husband and four kids); my little brother, Oliver, was the creative one. (He's now teaching yoga on an ashram in India — he evidently has a Twitter following of over 100,000 people, which I point out to Raina seems counter-intuitive to a devoted yogi, but what do I know?)

But me, I was never really anything. I was

William who should have been Willa. I wasn't Nicky, all shadows, so many question marks, but I had my own shadows all the same. I wasn't popular; I wasn't unpopular. I wasn't smart; I wasn't unsmart. I was pretty enough with brown hair and big eyes but not really pretty in the way that mattered, and my breasts didn't come in until way too late, so I didn't lose my virginity until November of my freshman year in college. By then, I'd met Vanessa, and she told me who I should be, and so I listened. I wore Doc Martens (until they were no longer cool); I decided that Amstel was way more awesome than Zima (even if I actually secretly preferred Zima); I learned to dance to Prince and smoke a cigarette without coughing and kissed enough boys that eventually, one of them slept with me.

But at twelve? Who knew who I was. For my twelfth birthday, my mom and I flew to Disney World. I was too old for it, but she offered, and I'd never been, and besides, I never got alone time with just her, so I acted excited and clapped my hands and hugged her tightly when she suggested the trip. On our first day there, right as we were about to fly down the ramp on Splash Mountain, the ride broke. Actually broke. Broke long enough that we made the national news.

We were stuck up there on the precipice for nearly five hours — teetering, not going up, not going down — and at about hour four, the guy behind us, a newlywed from Kentucky, started screaming about suing Walt Disney. His bride kept yelling things like, "Yeah!" and "You fucking tell them!"

The quartet in the car two cars in front of us was close enough to the splash pool that they gave up and jumped, and though I saw three of them pop up from the water for air and scramble to the ledge, the fourth took longer, and I watched and watched and watched, holding my breath, wondering if this was going to be that woman's fate: that she would jump from a broken car due to a blown fuse on Splash Mountain and land on the cement floor of the tide pool and drown. Eventually, she bounced to the surface and started screaming about a broken ankle, and another man threw himself into the water to rescue her and drag her over the side. My mom watched all of this with a certain stoicism that I'd inherited from her — part fascination with what would happen next, part uncertainty at her own fascination — and looked at me with a shrug.

"I'm sorry your birthday was the pits," she said.

"Don't be sorry. You couldn't have known."

"Maybe," she said. "But it's the pits all the same."

We finally got moving after hour five, and we were offered vouchers for a midnight buffet and another voucher for free lifetime entrances to the park. But my mom and I, we weren't up for the adventure, so we took a taxi to the airport the next morning and came home early. My dad had seen the news report, so he just laughed and handed me a skateboard with a bow on it. As if I'd ever wanted a skateboard or as if he'd ever paid attention to what I'd wanted anyway.

"I'm not William," I said to him. He looked at me with a cocked head and wrinkled brow, so I just sighed, then tossed the board in Oliver's room on my way to shut my own bedroom door.

Nicky returns with a pepperoni pizza and Tropical Skittles, which sound awful but work fairly well as an appetizer if you want them to.

"It's cool," he says. "My mom never lets me get shit like this. She's totally organic."

"I should go organic," I say. "They say you can add three years to your life." I lick the grease off the pepperoni and stick the disc to the roof of my mouth. *Organic or not, it doesn't really matter.*

"Or you could get hit by a bus tomorrow."

I nod my head in acknowledgement and wonder if he's thinking about his dad like I'm thinking about his dad.

"Getting hit by a bus wouldn't be that bad," he says, dribbling a long string of melted cheese into his mouth. "I mean, in terms of ways to go. Boom. That's it."

"I got fired today." The pepperoni grease oozes down my throat.

"That blows."

"You're the first person I've told. Which is sort of screwed up."

"Yeah," he says. "Where's Uncle Shawn?"

My phone lights up with a text, and like a Pavlovian rat, I reach for it.

"This might be him."

FACEBOOK ALERT

THEODORE BRACKTON HAS ADDED YOU AS A FRIEND

THEODORE BRACKTON HAS SENT YOU A MESSAGE

"Shit," I mutter, then feel Nicky's eyes on

me. "Sorry. I shouldn't have said that. Shoot. Shoooot."

"I say 'shit' all the time."

"You shouldn't. Why isn't your mom telling you that you shouldn't say 'shit' all the time? Like, if you have to go to a college interview, and you say 'shit,' you won't get in."

I head to the refrigerator in search of some wine. There must be wine somewhere in the house.

"I'm a 9/11 kid. I could say, 'Your mother is a total piece of fucking shit,' and they'd let me into Harvard."

I stop my excavation of the fridge abruptly and face him.

"First of all, that's a terrible thing to say. Second of all, I doubt that's true. Third of all, you should have some standards for yourself, even if it were true."

"I do have standards for myself," he says. "My teacher said I have the best imagination in my English class. That I could be a writer someday."

"Really?"

"Why are you so surprised?"

"I'm not surprised." I refocus on the bottom shelf of the fridge, where I find no wine but do find a beer that was likely abandoned two Super Bowls ago, but what the hell.

"I've never seen you drink a beer." Nicky smiles. "I mean, you are such a white wine sort of person."

"Are you twelve or are you thirty-seven? Because you're very weird."

"Birds of a feather flock together." He laughs.

"Are you suggesting that I'm weird? I'm a lot of things, but I don't think I'm weird. I'm Switzerland."

"People who are really weird never realize what weirdos they are," he says. "Like, ignorance is bliss, you know?"

"Well, that's true. It is. So cheers." And I clink my bottle against his Coke.

Theodore Brackton
321 friends
Hometown: Seattle, WA
Relationship Status: It's complicated

Message header: Feel free to ignore me
Dear W,

I can't decide if I should write or not. I'm writing. But I can't decide if I should send it or not. Funny, right? No, it's not funny. I guess it's ironic. But still. I find myself in a quagmire, and even I don't know how to get myself out of it. Who'd have thunk?

(Did I really just type 'thunk'? I guess so. Forgive me. I really don't know quite what to say. Also, I'm nervous. And terrified.)

Anyway, I know it is weird that I'm writing. I mean, the last time we saw each other wasn't exactly ideal and you probably hate me. I understand why you would.

So, the thing is, I was recently diagnosed with testicular cancer. I know, can you believe it? I guess my balls got sick of me using them so often and decided to pay me back. (Okay, you know I'm joking right? I am really bad at this.) I'm going to be fine — minus a nut, but otherwise fine — but this type of thing makes you think. Makes you reconsider choices you've made in your life and choices that maybe you thought you were going to make in your life. Does that make sense? I know that I'm the last person who ever would have found myself stuck, but when they took me into the OR a few months ago, all I could think of is, "Why did I screw it up with Willa, and what can I do about it now?"

So anyway. Wow. That's a lot of information for a Facebook message. This isn't like a "please leave your husband" email or "please feel sorry for me" email. I just . . . wanted to let you know.

xo
T

I knew I shouldn't have opened it.

I tell myself this as I lie on the bathroom floor, my abdomen in cramps brought on by nerves, by adrenaline, by Theodore, by the Pandora's box of Facebook.

Why did you open it?

I need to call Vanessa, who will tell me to write him back. Or maybe Raina, who will tell me that I'm a total idiot regardless.

Oliver once showed me how to breathe when I felt a panic attack coming on, so I crawl my way into a sitting position and force my diaphragm outward, then inward, then outward again, the air through my nose whistling and mocking me.

I think of Theodore and regret, and how my dad says that regret is just misplaced nostalgia. That you can look back fondly or even wistfully on pieces of your life and hound yourself with endless what-ifs, but nothing will change. The present will still be the present. The future will still unfold as it's meant to.

My stomach clenches again, and I attempt to spurn my own nostalgia . . . that maybe I should have told Theo "yes," that maybe he was my own Switzerland, that maybe I should have taken a closer look at the map. I know it's silly, I know that it can't be undone, I know that Shawn is my meant-to-be. But regret and nostalgia and what-ifs have a way of taking on a life of their own, even when you know better.

I grab the top of the toilet and throw up.

Then I shuffle to the sink, splash my face, and resolve to my reflection in the mirror to tuck this part of my life as far away from my current life as possible.

I flush the toilet twice to be sure that everything has washed away. It appears to have, but then again, and I should know this by now: nothing is ever as it seems.

"You've been working late a lot," I say to Shawn later that night, when he is finally home but checking email on his phone, and while Nicky flips through the pay-per-view channels, even though it's probably past his bedtime.

"Uh-huh. Getting slammed."

"Is it the new project?"

He leans against the refrigerator, only half-listening.

"What?" He looks up. "Oh, no. I mean, yes, but tonight the guys and I went down to the driving range."

"The driving range? You don't golf."

"I'm trying to learn." He glances toward the TV, his eyes suddenly wider. "Oh, oh, oh stop," he says to Nicky. "*Die Hard* is on!"

Grape! Golf!

Shawn jumps over the back of the couch and bounces into a seat. He's not a man who jumps over couches. Though he is naturally lean, he still adheres to coding-geek mantras that "typing burns calories," and "exercise your brain, not your body, dude!" (One of his friends actually has a bumper sticker with this quote.) I watch him watching Bruce Willis and wonder if he's been working out without me (jogging three miles used to be part of our weekend routine together until we decided that jogging zero miles was actually a lot more relaxing, and weekends are meant for relaxing), and if so, why. Or for whom.

"This guy is now like, a hundred," Nicky says. "And he's bald."

"You need more male role models," Shawn answers. "John McClane rules."

"Speaking of male role models," I say. "Don't forget, we have dinner with my parents tomorrow night. Nicky, you're invited."

"I thought we agreed to cancel that?" He doesn't turn around.

"It was too late, the restaurant would have charged their card."

Shawn says nothing for a breath, and then: "Oh. I kind of bought tickets to take Nicky to the Yankees game."

"You kind of bought them or you actually bought them?"

Now he looks my way. "I actually bought them." He gives me this pseudo-cute apologetic smile, and if not for *Grape!* or golf or couch-jumping or Switzerland-defecting, I might have smiled back and let it go.

Instead, I grab a carton of ice cream from the freezer and slam the carton on the counter. The plastic seal refuses to tear away, so I stick the pint between my thighs and wrestle it open. Shawn never makes plans like this without first flagging me; we are the couple who uses the *Together To-Do!* app, so we're always in sync. (FYI, it is a very handy app that allows you to drop in to-do items for your partner, and they simply pop up on said partner's own list. And I'm not just saying this because I worked on their ad campaign.)

I wedge the scooper into the rock-solid ice cream (reminder: put "adjust the goddamn freezer temperature" on Shawn's to-do list) and grunt, my bicep and forearm pulsing with effort. Baby sweat beads announce themselves on my forehead, and I push harder, then harder still into the chocolate chocolate-chip goodness. I manage to carve out a tiny wedge, a little turd of a piece of ice cream, and I should really drop it into the bowl I'm making for Shawn, but instead, I pinch it up and place it right in my mouth.

Ah yes. A perfect blend of sugar and vindictiveness.

I plunge the scooper back in, losing myself to the task, trying to ignore my irritation, trying also to ignore Theodore's Facebook email, because I am very good at ignoring things.

This one, however — Theodore — proves too wormy and keeps creeping its way in.

I exhale after I manage to grind out a particularly healthy-sized scoop.

Why did I screw it up with Willa?

I remind myself to google testicular cancer later, once Shawn is asleep.

6

Raina agrees to accompany me to dinner the next night. She picks me up in her Escalade at exactly 6 p.m., ushers me in the backseat, then waves her driver on. Then she leans back and assesses me.

"Before you say anything or suggest ways that I should improve my hair or make my skin more glowy, just know that I lost my job yesterday," I say as we stop, start, stop, start, stop, start our way down Fifth Avenue.

"Cliff, I'd really take Park," she offers.

"Don't tell Mom and Dad," I say.

Cliff brakes too abruptly, and the seatbelt digs into my collarbone.

"I'd never say anything about your hair." She smiles, then frowns. "You got fired?" She tries to look concerned but her eyebrows don't move enough to express it.

I stare.

"Yes," she says. "I caved and got Botox . . . Don't tell Mom and Dad."

"I don't think I'm going to have to. It's kind of obv . . ."

"Shut up, Willa," she interrupts. "It will wear off."

"Sorry."

"Do you want me to ask around at the firm?"

"About your Botox?"

"About a *job,* Willa. And please. I have four kids under the age of seven. And I'm one of three female partners. And I'm not getting any younger. The Botox was my gift to me."

"I thought that was your trainer."

"He is my gift to me too."

"Hmmm," I say. "That doesn't sound right at all. Does Jeremy know?"

"Oh *shut up.*" The SUV finally lurches forward and we cruise two blocks without stopping. Then she says, as if she's given this a fair amount of thought: "Besides, I'm pretty sure that Nicholi is gay." She sighs. "But what happened at work? And do you need my help?"

"Adult Diapers happened, that's what happened."

"What?"

I start to explain adult diapers and sexiness and how I was texting Vanessa because she could have actually saved the day in the way that Vanessa tends to, but it all feels pointless, and besides, her own phone beeps right then anyway. She glances at it quickly, then shuts it off.

"Jeremy swore he could handle all four tonight. What he meant by that was handle them while texting me constantly with questions. *Dear husband: I'm pretty sure that if you look in her underwear drawer, you will find Eloisa's underwear.*"

"Where's Gloria?"

"I'm giving her Saturday nights off two times a month."

"That's generous."

"Jesus, Willa! I know, I know. I am a pampered working mom with full-time help, and I'm spoiled and gross and all of those things to you. Seriously. I get it! But you asked me to rearrange my night to come to this dinner with you because your husband has broken the sacred rules of Shilla . . ."

Cliff glances in the rearview mirror, then quickly averts his eyes.

"What's Shilla?"

"You've never heard that? It's what we call you guys — Shawn and Willa. You know, your celebrity name. Because you guys never do anything apart." She smiles because she knows that it's a little mean but it's also a little true.

"Shilla?" I ask. "It sounds like . . . an Eskimo town in Alaska or something."

"Well, you're not Brangelina."

"We could be Brangelina."

"You're not Angie," she says, and then wavers. "Sorry. That was said out of jealousy. I take it back. You could be Angie."

We both know I could never be Angie, but it's nice of her to say all the same.

"I don't get it. What are you jealous of?"

"You guys do everything together. Remember that time a year or so ago when we went to get a manicure, and Shawn actually came along just because he didn't have anything to do that Sunday?"

"When you put it that way, it sounds really pathetic." Did he really come along because he just didn't have anything better to do that day?

"No, it's sweet, actually. Of course, it's also little sickening," Raina laughs, then examines her own manicure, lost in a tail end of a thought. "Do you know the last time Jeremy voluntarily spent time with me?"

"Don't say that," I say. "He loves you. And besides, Shawn's not here tonight, so we can't do *everything* together." *Because he's too busy at* Grape*!? Because he's too tired to run down to* Hop Lee *and French kiss me for*

83

free egg rolls!

We stop again at a light, the rush-hour traffic at a standstill, the taxis honking their horns, the pedestrians rushing through the streets, weaving through the cars, paying no mind to the sidewalks or the crosswalks or any of the rules set in place.

I roll the window down and yell, "There are rules set in place, you know!" An angry-looking twenty-something woman likely on the way home from her lousy magazine job gives me the finger. My cheeks feel hot, and I immediately press the window button back up.

"I don't know why I did that," I mutter.

"Anyway," Raina sighs, "please don't give me crap today. I have enough. And you have Shilla."

"I'm sorry about the Botox comment," I say, both because I am and because I also don't like arguing. "I'm being a bitch. I got fired, and I think that Shawn is having some sort of early mid-life crisis-slash-possible-affair, and I'm having weird fantasies about Theodore Brackton . . ."

I drift silent. Cliff turns up the radio to fill the space, and some mind-numbing hip-hop artist comes on, the bass blaring, his words unintelligible. Raina bobs her head — she probably knows this song from Soul

Cycle or something — and fishes in her purse.

"Here." She holds out a pill.

"What's this?"

"Xanax." She shoves one in her mouth.

"You're on Xanax?"

"Oh William, everyone's on Xanax." She pinches the bridge of her nose. "You always were the last to know."

My parents are waiting for us at the Four Seasons when we arrive. I see them before they see us, my mom dabbing the sides of her mouth with her napkin, my dad perusing the menu as if he's reading it for the first time. The Xanax has blunted me, dulled the edges, and though there's normally a slight beat of — of what? anxiety? tension? desire to please my dad? — tonight, I just let that flow over me, as if immune to them all.

My mom waves, then registers Raina beside me, and her face shifts, from pleasant to overjoyed. The firstborn. The prodigal daughter. And then there's me. The kid who was supposed to be a son.

We weave our way to their table, and my mom stands, clasping Raina's cheeks in her palms, kissing her on each side.

"Now this is a surprise. Both of our

children at once."

"There's a third child too, Mom," I say, as the waiter pulls out my chair, and I sit.

"Oh well, Oliver. The only way that I know anything about him is that Tweeter."

"Twitter," I say.

"Oh, yes, that!" she answers enthusiastically.

"Hello girls." My dad reaches for my hand and kisses it. "Raina, what brings you here? I thought you were preparing for a trial."

"Shawn is at the Yankees game with Nicky. Last-minute sort of thing."

"I do have a trial, but I made the time." Raina talks over me.

My dad motions for the waiter. "It's just as well," he says. "There are things we wanted to talk about with just you."

"Just me?" I'm unsure if it's the Xanax that has me confused, or if he's intentionally being vague.

"Just our children," my mom replies, pursing her mouth, her ruby red lipstick sinking into the fine lines just above her lips. She looks tired, more worn than the last time I saw her, even though that was just last month at this very same restaurant at this very same table.

"Is one of you dying?" Raina asks with genuine concern. I can tell that she's adjusted to the pill, the brain-softener; that this is a regular habit, like candy, like a glass of white wine. She's lucid but soft, softer anyway, at least for Raina.

"Neither of us is dying," my mother says, though she fiddles with her fork and doesn't meet either of our eyes.

My dad offers: "Let's order dinner. I'm starving. I've been on CNN all day and their green room is for amateurs."

"That was very adept," Raina says. "That humblebrag you just pulled off."

"A what?" My mother looks confused.

"Forget it," Raina says.

"Don't talk to me that way, young lady," my dad snaps. "Whatever 'humblebrag' may mean, I do not like your tone." He raises and lowers his hands to form air quotes, which strikes me as really odd, like he's trying to be a teenager or something, but then I reconsider. My dad was happy to put quotes around just about anything: it was his way of rewriting someone else's story.

He presses on: "There was an earthquake in Burma today, and a lot of people lost their lives, and I was only trying to lend my perspective on air. They had me on for the entire span of the news rush."

"I know, Dad," Raina says, mostly just to placate him. And since the waiter has now poured the wine, she reaches for it and rather than speak further, takes a generous sip.

I smile a crooked, partially-lobotomized smile. I'd forgotten how feisty Raina could be; how she refused to accept my father's prophesies, how she'd found a way to discover her own voice, her own perspective, even if that meant drowning herself in law school and work and children and then more children and charity and Escalades and a live-in nanny who now evidently got Saturday nights off as Raina searched for that ever-elusive thing that all moms search for: balance. Oh. And also, a Xanax dependency. But still, she didn't take shit from my dad, and that might have qualified her for a very unique club of one. Well, and the Nobel Review Board, if you count those five gentlemen, which surely my dad does not. (And Punjab Sharma too, of course.)

"Listen, if one of you is dying, please just tell us now," I say, my eyelids feeling unusually heavy, my mind feeling unusually light. It's not so bad, this floating. I think about Theodore, and how maybe I should write him back. I wanted to trust myself enough to, but then there was that tricky part about not trusting myself to at all. I was always doubting everything, even though I was also always placing my faith in the meant-to-be. My brain was at constant odds with itself, a bubble of confusion fostered by my father himself, and then nurtured by my paralysis in making any defiant moves against his philosophies.

Theodore knew this because he knew me as well as anyone had, though who I was at twenty-five and who I was now were hopefully different enough that he couldn't actually know me that well anymore — it had been seven years. A lifetime. Or part of a dog's lifetime anyway.

I close my eyes and listen to the clinking of forks against plates, the waft of conversation, the piano dimly floating out of the restaurant speakers. And then I consider that I may have gotten married and worked my way up the agency and found a different apartment and become a step-aunt and peed on a bunch of pregnancy tests, but really, I'm sitting here with my parents at the same restaurant we always sit at, and my sister is bickering with them, and my dad is the same old megalomaniac, and my mother is enabling it all, and Shilla (the name is growing on me) is perhaps very acutely imploding. And then I realize nothing has really shifted too much at all. That who I was at twenty-five is actually very akin to who I am now.

My dad always says that we can't change, and by God, if my thirty-two years are any indication, he's right. *Jesus.*

I open my eyes in time to see my mom settle her napkin in her lap and move it just so. "Let's just enjoy the sea bass," she says.

I am happy to just enjoy the sea bass if I'm being honest, but Raina coils up her face like a corkscrew, and since she has armed me with this unusually pleasant sense of nirvana, I feel the need to stand strong with her.

So I say: "We can't enjoy the sea bass if one of you is dying."

"If one of us *were* dying, I would hope that you wouldn't treat it as lightly as you are now," my dad says. "Even though" — because he can't help himself — "it would be whatever was meant to be. If either your mother or I were to die unexpectedly, I hope you know that I wouldn't want a big to-do."

A muscle in Raina's jaw flexes, and she stretches her neck to one side, the *pop!* audible across the table.

"So what it is?" she says. "Because once we know, *then* I certainly will enjoy the sea bass."

My mother clears her throat and purses her lips once, then twice. She eyes my father but then glances away, and he is no help (of course).

"Okay fine, I'll just come out with it." My mom reaches for her wine before continuing. "Your father has had . . . a difficult year. With . . . the Nobel . . ."

"Dad, you realize there are worse things in the world than being on the short list for a Nobel, right?" Raina says.

"Well, it was very devastating for him," my mom interjects. "And then there was that unfortunate restraining order."

"Punjab had no right! No claim!" my father cries, a shard of bread flying from his mouth and landing unceremoniously in the olive oil on my own bread plate. My mouth curls down, and I inch the plate toward the center of the table.

"Well, with all of that happening, your father came to some decisions. And I don't necessarily agree with them, but . . . well . . . you know." My mom waves her hands, as if this explains it. *Well . . . you know.* It does explain it though, as good enough shorthand as any in this family.

My dad dislodges the mucus in his windpipe, then announces:

"What she is trying to say is that I intend on taking a lover."

At this, Raina spits her wine back into her

glass. And though my head is cloudy and buzzy and thick, even I sense a widening of my eyes, a slackening in my face.

"Jesus, Dad!" Raina folds her hands over her face and drops her head. "Honestly! Just . . . Jesus Christ."

"I'm glad I didn't order the sea bass," I say.

"Well girls, let's be fair about this," my mom suggests, like she needs to defend him, like her staying with him for four decades hasn't been the greatest gift she could give him. "Your dad and I have been married for a very long time, and it's normal to consider other options. And well, he came to me and presented this in a reasonable way, and now I'm thinking that I might just go get a lover too!"

The waiter has arrived to take our order, but stops short and then turns quickly to a neighboring table.

"Mom!" Raina snaps. "Oh my God!"

"Honey, you're almost forty. I should be able to tell you the truth."

Raina fishes in her purse for her phone.

"I should check on the kids. Excuse me. And I'm not even close to forty."

She stands abruptly, and we all fall silent watching her flee.

"She always was a rule follower, Willa. Not

like you," my dad says, his eyes still on her until she disappears out the lobby. What he means is: she never quite came around to my way of thinking, which also means: she never loved me as much as you did.

"Oh please. Shut up." I can't even bear it.

My father's chin remains stoic but I can see his pulse throb in his neck.

"Willa." My mom moves her hand over mine.

"Mom," I say, my eyes suddenly full.

She leans in close enough that I can smell her Chanel perfume, a memory of my childhood, of complicated nostalgia, and then she says: "Don't be sad. If anything, after forty years, it's a bit of a relief."

7

Shawn makes eggs for breakfast. It's one of our things. A thing that Raina would add to the list of "Shilla things," like our joint manicures, if she were to make such a list. (Which she might.)

The smell of the grease doesn't wake me, but the doorbell does. The Xanax rendered my sleep a blackout, dreamless, and I wake disoriented, my lids crusty, my mouth tacky as if I'd eaten glue.

There's a knock on the bedroom door, and then Vanessa pokes her head in.

"Nice," she says, like I should've known she was coming over, and I should've been better prepared, should've been gussied up.

"What are you doing here? It's . . . like, 8 a.m., and I'm unemployed. So . . . go away. I want to sleep."

"It's Sunday, so unemployment has no bearing. And you said you'd come to the free fall with me. The warm-up for the *Dare*

You! book."

I'd forgotten. In order to boost tourism in the city, the mayor's office had implemented a simulated free fall off the Brooklyn Bridge. It was basically an over-hyped bungee jump, and if the mayor ever bothered to go to 42nd Street, he'd see that we should actually be attempting a mass exodus of tourists, not inviting more in. But still. The *Dare You!* producers set it up to announce the book deal: blasting out a press release to the trades wasn't exactly their speed. Throwing their writer off a bridge was. Vanessa had asked me to tag along because she grew paralyzed when transported to any level above five floors, though her paralysis wasn't enough to scare her off the job or off anything really. It never would be.

I probably put the free fall in the *Together To-Do!* app, but I hadn't checked since spiraling down my Xanax haze. I reach for my phone on the nightstand.

Together To-Do! has one notification:
Bungee with Vanessa: book deal announcement!!!!

"Ugh," I croak. "Okay. Hang on. Give me ten minutes."

She slides the door closed, and I stretch up, my back cracking, my mind gray. I sit on the precipice of the mattress until I can physically will myself to the bathroom, brushing my teeth, splashing water on my cheeks, grabbing sweatpants and a tank that were abandoned on the floor at some point earlier in the week. I gaze in the mirror — I am wrinkled and pale and borderline inhuman — until I have nothing left to do but get moving and stomach the day.

"You lost your job?" Shawn says when he sees me. I was deep into REM when he and Nicky got home from the Yankees game. He must have slept on the couch again. He's still wearing a Jeter jersey.

I glower at Vanessa. "You told him?"

"I didn't tell him anything. I'm just eating eggs. Minding my business." She flourishes her fork in the air and takes an overzealous bite as if to make a point.

"Nicky told me. Were you planning to?"

"I *was,* of course."

I pull out a stool, and out of habit, like an assembly line technician, he sets a plate in front of me. He has made eggs every Sunday morning since we moved in together. When we first married, he would place bacon in the shape of a smile at the base of the plate and two little strawberries up top — a face to greet me to start my day. Now — I eye the eggs with distrust — now, they're just a plop of *eggs.* I should be grateful that he's still honoring our Sunday ritual, that he hasn't insisted on, like, brunch at some hip place in Williamsburg or bought a crepe maker from *Sur La Table* or something, but the gratefulness is seeping out of me now, slowly, like my appreciation has been dumped into a sieve. I move some of the eggs around with my fork, buying my time.

"I was planning to tell you," I say finally. "I just really haven't seen you much alone since it happened. But now you know. Hannah was all coked up and made me do Adult Diapers by myself, and I told you that the meeting was disastrous, and so they dropped us as a client, and then she got fired, and then I got fired. And you know, it's all live free or die, Shawn! That's what it's about! *Live free or fuckin' die!*"

Now it's my turn to take an overzealous bite of eggs, as if stuffing them in and bulging my eyes is the exclamation point for my story.

"What does that even mean? What are you even talking about?"

"It's the goddamn universe, Shawn!" I bark. "Like, what the hell was I supposed to do anyway?"

Vanessa sighs audibly and Shawn scowls. "Why are you taking that tone with me? I'm not to blame here."

I swallow and drop my forehead to the counter.

"I'm sorry," I look up at him. "I should have told you. And I'm sorry for my tone. I'm resolving as of this moment to stop being mad at you. Anger is pointless."

Vanessa makes a face like she bit into a sour grapefruit.

"I didn't realize that you *were* angry with me," Shawn says.

He dumps the remaining eggs in the pan onto a spare plate and sets them aside for Nicky who will likely make a gagging noise at the sight of them and just ask for, like, some Pop Rocks and Sprite for breakfast. Which we'd give him. (That kid from the '80s' stomach totally didn't explode, in case you were wondering about our parenting. I googled it.)

"I'm thinking we should get going," Vanessa says. "I have to be there by nine — they have a camera crew there, so I need make-up, which is sort of ridiculous since they better not be doing a close-up of me hanging upside down with my face all morphed and bulging." She scrambles off her stool. "And also, I don't know why I just ate these since I'm probably now going to throw them up before I jump. The whole theory of what goes down, must come up."

"Wait," Shawn says to me (not Vanessa, who is shoving the last bites in her mouth too quickly). "Seriously, why are you mad at me?"

"When did you take up golfing?" my tone is a little too forthright to be casual, a little less kind than conversational.

"I . . . I don't know. I'm trying new things. Recently."

"And that jacket over there . . ." I gesture to a motorcycle jacket that I am only now noticing thrown over the couch. "What is *that*? Do coders wear that?"

"Ooh, that's actually really nice." Vanessa gets up to paw it. "This isn't ridiculous. This is the real deal. Varvatos. What did this set you back?"

"Oh Jesus, Vanessa, can you please pipe down for once?" I say, then immediately follow with, "Sorry. Shit, sorry. I don't know what's wrong with me."

"Hey, no flies on me. I'm gonna do this thing without you. You guys keep going. Just call me. Coffee later."

She quickly kisses my cheek and breezes out the door before I can beg her not to leave without me. Shawn and I are left alone, flanking each other in the kitchen. He pours himself more coffee, making a big show of the silence, dropping in his first plop of milk, then his second, then one last splash, as he does every morning, and for the first time ever, this makes me insane. I don't want my husband to make me insane, I want Shilla! But then I remember *Grape!*, and that I'm not exactly the one who might be cheating on us.

He sprinkles exactly half a packet of Splenda in, then stirs, then sips, and then sighs. Then he unspools the plastic wrap and envelops Nicky's plate as carefully as parents would swaddle their newborn. Finally, he turns back toward me and says:

"Why are you so mad at me?"

"I'm not mad at you."

"You're mad at me. You said, and I quote, 'I'm resolving as of this moment to stop being mad at you.'"

I'm about to shout out: *Grape!* when his phone vibrates on the counter, and he grabs it.

"Hey," he says, then wanders to the couch and perches on its arm. "Oh. Okay. Sure. For how long?"

A long pause.

"Um. Okay. No, no, that's fine. I mean, I have to talk to Willa." He falls silent.

I can feel my nerve ebbing out of me. I can't talk to Shawn about *Grape!* now. That might undo everything — set something in motion that I'm not ready to face. And besides, now, he has something to talk to *me* about. My thoughts turn to static. I try to catch my breath — breathe in and out, like Oliver showed me — and not totally come undone with the notion of what Shawn needs to talk to me about — affairs, divorce, one-night stands — and to whom he's saying all this. Please, universe, do not betray me. Please do not make Shawn be like that Goldman guy who slept with Izzy's friend, Candice.

Shawn says to his phone: "We'll figure it out. Sure, sure. No, I get it. I'm sure that Willa will be fine with it."

I allow myself a little more air because he must know that taking a call from some floozy whom he met at *Grape!* or at golf or whatever is not something I'd be fine with. I look at him sideways now, but he's focused on the long view out the window. Who knows what he sees out there in the distance. But it's not me.

"He's still sleeping," Shawn says. "I'll have him call you when he's up."

Another pause.

"Okay. Be safe. No, I understand."

He presses the off button and stares at the floor for a moment, then seems to remember that I'm sitting there with my runny eggs, that we were in the middle of something, that there were things to be said.

"That was Amanda." He rises slowly, like he threw out his back while talking.

"Okay."

"She needs us to watch Nicky for a while longer." He doesn't make eye contact and instead reaches for his coffee.

"Well, that's fine, I guess. How long?"

"Um, most of the summer."

"Most of the summer?"

"She was up for this position in Tanzania, and she got it. Which is great, by the way. I mean, she's out there making a difference."

"No one said she's not." I can't help but wonder if he doesn't mean that coming up with sexy ad campaigns for Adult Diapers is not exactly out there making a difference. *Hello! I'm well aware that it might be the dumbest thing on the planet. Why do you think I was texting Vanessa in the meeting in the first place? You try to make an incontinent Indiana Jones sexy!*

"Well, you know," Shawn says. "Where she's going to be isn't safe for Nicky right now, and this job is pretty much all she has other than him, and it's only until August."

"That's our whole summer, Shawn! I thought we were, like, trying for a baby!"

"We can try for a baby with Nicky here,

Will. Come on."

"You know what? Let's not try for a baby right now," I glower, raising my voice a little too loudly. "I don't think I want to."

A wild overreaction to be sure. But also, a wee relief. As soon as I say it, I feel it in my guts, deep on my insides: a weight lifting, a release from the burden that has been pressing me so very far down. Maybe @nurseellen at BabyCenter was right. Maybe I owe her an apology. Maybe some of us just aren't cut out for offspring, and if that's what God's plan is telling us, then maybe we should lean in and listen.

"What?" Shawn reacts. "Now we're not having a kid?"

"You heard me! The kid is off the table! I mean, we can't even have one anyway, even when we're actively trying! I'm not pregnant again, and maybe it's just a goddamn sign!"

"Where's this coming from? Because Nicky will be sleeping in our spare room?"

"No!" I shout even louder. I breathe in, breathe out through my nasal passage, just like Oliver showed me. ("This is called pranayama breathing," he said. "I know master yogis who can orgasm from it.") I feel my pulse slow, then say hesitantly, more quietly:

"It's coming from . . . golf . . . and the

Yankees . . . and . . ."

I try to say it, I try to actually be forthright and confront what needs to be confronted, but I can't. My dad would say it's because my conscious mind is too scared to set something in motion that I don't want to set off, but he'd also tell me that it wouldn't matter: if disaster is impending, it's a-coming anyway. But I'd say that it's probably something simpler: that I don't want to say *Grape!* because of the simple truth that I'm a coward who never wants to rock the status quo.

"What the hell, Willa?" Shawn snaps, still a decibel too high. "You don't want to have a kid because I'm taking up golfing? What does that even mean? We're supposed to have a kid now. We agreed that we were having a kid now! It's part of our plan!"

"Well, now that you put it that way, let's definitely have a kid! Let's have twins!" The pranayama breathing is of no use. (Orgasm? Really? From breathing? Not buying what you're selling, Dalai Lama.)

The guest bedroom door opens and Nicky wanders out, his hair a bird's nest from behind, his skinny legs gawky in his boxers.

"What the fuck, you guys?"

"Don't say fuck, Nicky," I say back.

He shrugs.

104

"These for me?" He spies the spare plate of eggs on the counter. Shawn nods yes, so he scrambles up on the stool, unwraps the plate, and digs in.

Shawn sees his opportunity to deflect.

"So your mom called . . . we should talk, dude."

I consider if this is the first time Shawn has ever called anyone "dude," and if he realizes what an idiot he sounds like. And then I hate that I've even thought this. I want to scrub the notion from my mind: that my husband sounds like an idiot, that I'm the type of wife who would ever see him as such a moron.

"Whatever," Nicky says.

"Whatever," I say.

"Whatever," Shawn replies in return, which is not the white flag I was hoping for.

I grab my purse and turn into the foyer, then out the front door. The door slams behind me, and then the latch clicks, and as I wait for the elevator to come and take me away from this mess, I try to muster the courage to go back in and apologize. I count to twenty in my head.

If the elevator dings before I reach twenty, I'll get in and go meet Vanessa. If it doesn't, I'll go back.

I don't even get to eleven.

The door opens, and I step forward. The universe gave me a sign. I'm just listening.

The taxi drops me right at the foot of the Brooklyn Bridge, from which an enormous banner hangs. *DARE YOURSELF TO A BETTER LIFE!* It's red and bold and unavoidable, and all around me, pedestrians stop to gape and wonder, perhaps, if they can indeed dare themselves to a better life. Maybe it's that easy, the girl to my left considers — *dare yourself!* — and she can finally meet a guy who calls her after sex. Maybe that's the answer, the chubby guy next to the girl thinks — *dare yourself!* — and he can finally stop inhaling éclairs at midnight and lose the twenty pounds he's convinced are keeping his life, his entire life, in a rut.

I peer toward the bridge, right in time to see Vanessa catch air. She hesitates just before jumping, and I know it's to swallow down her fear, but then she closes her eyes, counts to three, and throws herself forward. I can hear her shriek all the way from where I am on the sidewalk, but then I also hear her scream, "Holy shit! This is amazing!" And I watch her fly, soar, float through the air on her way down. The gathered crowd erupts in spontaneous applause, and Vanessa pumps her fist in reply. She bounces twice at the bottom, and then starts to hyena-laugh at what she has done.

I stand there watching, my heart in my throat, my breath quick and measured, and I start to weep. For her bravery, for her leap. For something that I could never do.

And then, as they pull her up, she must spy me, even from her upside-down angle, and she yells, "Willa Chandler-Golden! I dare you: you're next!"

And we both laugh because we know that I'm not.

Vanessa insists that we walk home, though it's over five miles and the June heat wave has continued, and I'm already feeling damp. I wrap my hair up in a bun and tug my tank top away from my chest, but I'm too late: already, tiny pockmarks of sweat have seeped through.

"You should tell Hannah to get into bungee jumping. It will goddamn blow her mind!"

We're weaving our way through China-town, which is vibrant, too awake on a Sunday morning. Chickens hang in windows, knock-off handbags spill from corner vendors, tourists push and elbow their way through. Vanessa's practically levitating, amped on high from the adrenaline of the leap. A guy tries to sell me a fake Rolex but I contort my face *no* and say to Vanessa:

"Why would I try to get Hannah into bungee jumping? Also, I'll probably never speak to her again."

"Because this is probably exactly how coke feels, but it's better for you. And you never know. Don't burn a bridge."

"Just jump off one instead?"

"Hardy-har," she says.

We point ourselves north through Little Italy toward Soho, the demographics shifting with each passing block.

There's a hot new yoga studio on the corner of Broadway and Houston — *Yogiholics!* — and throngs of skinny women in black capris and Lululemon tanks emerge. They slide on their sunglasses and make plans for brunch. Vanessa and I stop on the corner alongside their pack, as the skinniest, tallest one of them says:

"God, is Oliver not the best teacher in the world? I swear, his pranayama breathing turns me on."

The light changes and they charge forward, giggling, gossiping, mostly happy, though also probably with a secret Xanax habit just like Raina.

"That's weird," I say. "Her yoga instructor

is named Oliver. How many hot yoga instructors are named 'Oliver?' "

"Isn't yours in India? I checked his Twitter feed last week."

"World's most famous yoga guru is addicted to Twitter. How ridiculous," I say, a little too spitefully.

Vanessa's eyebrows skewer inward. "Oliver isn't hurting anyone, even if he is a little ridiculous."

"You're right," I concede. The blood moves over my cheeks. "I'm just having a bit of a shit life moment." I explain Nicky, and my dad's *lover,* and Shawn's disgusting eggs and coffee and "dude." Not to mention our argument this morning, to which she was witness. "Shawn and I don't argue. I mean, we don't have shit moments."

"I guess you do though."

I want to slug her for being right, but instead, I mutter: "Well, I don't know."

And she says: "It's the not knowing that will kill you."

And I retort: "I'm pretty sure there are other ways to die."

And she answers: "Of course there are. But at this rate, I wouldn't count on it."

OLIVER CHANDLER
Yogi, life-lover, naturalist, vegan, student,

teacher, wanderer, admirer of beauty. Namaste!
Following: 121
Followers: 104,531

Amazeballs power vinyasa class today at Yogiholics! Thanks ladies for getting your om on! *(1 hr)*

> *@RainaChandlerFarley* Are you serious? You're in NYC, and this is how I find out? *(3 hrs)*
> Best cure for jet-lag? A green smoothie from Juiceriffic. Thanks, Juiceriffic! Twitterphoto.com/oc1842 *(1 day)*
> *@savvylady* A little birdie tells me you're coming to town. Buzz me. *(2 days)*
> *@alliebaby* Yay! Can't wait! Like old times. Balthazar this week? *(2 days)*
> We are all only one with the universe when we let the universe be one with us. *(3 days)*
> Sometimes bad news is actually good news. You just have to dig deeper. (Shout-out to my pops.) *(5 days)*
> Absorb what is being said to you. Listen, and you will hear. *(1 week)*

"Well, he's evidently in New York," Vanessa says, clicking onto her home screen on her phone.

"And evidently, still as full of shit as before."

"You should join Twitter," she urges.

"Why?" I reply. "I never have anything interesting to say."

Two hours and five miles later, I am back at my apartment, though no more ready to go inside. I know that it will likely make no difference, my entry, my refusal to say *Grape!* That whatever will be, will be — we will fight (we never fight), we will say things (though we never say things), we will dance around this and then we'll move on to wherever we're supposed to move on to. The thing about half-believing in my father's philosophies is that they lend themselves to passivity: why bother fighting, why bother speaking in truths when maybe those truths don't matter. Can't we just fast-forward to when we're happy again? Because if we're going to be happy again, none of that in-between stuff matters.

I insert my key and rotate the doorknob. *None of this in-between stuff matters. Apologize.*

Shawn is on the couch, a sweat ring around his neck, his workout clothes soaked. He flips off the television when he hears the door open, then swing shut.

"Nicky went to a friend's for a few hours," he says, not turning around.

"You went running?" I linger in the foyer, unsure about stepping forward.

"I did go running, Willa. Is that okay with you?"

"What? I was just asking."

Shawn sighs like this is the most exasperating statement in the world and finally looks toward me. "I don't want to fight with you."

"I don't want to fight with you." I feel the bubble of tension ebb from my body. My stomach unknots, my adrenaline slows. *None of this in-between stuff matters. We'll go back to where we left off. Of course we can do that. I was silly to think that we couldn't.*

"But . . ." he starts, then stops. "But . . ." he starts again.

Shawn, for all of his strengths — and he has many — is no better at this than I am, and my resolve crumbles all over again. Something is wrong here, very, very wrong, and whether or not I should listen to my instincts (and my father has taught me not to), I can't help but sense that we are about to make a very abrupt, very hard turn into the unknown.

He glances at his hands, shakes his head, and then, quickly, like he's about to lose his nerve, says:

"Wired2Go wants me to come spend the summer at their corporate office in Palo Alto."

I exhale. This isn't devastating. This isn't an abrupt, hard turn. I mean, it's not in the diagram that we drew up three years ago, but I can manage Palo Alto for a summer.

"I'm sorry about before. I should have told you about my job."

The apology bounces off him, barely registering, like he just needs to say what he has rehearsed, to get it out while he has the will to.

I continue: "Anyway, I guess that sort of sucks, but you can fly back for weekends. Or I could come visit. I don't have a job or anything. I guess I could go with you." I squint and try to imagine myself in Palo Alto.

"No, that's not what I mean. I suspected you wouldn't be excited."

He sighs again. Then looks at me, really, really looks at me, like it's the last time he might see me, might take me in. I take a step closer but then stop when he offers: "Willa, don't you ever feel like . . . like . . . like you're stuck?"

"Stuck? Not really. I mean, no."

"Well, I guess I do."

113

"You feel stuck?" I ask. "With . . . me?"

"Yes," he answers, then covers himself with: "No. No. No, that's not what I meant."

The room spins, and I press a palm against the wall to steady myself.

"Is this about *Grape!*?" I whisper when I feel like I might not pass out.

"Grape?"

"*Grape!,* yes, *GRAPE!* The club you went to when you were supposed to be at basketball with your brainiac squad who worship you because you happen to have been blessed with better cheekbones but are still a wolf in sheep's clothing." I pray that he doesn't mock my stupid metaphors. Why did I choose such a stupid metaphor?

"How do you . . ." He doesn't finish his sentence, and I realize that he thinks it doesn't even matter.

"Are you cheating on me? Seriously? *Are you fucking having an affair with some girl from* Grape! *who has, like, a fertile uterus and better boobs?*"

"What? No!" He stands now, but doesn't move nearer. "I'm just . . . what?"

I ask him again, more quietly now, because I have finally said it, and I need to hear the honest answer, not the first denial.

"Shawn. Just tell me. Are you cheating on me? Am I not enough?"

"No!" he snaps, too loudly, setting me off again. "I'm just . . . ugh. Listen, Willa, this is hard."

"What's so hard? Your affair? Your stupid leather jacket? Your discovery of golf . . . or . . . or running on Sundays without me? What?"

He sits back down.

"Shit. I don't know."

We stay on pause for a few minutes, him staring at his hands, me pressed against the foyer wall, unable to find a way to say whatever it is to mend this. His phone buzzes — I can hear it in his pants pocket — but he doesn't pick it up. When I can no longer bear it, I say:

"So . . . what? I don't get what you're saying."

"I guess what I'm saying . . ." He cracks his knuckles. "Is that I'm trying to make life more interesting. I'm not cheating." His voice breaks here, and I can't help but feel something splinter inside of me too. "I went to *Grape!* because it was different, because, well . . . it was fun. The guys wanted to, and *Jesus,* I wanted to. Go out, do something new, *try* something new. I mean, I love you. I do. But I kind of feel like my life is one fucking *Together To-Do!* app." He sighs. "I'm in a rut."

"So get out of it."

"I'm trying! Don't you think that's what I'm doing?"

A rut. It's only that he's in a rut.

"So what does Palo Alto have to do with this?"

He doesn't answer right away. His phone beeps twice again in the silence. Then he says:

"I was just thinking, you know, maybe I could go by myself. Or take Nicky for a while."

"Maybe you could go by yourself?" Bile rises up from my stomach, my easy gag reflex announcing itself at the first sign of trouble. I swallow deeply, but the wave of nausea doesn't pass.

"You know . . . like . . . a break or something?"

"Like . . . a break or something? From . . . me?"

"From us. Not, like, anything legal. I mean, I love you."

"I don't . . . where is this coming from?" I slide to the floor and cross my legs, tucking my head down so the room stops spinning. Xanax. That's what I need. I remind myself to call Raina, to start seeing her more regularly. "I can learn to play golf! I can, like, go to a Yankees game!"

I hear his footsteps, and then he's above me.

"Do you really want to be Shilla forever?"

I look up at him.

"You know about Shilla?"

"Yeah, why wouldn't I?"

"I hate baseball, but I mean, I'd go with you," I start to cry now. I remember that he bought me a gift certificate to golf lessons a few months ago, but I tucked it into a drawer at work and promptly lost it. "I'll learn how to golf."

"But you don't need to go with me; you don't have to learn if you don't want to," he says. "That's kind of the point. That I need to go without you, but that you don't want me to go."

I feel the snot running down my upper lip. "What the hell is wrong with Shilla anyway?"

"Nothing's wrong with Shilla." He's quiet. "But maybe we need a little distance to start being Shawn and Willa again. I kind of liked us from before."

I don't reply, so he says:

"I reread your dad's book, and the tenets of it make a lot of sense." He rattles off the table of contents. *"Embrace the Master Universe Way. Accept inertia. Close your eyes and follow the map. Be what you already are.*

Set yourself free."

"What the hell are you talking about? Those are words that wrap up his philosophies in neat little packages. They're *words*. They don't mean anything." I'm surprised to give voice to this notion. "And you're not, like, accepting inertia. You're changing it! You're screwing up our plan!"

"It's like the epigraph in the book says," Shawn continues as if he hasn't even heard me. "'If you love something, set it free. If it comes back to you, it's yours forever. If it doesn't, it was never meant to be.'"

I say nothing, so he suggests:

"Maybe it's something like that. Maybe you and I are something like that."

"So you're setting me free?"

"Maybe not for forever."

"Forever doesn't matter. Now is the only thing that does."

"Well, then for now," he says.

And he sets me free.

8

THE RULES OF SHAWN AND WILLA'S PSEUDO-SEPARATION

as agreed to on June 12 and to dissolve on agreed-upon date in August

1. Shawn and Willa will have no contact — barring an emergency such as death — during the designated time period.
2. If one party does contact the other, the contactee is under no obligation to return the engaging party's email/phone call/text/Facebook message, etc.
3. Within the designated time period, the named parties can behave as if they are single.
3a. This means that should anything physical happen with a new party, there will be no repercussions in the

union should the named parties decide to remain married.

3b. It is also understood that should sexual relations occur, the sexually active party *must* use protection.

4. While neither party can be prevented from googling/Facebook-ing the other party, this is highly discouraged.

4a. However, both parties agree not to change their Facebook status to "it's complicated" without consulting the other party.

5. Should the need for communication arise but is non-urgent, for example, about Nicky's whereabouts, each party can check a mutually agreed upon email account: shawnandwilla@gmail.com.

6. Have fun!

9

Shawn leaves on a Wednesday. An average Wednesday by anyone else's standard but anything but average for me. We said our awkward goodbyes *("Speak to you in August!" "Don't do anything I wouldn't do — ha ha ha!"),* and then he goes to kiss me, but I turn my head, so we sort of bump noses while our lips pass over each other.

Nicky stands in the living room and makes an explosion noise with his cheeks, then his hands follow — his fingers mimicking a grenade, and Shawn says:

"Come on, dude, don't be like that. I'll see you next week in Palo Alto. Wired2Go has the coolest office ever. You can zipline from one floor to the next. You'll love it."

"Sounds cool," Nicky says, then heads to the guest room and locks himself inside.

"They also have Pac-Man and Donkey Kong in the common room!" Shawn calls after him. He rubs his forehead and says,

"Shit. Like this is one more thing he needs."

"Another child of divorce," I say flatly.

"We're not getting divorced, Willa. And I feel terrible for him." He pauses and I wonder if maybe he won't change his mind, if maybe Nicky is the one he'll stay for, but I can be the one he discovers he needs. I should say this — I should scream *please don't go!!* but my old habits get the best of me: why fight it when whatever will happen will happen? In this moment, I hate myself for my passivity, so I offer:

"Nicky might hate you for doing this."

And he looks like I've pierced his heart, which is exactly what I hoped for.

"I've done everything in my life for him." And this isn't untrue: though we hadn't yet met, I know that Shawn moved in with Amanda after Kyle was killed. He was in the delivery room; he took Nicky to his first day of preschool; he trekked out to the suburbs for Little League games on Saturday.

"Well, he still might hate you." I'm pretty sure that's not fair, but it's easier to talk about Nicky's feelings than mine.

"This has to be about me," he says simply, zipping his heart back up.

I open the door for him, hurriedly trying to get him out now before he (or the universe) can inflict more anguish.

"Have a safe flight." As if anyone can actually determine whether or not their flight will be safe, and if it isn't, as if anyone can do anything about it anyway. United 93. How many of their spouses said, "Have a safe flight," or "Safe travels," or "Be careful." Like that amounted to anything.

But Shawn just wheels his roller suitcase out the door and says:

"I will."

Not giving destiny a second thought.

Raina's two older kids were at day camp for the summer, but her younger two, the identical twins, Bobby and Greyson, were left in the care of Gloria, the super-nanny, during the long summer days. To everyone who knew them, they were known as "the twins," and Raina sometimes worried to me (when she had time to worry about such things) that they'd never form identities outside their twindom. From a distance, and even mostly up close, you honest to God couldn't tell them apart: tow-headed, impish, both with a splash of freckles across their cheeks, exactly the same height, exactly the same weight . . . it was as if your mind were playing tricks on you. That you were seeing double (you were), but not in a literal sense, only as an illusion. Raina insisted on dressing them differently, so if I ever got confused, I just remembered that Bobby wore the graphic tees and Grey went for preppy chic. Also, Bobby fell off the jungle gym four months ago and knocked out his top right tooth, so when he smiles, I always have a second of clarity: "Ah, that's Bobby."

Identical twins freaked me out a bit, not just because they were really strange to look at but also because they felt like official confirmation of my father's prophesies. If Raina's egg hadn't split, only one of them would be here. They wouldn't have these tangled identities, they wouldn't have the other half who could occasionally read the other's mind or know what the other wanted before he even knew himself. There would just be one. Bobby. Or Grey. Which one would it have been?

Today on the subway, Bobby swats Grey across the face for no particular reason. Grey was annoying him, I suppose, just for being there. Grey starts shrieking, his pale cheeks now a shade of brighter pink, and Bobby grins up at me, half-toothless, like I'm in on the joke. Like he's saying, "Yeah, bitch, so what? I'd have been the twin who would have survived."

Though Nicky is eight years older than

the twins, it was his idea to invite them to the *Bodies* exhibit down at South Street Seaport. I asked him twice if he were sure that he wanted two sweaty four-year-olds along because frankly, I wasn't even sure that I wanted two sweaty four-year-olds along, but he looked at me like I had three heads and said, "Yeah, of course. They're cute. Don't you like kids or something?"

I didn't have a response quite prepared because who the hell knew if I really did like kids? I barely liked myself. And while Nicky had grown on me in the four days since my husband had opted to zipline from office to office rather than honor 'til death do us part, I wasn't exactly about to pledge undying maternalism to the twelve-year-old either. For one, puberty was doing really strange things to his sweat glands, and for two, his 9/11 status aside, he really was a little disturbingly consumed with death. Which is how we ended up at the *Bodies* exhibit in the first place.

"Can't you just ask if they can come?" he whined.

"I really don't think this is appropriate for four-year-olds."

"Everyone dies, Willa," he said. "Facts are facts. Even four-year-olds need to know that."

I was going to argue, but I found myself too tired to, so I texted Raina to inquire. And she immediately texted me back and said:

GRT!!!! Gloria will have boys rdy in 30.

On the subway now, Grey finally stops crying and turns his sad face into a furious one. He stares at the grimy floor, biting his lip, and flaring his nostrils.

"He's a little touchy because his fish died this morning." Gloria kisses his head.

"Frank died," Bobby echoes matter-of-factly.

"Everyone dies," Nicky says. Then to me: "See, I told you."

"We woke up and he was floating in his bowl," Bobby clarifies, his little reedy voice carrying all throughout the subway car. He pronounces "floating" like *fwoating,* and a small part of me wishes in that instant that he were mine. Raina has told me motherhood is like this: a series of tiny moments that add up to an enormous love, with lots of other moments of frustration and misunderstanding and complexity woven in between.

"That must have been sad. Did that make you sad?" I crouch down to his level.

Bobby shrugs. Grey says nothing, though his nostrils still flare, his lips still purse. He holds a grudge, I can see, just like his grandfather. *Punjab Sharma!*

"Grey, your Aunt Willa asked you a question," Gloria says.

"It's okay, he doesn't have to answer. I get it." I right myself upward.

The subway jolts and on instinct *(ignore your instincts!),* we all reach for a pole, a shoulder. Grey reaches for Gloria. Then he looks at me.

"Frank didn't die. Bobby killed him."

"Did not!" Bobby yells.

"Did too!" Grey shouts back. He curls up his tiny fist, anger churning through him.

"Did not!"

Before Gloria can even stop him, Grey's arm is in the air, his knuckles aimed squarely at Bobby's remaining upper tooth. But then fate intervenes — or the train conductor just hits the brakes too quickly — and we all heave forward unexpectedly. Bobby falls atop Gloria's knees, and Grey, poor Grey, trips backward and lands squarely, firmly, on his bottom.

Who knows why it plays out this way, with Frank dead and Bobby triumphant and sad little Grey on the disgusting floor of the train where various forms of bacteria could be infesting him even as we speak.

I look down at him, the defeat on his face,

and I offer him a hand, pulling him up.

"I'm okay," he says, though his full eyes and trembling chin betray him.

"I am too," I reply. Though I have my own laundry list of betrayals too.

Vanessa meets us at the exhibit, her exuberance dialed up to ten, which I find a little disrespectful in light of my current life situation, not to mention the countless dead bodies on display.

"I have an idea," she says to me, as we stop to stare at some poor guy's muscle tissue. "And it's an awesome fricking idea."

"Do you think that when this guy died, that he knew his insides would be on display for thousands of people? Like, do you think that's what he'd want?" I ask, ignoring her, moving closer, my nose close enough to the glass that mostly I can just see my own reflection.

"He's dead," Nicky says behind me. "It's not like he knows."

"You're a real downer," Vanessa retorts. "Are you like this all the time?"

"My mom blames puberty," he shrugs. "I think the terrorists could have something to do with it."

He walks off to the next encasement.

"Wow," she says.

"Tell me about it. Though actually, he's got a point." The kid is really growing on me.

We pass under a sign that reads, "The History of Anatomy," and Bobby scrambles over to the next body.

"Penis!" He screams, then starts giggling wildly.

Grey stands on his tippy-toes and points to another body.

"Boobies!" He matches Bobby's laughter.

"Boys!" Gloria reprimands.

A woman turns to Gloria and affirms:

"Oh, boys will be boys. It's always the same."

And Gloria nods her head and offers a smile because she knows that to be true. That running around shouting *penis* or *boobies* really isn't the end of the world. She needs only to look at Nicky to understand what the end of the world really is. Gloria nudges the boys away from the glass, and they gleefully run in front of her, chasing their discontented second cousin (by marriage) down the hallway.

I watch them for a hopeful beat.

Stay four, I think. *Don't grow up into twelve.* I think again. *Don't keep going to thirty-two. It's all so much more complicated.*

"Before we get to my grand idea, I want

to talk about Shawn," Vanessa starts. "You've been ignoring the subject since Wednesday."

"I'm not ignoring the subject. It is what it is. A break. An intermission. He's in Palo Alto, and I'm here. What can I say about that?"

"A lot. There's a lot to say about that."

"Telling me that he's an asshole doesn't help. Up until this moment, Shawn has never been an asshole. I love him, you know."

"I'm sorry, Willa. But in this moment, he's a real asshole."

We wander toward the children who have rushed far ahead, but we stop, start, stop again, stare some more at each piece of flesh, each part of the human body that is tucked somewhere inside of us but seems completely foreign all the same. The kidney. The liver. The pancreas. The lungs. I have these things?

"Okay," Vanessa begins again. "Let's not talk about Shawn. Let's talk about you." She touches my elbow, slowing me.

"I'm fine. If this is what's meant to happen, this is what's meant to happen."

"Willa, that's ridiculous."

"What should I say? That I'm heartbroken? What's the point of being brokenhearted? It will all work out. I really believe that in August, it will all work out."

"That doesn't mean you can't be heart-broken." She pauses. "Besides, that's what you want? For it all to just work out in August?"

"Of course that's what I want."

"He just unceremoniously took a break from you."

"I know what he did!"

"Then why not reconsider what it is that you want?"

I drop my head. "I don't know. I don't know what to say."

"Why don't you though?" She turns to look at me, to really meet my eyes.

There's nothing to answer in reply, so we start back toward Gloria and the boys, but find ourselves thwarted behind a tour group of French Canadians. So rather than push forward, we study the display in front of us.

The Human Heart.

The heart weighs between 7 and 15 ounces (200 to 425 grams) and is a little larger than the size of your fist. By the end of a long life, a person's heart may have beat (expanded and contracted) more than 3.5 billion times.

I inhale and think of Grey's little fist. I think of how many times Nicky's dad,

Kyle's, heart must have beaten. Not 3.5 billion.

"So I have a proposal," Vanessa says. "I met with the *Dare You!* team and my publisher this morning."

"If you want me to sign a waiver to be your next of kin because they're requiring you to skydive without a parachute, I'm going to have to draw the line."

"No," she says. "It's nothing like that." Then she reconsiders. "Well, it's sort of like that."

The French Canadians filter down the hallway, but we stay put, still staring at the human heart, at its power, at its ability to grant life and to take it away.

"What if I told you that we had the chance to prove once and for all that your dad isn't right? That you don't have to sit around and wait for August for your life to begin?"

"Can we get off the subject of August? I really don't want to delve into it right now."

She waves a hand, dismissing me. "Okay, what if I told you that we are the masters of our fate, that life is what we make of it?"

"I'd tell you that the Nobel Prize committee would disagree with us."

"Fuck the Nobel Prize committee."

"Actually, my dad would say the same thing."

Vanessa smiles, so I gather the strength to smile too.

"I pitched my editors a new idea. A better idea. And they love it. I told them that I found the loophole in your dad's theories."

"There isn't a loophole, Vanessa. Part of the reason it's so brilliant is that you can't *disprove* that something didn't happen on purpose. You can't disprove an intangible proof."

"I believe that you can. But I need you to trust me."

"V," I say, "You know that I trust you, but I'm not really interested."

She grabs my wrist and forces my gaze.

"Willa, don't you ever wonder what would happen with your life if you hadn't been born William, if you'd actually been given a chance without your dad?"

Every day, I think. Though that's not necessarily true. Some days, and even then, it's exhausting to consider the alternatives, so mostly, I don't.

"Please, come with me. Write this book. Tell this story. At the very least, we might change our lives."

I can feel my own heart, just like the frozen one on the pedestal in front of me, come to life, beating with anxiety, beating with fear, beating from the utter terror of

133

taking a leap that might change everything.

"I like my life," I say finally.

"Actually," she reminds me, "you sort of don't."

10

Google.com/search
Search terms: Theodore Brackton
Search results: 17,192 hits

Theodore Brackton — Wikipedia, The Free Encyclopedia
Preview: Theodore Brackton (b. April 14, 1978) is the successful founder of the firm: Y.E.S., also known as Your Every Success. Since its inception in 2008, Brackton has helped thousands of CEOs and major power players assess the odds of successful decision-making by analytic research, as well as what *Time* magazine cites as "one of the best gut-checks in the business." It was rumored that President Obama personally . . .

Time — Is This the Face of Our Future?
Preview: Deep inside the Go Room in the Seattle office of Y.E.S., Theodore Brack-

ton is splayed on the conference table, staring at the dimmed, recessed lights on the ceiling, tossing a stress ball up and down, then up again, catching it effortlessly in his left hand while his staff sits and waits, watching both him and the newsfeeds that are muted on the various televisions on the walls. Finally and without warning, Brackton sits up sharply and shouts, "Yes! I have it." What does he have? The solution to a sexual harassment suit against the president of a major movie studio, who we . . .

Seattle Social Diary: The Engagement Party of Theodore Brackton and Sonya Nordstrom

Preview: A hundred of the who's-who of Seattle's hipster, fashion and tech scene mingled last night at Tom Douglas's hot spot, Seatown. There wasn't a hotter invitation in town as everyone who's anyone clamored to get a peek at the 33-year-old whom *Time* magazine called "the face of our future," and his future wife, the current COO at Nordstrom and daughter of the mogul John Nordstrom. The two met by accident — she had inadvertently taken his seats at a Mariners game, and last night they joked that they may be the only two people in the world who are grateful for the team's abysmal 2011 season . . .

The *New York Post* — Page Six
Preview: We Hear . . . . . . That a certain hot prospect (and hot-bodied!) CEO and face of the future is about to become very single. It seems that a recent health scare has jolted him into reality, and that his supposed wife-to-be will not be saying Y.E.S.! We're betting her daddy won't accept him for return, even if he comes begging for her back, despite his very generous return policy.

"Here is what we're going to do," Vanessa says later, back at my apartment, once we are done looking at dead innards, once I can stop gazing at the human heart, wondering how many heartbeats we all have left.

As she speaks, I snap my laptop shut quickly — I hadn't even meant to google Theodore. I find myself doing that too often these days: thinking of him, wondering if he's out there in the world also thinking of me, waiting for me to respond to his email and reignite our closed connection. I inch the computer to my left on the counter, as if hiding it, exorcising it from my sight line will allow me to exorcise him *(the face of our future!)* from my mind.

Vanessa rises from the stool in my kitchen and pours herself a bowl of cereal.

From the couch, Nicky says while completely focused on the TV, "Can you make me one too?"

"So here's what we're going to do," she repeats, reaching for a second bowl. "I have this theory — the theory of opposites."

"Like, opposites attract? Is this going to be some psychoanalysis of my relationship with Shawn? We're not opposites, so I can stop you right there."

"My mom and dad were opposites," Nicky says, tearing himself away from the TV. "That's what she tells me anyway. That they were always learning something new from each other." He glances away, his moment of vulnerability gone as quickly as it came.

"That's sweet, Nicky," I say. "I didn't know your dad, but from everything I know about him, I bet he was totally crazy for your mom."

He doesn't answer, already wrapped up in some HBO movie that seems upon quick glance — the actor on screen is snorting cocaine and then punches another guy dead in the nose — completely ill-suited for his age.

"No, my theory of opposites has nothing

to do with you and Shawn. It's this: what if we did exactly opposite of your dad's advice? Like, what if, every time you listened to your instincts, you did the opposite?"

"You know I have terrible instincts."

"I do know that. Which is why you're the perfect person to write this with me." She passes me the cereal box, and I scoop some into my palm. "You're someone who has no baseline, no real gauge of your gut. For which we can firmly blame your dad. But I think. . . . I think it's time you stopped blaming him for everything too."

"I don't blame him. This is just my life."

"God, you're frustrating," Vanessa states, which she's allowed to because she's known me since I was eighteen, and also, because I am.

"I read your dad's book, by the way," Nicky says. "I can't believe how many people believe that shit."

"Don't say 'shit,' Nicky," I say. Then: "You read his book?"

He doesn't reply at first, the action on screen in this terribly inappropriate movie too engaging (several Asian men being shot by a drug lord as he breaks into their compound in Barbados), but after all of the characters are sprawled in pools of their own blood, he says: "Yeah. My therapist

139

thought it might be helpful for me to understand the shit with my dad."

Vanessa chews her cereal.

"Did it help?" I ask.

"What do you think?" he says. "Maybe I'm not dumb enough to believe that stuff though."

"Lots of smart people believe it."

Vanessa rolls her eyes. "Well, I think that the more moronic you are, the easier it is not to question his philosophies."

"Come on. There's a lot of science behind his book." I find a mug that's been left on the counter and fill it with water, programming the microwave to "tea." It beeps and breathes to life.

"There is less science than you think," Vanessa says. "Have you read it recently? *Accept inertia! Follow the Master Plan Way!* Sure, he ran some lab rats in a maze and followed a few sad sack families for a decade or so, but . . . I mean . . . it's hard to argue against the fact that there aren't any accidents, that randomness doesn't exist."

"Because you can't disprove the disprovable," Nicky says. Then grins. "See, I ain't no moron."

Vanessa runs to him and pinches his cheeks.

"You are my little protégé!" she teases him

until he slaps her hands away and pretends to hate her affection. "But Nicky's right, which is where my idea comes in. Your dad's entire book is built on swimming downstream . . . letting life take you wherever you were meant to float."

"Not taking a left when you've already taken a right," Nicky says.

"So let's take lefts. Let me tell you when to turn left," Vanessa adds.

"I . . . don't get it." I really might be the moron here. I can't admit that I never actually read the book in its entirety. There never was much of a point. I lived it. I was there. The words on the pages couldn't tell me anything I didn't already know.

"It's the Theory of Opposites." Vanessa's voice spins up a decibel in excitement. "We'll disprove his own theories of inertia and 'it is what it is' and 'everything happens for a reason' because we will run counter to all of these things. We'll purposely *choose* to live life on the high wire, on the fine line where life actually becomes alive."

I chew on my lower lip. I don't like it when life actually becomes alive. I much prefer it in its safe, happy, comfortable space. I'm goddamn Switzerland, after all!

"I know that you want to say 'no,' " Vanessa says. "Which is exactly why you

141

need to say 'yes.' Start disproving him *now*. Let me dare you. I dare you, Willa Chandler-Golden, to try to live life on the outer edges. To fight so hard against your original instinct, *to change your fate by making choices that you never otherwise would make.*"

"I don't know." I chew on my thumbnail cuticle.

"You never know," she exhales. "Which is why you have to trust that I do. I do know. Come on, Willa, I'm your best friend. Unexpected things are bound to happen when you remove the baseline of predictability. It's the Theory of Opposites. And this is exactly what we'll prove."

"And you don't think my dad accounted for that — this theory?"

"Actually, he didn't. He concentrated on intentional choice, not purposely choosing the opposite of that choice."

"Hmmm," I say.

"That's fucking brilliant," Nicky chimes in.

For once, I don't correct him.

Email from: Raina Chandler-Farley
To: Willa Chandler-Golden; Oliver
    Chandler
Subject: Our Parents

I think that we need to convene to discuss the current mental status, not to mention marital status, of our parents. I suspect that dad is finally having his psychotic break, and that he is taking Mom down with him. Oliver, a quick check of Twitter tells me that you are in New York City — I sent you a tweet, did you not see it? — and while it would have been nice to get a personal hello, I expected nothing else. However, since you are here, and we are all in the same city, perhaps we can meet at the Pain Quot on Madison on Monday for lunch — the office is closed to repair the air-conditioning system. Jeremy will watch the kids. Though they would love to see their uncle, too.

Please let me know.

Raina

RAINA CHANDLER-FARLEY, ESQ
PARTNER
WILLIAMS, RUSSELL AND CHANCE, LLP
EMAIL: RCF@WRC.COM

Email from: Oliver Chandler
To: Willa Chandler-Golden; Raina
 Chandler-Foley
Subject: re: Our Parents

Darling sisters! Namaste! How are your glorious lives treating you these days? I hope with a little touch of beauty and a lot of touches of love. Indeed I am in town attending to some unexpected personal business, and nothing would make me happier than to break bread with the two of you this Monday. I am now a raw food vegan (I cannot wait to tell you what this has done for my physical and mental form!), but I am sure that I can get something at Pain Quot, as a quick search of my Vegan For Life! app gives them three stars and calls them a "friend to the local vegetable." I am staying downtown at the Tribeca Grand, but I will make my way up there by 2 p.m. Save a bench in the sun for me! Namaste!

Email from: Willa Chandler-Golden
To: Raina Chandler-Foley; Oliver
    Chandler
Subject: re: re: Our Parents

Raina — you have Twitter? Why am I always the last to know?

11

Raina and I arrive on time. (Of course.) Oliver, however, does not. (Of course.) I expected Le Pain Quotidian to be empty at 2 p.m. on a Monday, but it seems that there are plenty of other unemployeds out in the world too. I nod at them as I weave through.

Hi, yes, I lost my job too.

Hello there, is the Ellen Show *the highlight of your day as well?*

"Oliver keeps to a world clock," I say to Raina as we settle ourselves at the farmhouse table in the back corner. She rolls her eyes and goes back to typing angrily on her BlackBerry. I peruse the menu and wonder if I'm someone who would enjoy quinoa or just start eating it because it's part of the trend, and then watch Raina for a second. Her Botox has warded off her scowl, but still, her face is pressed downward, her lips tense, her chin drawn. For someone who is one of only three female partners at her firm, she doesn't seem to enjoy her job all that much.

"Do you like your job?"

"Huh?" she answers, still typing.

"Your job? Do you like being a lawyer?"

"What?" She looks at me vaguely. "What? Oh, I don't know. Sure. It's fine."

She returns her attention to her phone.

I order a mint lemonade (it sounds like a healthy match to my quinoa) from the waitress, and Raina asks for a double espresso. Finally, she beats her BlackBerry at its own game and tosses it across the table.

"You would think that we were saving lives or something here," she exclaims.

"Speaking of saving lives!" a voice booms from behind her, and we both look up. The legendary Oliver Chandler, homeopath, vegan, super-yogi to the stars, and current resident of Mumbai, in the flesh. He is practically glowing, literally, like a glistening of sweat is encasing every inch of his skin, but somehow it adds to his handsomeness, like he intuited just the right amount of sheen for the afternoon and his body complied. His brown hair is richer than mine, his eyes darker too. Jesus, he was good at everything.

"You're saving lives these days?" Raina

asks. She stands to hug him.

"Give me an hour with you, my darling sister. Yours will never be the same." He leans over and kisses me, then sits.

"William, no offense, but you look like shit."

"And it's nice to see you too, Ollie."

"Listen, if a brother can't tell a sister when she looks like shit, then the system is broken."

"My husband left me."

"All the more reason for you to look fabulous. There are other fish in the sea."

I think: *Theodore.* And then I regret thinking that because I also want Shawn to throw himself on his knees in front of me and beg to set things right, set them exactly as they were before.

"Oliver," Raina interrupts. "We haven't seen you in over a year. I had to check your Twitter feed to discover that you were in town."

"It was last-minute." He grabs a menu. "I've heard raves about their quinoa salad. Gaga told me I had to order it when I told her we were meeting here."

"Lady Gaga does yoga?" Raina sounds dubious.

I can't decide which I'm more impressed with: that Oliver trains Lady Gaga or that

Raina actually knows who she is.

"Lady Gaga does everything," Oliver says, like we're supposed to know what that means.

"How's India?" I ask, resolving to forget both Theo and Shawn entirely.

"Hot as balls," he answers, waving down the waitress. "But you know, if you build it, they will come."

"I have no idea what that means," Raina says, ordering the tuna salad, no mayo, pesto on the side, and hold the bread too. I order the tuna salad with mayo, with pesto and with bread. The quinoa seemed like a good idea only in theory. Even if endorsed by Lady Gaga.

"The ashram. Did you see that it was written up in *Travel and Leisure* as the number-three yoga retreat in the world?"

"We didn't," Raina says.

"Well, it was," he shrugs. "So I built it. And they came."

"So then why are you here? Shouldn't you be saving souls in a tent filled with incense?" She sniffs. "Or pot? Because don't think for a second that I can't smell the pot right now."

"Raina, sister, I don't understand the hostility," Oliver says in this super-annoying tone that he must reserve for the end of his classes when everyone is all "oooommm," and "inner-peace," and "the light that guides me is the light that guides you." He continues: "And that's not pot. It's patchouli oil. It's good for my digestion. I'll bring some over for Jeremy sometime."

"There's no hostility," she says, though it sounds very much like there's a lot of hostility. "We just don't see you for a year, and William and I are left to deal with things like Mom and Dad taking *lovers,* and it would be very much appreciated if the prodigal baby boy were around to, you know, lend a hand."

"Not figuratively, of course. They have that taken care of." He laughs. Raina's nostrils flare.

"Why is everyone calling me William all of a sudden?"

Raina sighs and pinches her nose, just as her BlackBerry echoes again.

"Christ!" she yelps, then grabs it and walks toward the front of the restaurant while typing.

Oliver and I both fall silent for a moment until I say, "Ollie, really, what are you doing here? It's a little unexpected. And I know, like, I don't follow you on Twitter or anything, but you could have given us a heads-up."

He drops his chin to his chest.

"I know, Willa. Shit, I know."

When he looks up at me, his sheen is gone, his beautiful cheekbones suddenly looking skinnier and less beautiful than just a moment before.

"I'm in a little trouble. Just . . . I mean . . . it's nothing. I mean . . . it's something, but . . . well, don't tell Mom and Dad."

"Tell them what?" Raina says, already done with her mini-crisis. She reaches into her purse and pulls out a prescription bottle, unscrews the cap and pops a pill down the hatch. Then she empties another out into her palm and slides it my way.

"Self-medicating?" Oliver asks.

"No," Raina utters. "It's good for our digestion."

"I make no judgments." The waitress delivers him a hot drink that smells distinctly like a perfect blend of grass and urine. Oliver takes a long sip that appears to stir some sort of nirvana within. "Oh man, Will, have you tried this? It's exactly the cure for your skin right now."

I consider protesting the insult but that's just the family way, so instead I merely shake my head *no.* Also, it really does smell like the inside of a restroom in Central Park.

"Don't deflect, Oliver. What sort of

trouble are you in?" Raina persists. "Everyone else may buy this ridiculous Kama Sutra thing, but don't think you've fooled me."

"I'd be offended if I couldn't just breathe through that. I try to leave each person I connect with just a little better, a little happier, Raina. Can you say the same? Does the light inside of you shine like it shines inside of me?"

"Oh Oliver, cut the crap."

"Fine." His head droops. "Yogi Master Dari asked me to invest in the retreat, then find some other investors, who then had to find other investors . . ." He flickers his hand in a little spiral, as if to indicate . . . and so on. Or maybe it's to indicate that he's crazy. I'm not totally sure.

"A pyramid scheme!" Raina cries. "You're involved in a pyramid scheme!"

"Holy shit," I exclaim, and then reach for the urine drink because I need a drink and my mint lemonade was never delivered.

"It wasn't my fault."

"Of course not," Raina tuts. "In this family, it never is."

As we're leaving Pain, just as I am sliding into my Xanax haze, we run smack into Alan Alverson. He introduces himself to

Raina and Oliver as *Alain.* Naturally, I therefore call him Alan.

"I wish we were on better terms, Willa," he says. Then to Raina and Ollie: "I practically worship your dad. Willa knows. I would just love to be on better terms, to learn more about the man behind the miracle."

"He's not Jesus, you know," I say.

"I wouldn't call it a miracle," Raina adds.

"You guys," Ollie weighs in. "Don't be bitches. Dad's great."

Undeterred, Alan presses on. "Like, I know that it sucks that you got fired and everything, but it's like your dad says — if you hadn't been texting in the meeting and Hannah didn't have a coke problem, and Dependables didn't have totally unreasonable client expectations, and if it hadn't all imploded at the right time, I wouldn't have gotten the promotion. It's all part of the Master Plan Way! I mean . . . it's brilliant!"

"That's very noble of you, Alan."

"Not noble," he says. "Just the facts."

"Hmmm," Raina says.

"Cool dude, I get it," Oliver says. "I roll the same way."

He slaps Alan on the back, like they're comrades, like the little bastard didn't slide right into my job.

"Well, good seeing you, Alan." I step onto the sidewalk, my brain a little foggy, my limbs a little loose.

"Hey, did you hear? Hannah's in rehab."

"Really?" I turn around.

"Yeah, Meadow Air up in Connecticut. Evidently, she was way worse than anyone realized."

"Who's Hannah?" Oliver asks.

"My old boss," I say.

"Meadow Air is a good one," he replies, which seems totally normal coming from him.

"Anyway, you should write her. Or something." Alan makes a face like he doesn't care all that much.

"Have you?"

"Me? No. But we weren't friends. But you should. Everyone makes mistakes, you know."

"I thought no one made mistakes. Isn't that what my dad says?" I remember that sext of her boobs that she sent me, of the false EPT test, of Shawn leaving.

Alan scrunches up his forehead and stares at the sky, contemplating. Then his gaze makes its way back to us, and he shrugs.

"Hell if I know. I just like your dad's book."

12

"What is one thing you hate more than anything else in the world?" Vanessa asks.

It's Friday again, and we are power walking as if nothing has changed, even though everything has. That Shawn hasn't disappeared into the ether, that he and I haven't given up trying for kids, that my parents aren't having some sort of late-in-life sexual crisis, that my brother might not be indicted as the next (not-so-masterful) white-collar mastermind, and that adult diapers didn't ruin my life.

Nicky made it safely to Palo Alto two days ago, and now I've been left to face the utter aloneness of my situation. I wake up to silence; I make my coffee in silence; I check Facebook in silence.

Accept.

Ignore.

Deny.

I still haven't written Theodore back,

though I've googled "testicular cancer" enough to apply for a grant at the AMA.

I offered Oliver our spare bedroom but he grinned — evidently not too, *too* concerned about the FBI investigation into the funding of the Kalumdrali Retreat — and said the Tribeca Grand was comping him. All friends of Jennifer get comped, he said. So I took a stab in the dark and said, "Lopez?" and he said, "Aniston," and Raina said, "Of course."

Nicky emailed yesterday that Palo Alto was "kind of cool," but that there were a lot of people who thought they were really granola who drove Priuses but who also wore Rolexes and fancy yoga clothes all day, and "he found that kind of fucked up." I naturally responded and corrected his language, but he just replied and said, "Aunt Willa, this zipline in Uncle Shawn's office is fucking awesome!" And attached a picture of himself hanging ten while soaring over Wired2Go's open floor plan.

I didn't write back and rebuke him because I'm not the kid's mother, after all.

"Hello, are you listening to me?" Vanessa asks, as we stop at the crosswalk on Central Park West. It's a grim late June day in the city. All low clouds and gray lines, the humidity swaddling the hurried New Yorkers as they scatter every which way. But I didn't have anywhere to hurry to, no one to hurry with.

A red-faced toddler marches up next to me and punches my calf.

"Ow!"

I look down and see him, unrepentant. He narrows his eyes, like I've done something in his short, miniature life to offend him.

"Sorry," his mom half-heartedly apologizes. "You know how it is."

The light turns, and just before we step forward, the boy slugs me again.

"Jasper!" the mom reluctantly reprimands him as Vanessa and I leave them behind.

I glance back, just before we enter the park and see little Jasper screaming on the corner, his mother pulling him in for a hug. *Motherhood is complicated,* I decide. You can tell a kid not to use "fuck" all you want, but that doesn't mean it will change anything, that he'll actually listen.

"Seriously, Will, hello! Have you heard anything I've said? This is important." Vanessa is now a half-step ahead of me, her ponytail swooshing through the air to match her stride.

"What? No. I'm sorry."

She stops suddenly, and I lean over and

massage my calf.

"Willa, I'm serious: are you committed?"

I want to say: Committed? To what? Meadow Air? Can they find a spot for me? A nice bed to lie down on and sleep for a hundred years?

"To the book?" I ask instead.

"Yes, to the book. To embracing the 'theory of opposites.' To running counter to your dad's ideas. To daring yourself to run counter to them in the first place."

"I am," I answer, though I don't think either of us really believes it.

"So what is the one thing you hate more than anything in the whole world?" She resumes her pace.

"Pâté. I find pâté to be truly revolting. Also, recently, sea bass. Bad associations with sexual imagery of my parents."

Vanessa halts again, rests her hands on her waist and dips her chin to her chest.

"This is going to be much harder than I thought."

"What? You asked! I really, really hate pâté! And sea bass!"

"I had something else in mind." She squints toward the sun, the light reflecting off her cheeks like she's some sort of goddess. "Pack your bags. Be ready in the morning."

"Disney World? Because I've been surprised with that before. It's less great than you'd think."

"No." She shakes her head but smiles. "Come on, this book has nothing to do with fairy tales."

EXCERPT:
New York Times bestseller, *Is It Really Your Choice? Why Your Entire Life May Be Out of Your Control*

TABLE OF CONTENTS
SECTION ONE: EMBRACE THE MASTER UNIVERSE WAY

Summary: Throughout the book, you will hear me refer to what I call the Master Universe Way. Others will choose to call this "God's plan," or perhaps "divine intervention," or simply, "that what will be will be." Please know that while my preferred term is MUW, and should you choose to sign up for our online course — Master the Master Universe Way! — that you will be asked to use our preferred phrasing, any name or title or moniker that you choose to give this phenomenon of "God's plan" while reading this book is a-okay with me.

SECTION TWO: ACCEPT INERTIA

Summary: Do not swim upstream! Life already knows where you are headed. Do not fight the feeling of being pulled in the direction to which you are meant. No good can come of this. Only heartbreak and failure come from jumping off a cliff. (And smattered innards too!)

SECTION THREE: CLOSE YOUR EYES AND FOLLOW THE MAP

Summary: Once you have accepted that you can embrace inertia, that you can be pulled wherever life pulls you, merely close your eyes, and your perspective will change — your senses will be heightened, you'll no longer be afraid of the figurative dark! Once you stop fighting change, change will find you. You will feel calmer! More peaceful! As if you are being carried by both the stream and the wind, and you will land wherever these forces of nature deem fit. Let the map of life carry you . . . there is no need to get caught up in life's confusing (and useless) detours!

SECTION FOUR: BE WHAT YOU ALREADY ARE

Summary: We are who we are. The saying is true. I don't mean to imply that humans aren't capable of evolution, because we learn to outgrow diapers, and eventually we don't throw our food at the wall if we are displeased with it (though I have a few colleagues who do that too, dear readers!), but getting older should not be confused with getting wiser, and my research has shown me that who we are when we are born is more or less who we are when we die. All of which is an eloquent way of saying, I'm sorry to tell you that your stubborn mother-in-law will never change.

SECTION FIVE: SET YOURSELF FREE

Summary: No summary can be provided because no shortcuts are allowed on the road to self-freedom. Read the rest of the book (and of course, buy the workbook and corresponding CD set) to liberate your own true self!

"This is where we start," Vanessa says, pointing to the table of contents of my father's book that night. "This is where we run counter to his advice, where I dare you to try something different."

"Do I get to dare you to do anything? Because this seems a little unfair." I chew on the inside of my cheek and think: *this is more than a little unfair!*

"How do you run counter to ideas like 'setting yourself free'?" Oliver asks. "Don't get me wrong: I think it's brilliant, but . . . impossible."

Oliver has begrudgingly agreed to apartment-sit while Vanessa and I are away — she has booked two tickets to Seattle in the morning. Though he's also agreed to stay only if I allow him to rearrange the rooms to make them more in line with his feng shui. He adjusts an armchair in the living room, shifting it toward the window.

I flip through the delivery menus rather than argue with him. He's right: it's not the dumbest idea in the world — *set yourself free!* Who can argue with that? It's easy to see why so many millions embraced the book. Why Shawn cited it the day he left me. *Don't do anything — no hard work required! — and you'll be happier.* Yeah, sign me up too.

Oliver squeaks the armchair another twenty degrees left, the noise like nails on a chalkboard. He steps back and angles his head, then clicks his tongue in approval.

"What do you guys know about Mark Zuckerberg's wife?"

"Genius," Oliver says.

"Helpful," I say back.

"I know someone who knew her at Stanford. Why?"

"Just curious." I shuffle the menus. I can't

come out and say: "Shawn was tagged in a photo with her yesterday on Facebook," because I'm not supposed to be stalking Shawn's Facebook. But he was tagged with her, and so rather than stalking him, I googled her.

What would Mark Zuckerberg's wife order for dinner?

"Anyway, can we get back to what I was saying?" Vanessa interrupts. She grabs the Indian menu out of my left hand. "There, decision made."

Oliver tuts. "No way. I'm not having Indian, not after having authentic Indian."

Vanessa says, "Oliver, do you ever know how big of a jackass you sound like?"

He breathes in and breathes out before answering.

"Vanessa, I'm so sorry that you must be so angry inside that you feel the need to take out that anger on others. Also, for your information, I am currently being investigated by the FBI, and I'd rather not eat Indian food, which brings back so many memories of my time in India, for which I am now being unjustly prosecuted."

"What?" Vanessa says.

"The pyramid scheme. I only did it because my mentor asked me to invest! And told me that if I found four other people to invest, I'd make back $100,000! Which I'd planned to donate to Greenpeace, so it's not like the money wasn't going to a good cause. The Kalumdrali Retreat was named the third-best retreat in the world by *Travel and Leisure*! People were healed there. *People were saved there.*"

Oliver sits down in the feng shui-ed armchair triumphantly, but then withers just a bit.

"So, like, can I just order a pizza or something?" I ask.

"Anyway." Vanessa pivots toward me. "We're going to construct our book around your dad's table of contents. Instead of embracing inertia, we're going to resist it. Like that. The *theory of opposites*!"

She nudges the book across the counter to me. I skim it and bounce my shoulders.

"Whatever. Sounds good. I don't know."

She laughs, but then presses her thumbs into her temples.

"I swear to God, Willa, if you don't know *something* by the time we're done here, then maybe your dad will actually be proven right."

13

The first thing you see when flying into Seattle is mountains. Miles of snow-capped mountains, which then give way to meandering, lovely, lingering bodies of water, greenery for miles, and what looks like, even from above, a perfect landscape of a city. They call it the Emerald City, and it's easy to see why. Flying in, I felt a little bit like I was careening toward Oz.

"Remind me again." I clench Vanessa's forearm as we hit a violent pocket of air. "Why Seattle?"

"Because you haven't left New York in almost four years," Vanessa says.

"That's not true," I reply. That can't be true. Is that true? Shawn and I honeymooned in Hawaii. And then what? The air calms, and I feel my pulse slow, and I try to recall what other adventures I've tripped down since marrying Shawn. Finally, I remember. "We went to D.C. for that conference Shawn had."

"D.C. doesn't count. D.C. is an extension of New York, just with political junkies, not finance junkies."

"Fine," I say. "But still. Why *Seattle?*"

I want her to say it — *because of Theo* — but she shakes her head and offers something murkier: "Because if you'd been more daring, you'd have moved here in another life, in your other life. Maybe in your new life."

I'd never move to Seattle, I think. *It's too green. And there's so much coffee! And recycling! And . . . plaid!* At least, I think Seattle's all of these things. I really only know what I know from *Grey's Anatomy.* And from googling it. I've never been here, but it's not like I haven't googled it, haven't googled Theodore and wondered where he goes, what he does, what sort of company he keeps. (In fact, I googled him last night to see if our paths might cross, but the AP informed me he's in New Orleans working with the Saints on a sexual harassment lawsuit.)

He asked me to move with him from New York when he founded Y.E.S. — he thought that Seattle, with its up-and-coming tech community and its (arguably) better quality of life (if you like mountain climbing or bike

165

riding or boating or green markets or skiing or general outdoor healthful activities, which I do not), proved too good to pass up. But I was twenty-four and didn't trust myself. Seattle was too daunting, too far from my parents, too far from everything.

Theodore and I met the day after I graduated from college. Vanessa and I were unloading our station wagon, dragging our boxes and our books and our Doc Martens and our half-drunk bottles of tequila (because college students would rather pack that than throw it out) up four stories to our walk-up on the Upper East Side, and he stopped to offer to help. It was sort of a self-serving offer since he lived in the apartment below us, and it was only in his best interest to get us in as quickly as possible, but still. He cruised up the sidewalk on his street bike, slung the bike over his shoulder, and grabbed a laundry bag stuffed full of dirty clothes in his free hand. "Come on," he said. "Let me."

I liked him immediately, so when he invited us over for dinner that night, Vanessa begged off and insisted I go. He made gourmet omelets from a cookbook, which I thought was sort of charming, until they landed me in the hospital because he infused them with truffle oil, and I am actually one of the five people on the planet with a truffle allergy.

But I think about that sometimes: how he rushed me to the ER when my lips blew up; how he calmed me without really knowing me when my breathing grew labored; how he didn't even find me totally repulsive when my face developed a rash that can only be described as resembling the inside of a pomegranate. I think about it sometimes and consider that if he hadn't made me an omelet, if he'd chosen spaghetti or warmed-up soup or thrown a steak in the broiler, and if he hadn't dotted it with truffle oil, how I'd never have ended up in the ER and never fallen in love with him, right then, right there, with my lips the size of bananas, with my face dotted with a modern-day plague.

He sat with me in the ER and said:

"Maybe this is fate."

And I said: "You believe in fate?"

And he said: "Actually, I don't."

So I said: "Hmmm."

And he said: "But I do believe in truffle-infused omelets."

And I laughed (even with my banana lips) and said: "You're a jerk."

And he laughed and said: "Yeah, but you like me anyway."

And then, three years later, he moved to Seattle. Got funding for Y.E.S., and asked me to take the leap with him. But Theodore was big and brave and daring in ways I never could be. In three years, I'd never ridden a bike with him ("What if a taxi sideswipes me?"), never learned to cook because I could just as easily order in, never considered that saying "yes" could actually change anything, even though he built his entire life around it. So he asked me, and I did what I always did: I stayed the course, and he, knowing me too well, I suppose, didn't fight it. He left, and then I met Shawn two years later on Match.com, and then Theo got engaged, and then he lost a testicle and found me on Facebook.

And now here we are. In Seattle, where maybe fate has meant to bring us all along.

I stare out the rental car window.

"Are you ready for this?" Vanessa breaks the silence.

"For what?"

"To start scaling mountains."

"You're speaking figuratively, right? Because you know how much I hate the mountains."

She presses her foot to the gas. "Which is exactly why we're going up."

Email from: Richard Chandler
To: Willa Chandler
Subject: This book

Willa — I will get straight to the point. I have heard whispers (actually, Lana, my agent, has) that you are somehow involved in a book project that is intended to disprove my world-renowned theories and conclusions. Even worse, it is evidently tied to a REALITY SHOW!?!? Can this be true? Surely, it cannot be! Need I remind you that I was approached for a reality show by Simon Cowell, and that I turned it down after heated contract negotiations because reality shows are (I determined) the lowest common denominator in our society?

I assured Lana that she must be mistaken, that no child of mine, however doubtful, would seek out a reality show, much less set out to prove my theories incorrect. (Amended: Raina might perhaps, but not you, not you, William!) Anyway, if I am somehow wrong and you have plans to publicly publicize your issues with my theories, please take a moment and consider the harm this will bring me and our family. Perhaps this email is unnecessary, since I know that in the end, what will be will be, and of course you wouldn't put such a blight on my reputation (did I mention that CNN has asked me to be a full-time contributor! I am very excited — also Cowell has reapproached Lana with a much more lucrative offer, so we shall see), but I wanted to go on record all the same.

Your mother has retreated to Palm Beach for a few weeks, and I remain in New York City. I have recently joined Match.com, which I am finding so very fascinating! I think there could be an entire dating book devoted to the inevitability of finding one's spouse online. Would you be willing to contribute to it? The bounty of electronic dating is so plentiful! I find that my cup runneth over with prospects.

Your father,
Richard Chandler
RICHARD CHANDLER
AUTHOR OF THE #1 *NEW YORK TIMES* BESTSELLER, *IS IT REALLY YOUR CHOICE? WHY YOUR ENTIRE LIFE MAY BE OUT OF YOUR CONTROL*
AGENT: LANA DELANEY,
CREATIVE ARTISTS AGENCY
EMAIL:
LIFESPLAN@ISITREALLYYOURCHOICE.COM

■ ■ ■ ■

The *Dare You!* producers have put us up at a quaint, homey hotel that overlooks the Puget Sound. We arrive just in time to see the sun begin its descent below the mountainous horizon in the distance, and it's as remarkable as anything I've ever seen — orange and ruby and breathtaking and magical and ethereal and perfect. The sun rises and sets every day. We go round and round every day. We walk the same path, the same destiny every day.

Vanessa and I stand silent in the window, as the sun dips, then dips lower, then lower still below the jagged peaks of terrain, and I wonder just how impossible it is to change that — that path, that destiny, if it can even be changed at all. Even though I'm here, in Seattle, not there, stuck in New York, where I was a day ago, or a week ago, or a month ago . . . how hard must one have to work to shift the pieces in her fate?

"I hope you're not doing what I think you're doing," Vanessa says later, when she emerges from the shower, with a white robe wrapped tight and a towel like a turban around her head.

I shutter my laptop quickly. "I don't know

what it is that you think I'm doing, so I can't say."

"You're looking at Shawn's Facebook page."

I stare at my toes.

"The blue reflection on your face gave you away."

"I could have been looking at anyone's page."

"But you weren't."

"He's my husband. Did you know he knows the Zuckerbergs?"

"I don't care who he knows. You're on a break."

"Well, I could have been looking at Theo's," I say, as if that would have been any better. Ex-boyfriend, on-a-break husband. Really, it's splitting hairs here, in terms of google-stalking.

"Well, you *could have* been looking at Theo's, but you didn't reply to his email. So if you're looking at Theo's page and wondering if you should reply, then you should actually . . . you know . . . do something about it. *Resist inertia.*"

I sigh and collapse on the bed, pulling the pillow over my head.

"Look, can I just say something?" she asks.

"Go ahead," I answer from underneath the pillow.

"I know that Shawn's leaving gutted you."

"It did," I say, my voice muffled.

"But did it really?"

I sit up quickly.

"Of course it did!"

"Okay."

"Shawn and I did everything together!"

"Uh-hum."

"What?"

"That's a reason to miss someone, to be sure. That's not a reason to be married to someone."

"What the hell, Vanessa? Just because I don't, like, sit here and sob into my figurative Cheerios, that doesn't mean I'm not gutted." I sit up straighter. "He's my husband. He's basically my whole life. I pretty much counted on the fact that he was my meant-to-be."

"Maybe you counted wrong." She says this quietly, and if I listen closely enough, I can hear the devastation that the words imply.

Instead, I lean back against the headboard, and she moves next to me, shifting the computer to her own lap.

"We're just on a break," I say. "In August, everything could be different."

"You're right," she said. "But only if you open your eyes and write your own map instead of following it."

"Step three in my dad's table of contents. I get it. You don't have to feed me the self-help stuff. And when I said 'different,' I meant that maybe Shawn will reconsider."

"I knew what you meant." She scoops the laptop off the bed and rests it on the desk, out of my clutches. "But my point is that if *you* chart your own course, maybe you'll be the one who reconsiders first."

Bookmarked Favorites
Facebook/Login
Shawn Golden
Friends: 2254
City: Palo Alto
Occupation: Taking over the world!
Relationship status: Married
Religion: HTML

Shawn was at Chipotle Mexican Grill *(21 mins ago)*
(me: great, he's putting on weight!)

Shawn listened to Arcade Fire on Erica Stoppard's Spotify list *(3 hrs ago)*
(me: Arcade Fire? He doesn't like hipster music! And who is Erica Stoppard?)

Shawn changed his hometown from New

York City to Palo Alto *(1 day ago)*
(me: only temporarily, and that sort of violates the rules of our agreement!)

Erica Stoppard to Shawn Golden (2 days ago): S, it was so cool to meet the god of coding at The Wine Room last night!!! Don't be a stranger! Thanks for the friend request! So glad Cilla Z introduced us! *(me: WTF?)*

Shawn Golden is now friends with Erica Stoppard and James Pichard.

Shawn logged into JDate.com: The Place for Jewish Singles.
(4 days ago.)
(me: shit.)

Google.com/search
Search terms: Erica Stoppard

14

DARING YOURSELF TO A BETTER LIFE!
By Vanessa Pines and Willa Chandler
PART ONE: REVISING YOUR MASTER
UNIVERSE WAY

Welcome readers! We are so glad to have you along for our journey, our journey of dares, our journey of how we changed our own lives! We know that bookstores are littered with self-help books, and we're not going to make you promises (like they may) that by merely reading this, everything will change. No. Nothing is that simple. This isn't the quick fix. For the quick fix, we'll direct you to the book we are arguing against: Dr. Richard Chandler's *Is It Really Your Choice? Why Your Entire Life May Be Out of Your Control.* Why yes, we really did go and mention the competition. Why? Because we want you along for the ride only if you are *with* us. It is that type of book. You'll be dared to make hard choices. You'll be dared to reconsider old truths. You'll be dared to make yourself uncomfortable and maybe even temporarily unhappy. And if you're not interested in being this sort of daring, by all means, set the book down now and pick up Chandler's, which is on the display case at the front of the store (for those of you browsing at Barnes & Noble, not just downloading the sample Kindle chapter, unsure of making the commitment).

But if you stick with us, we will change your life. Chandler will tell you that you cannot change your life. But he's wrong. If you are daring enough to turn left when you always imagined you would turn right, if you swing for the fences when you'd much rather sit on the sidelines, if you *do the opposite of your own low expectations*, then you will change your Master Universe Way. Or as we prefer to call it, your master plan. Or how about, just . . . life? Destiny isn't something that just happens, as Chandler would argue. Destiny or fate or whatever is meant to be is something that you steer yourself.

Don't believe us? In the ensuing chapters, read about how we changed our own lives, and then come back here, to the bookstore, in this aisle, or log back into your Kindle, and dare to pick up the book and start a journey of your own.

Vanessa wakes me up early, too early, even though I am still on New York time. I haven't slept well, haunted by the notion of Shawn skulking around JDate, and skulking around Erica Stoppard, who has a remarkably light Google footprint, despite my better efforts at prying. I pieced together a few facts: that she may or may not have been from Chicago; that she may or may not have been a tech reporter of some sort, but even that proved thin — a byline here and there, nothing conclusive. She appreciated hipster photos — with odd lighting and skewed perspectives — as profile pictures, and thus I couldn't even assess if I'm prettier than she is. And she is friends with Cilla Z, who I have used my detective skills to identify as Priscilla Zuckerberg, Mark's wife. Well, great.

I marinated in all of this quasi-info through the night, sleep coming in fits and starts. I finally fell into a deep sleep at around 2 a.m., but was shaken from it shortly thereafter with a dream of Erica Stoppard, who was dressed as a tragic Brooklyn hipster — a half-skewed beanie atop her head, a worn peasant shirt draping her lithe torso, a wrist covered in prayer beads, a knitted scarf swirling around her neck — slowly smothering me to death with my pillow.

"It's six-thirty," Vanessa says, shaking my shoulders. "Get up. Come on, we have to go."

"It's six-thirty!" I mumble. "Who needs to be anywhere?"

"We're due on the mountain." I can hear her shuffling into her sneakers.

My stomach coils, and I pull my knees into my chest. I've had a near-paralyzing hatred of snow-capped peaks since childhood — ever since my parents took us on a day hike in the Alps when I was eight, and I wandered off and lost my way and couldn't read my map because it was in French. I cried for three hours on the path because I was convinced that my dad would leave me there "because this is what the universe dictated." Finally, a kind German couple wearing lederhosen walked me down and reunited me with my parents under the gondola. I was safe, and I had been found, true. But at eight, you don't forget that feeling of abandonment, that disorientation and the worry that your parents might not be out there searching for you anyway. That you might be the only one who was frantic. Even today, tucked under the duvet in my haven of a hotel room overlooking the Puget Sound, I can feel the panic weighing in my chest, the confusion, the total sense of loss that my eight-year-old self felt.

"Come on." Vanessa throws a pillow at my head. "My first dare for you: crack the code in the Master Universe Way."

"I don't really see how me climbing a mountain has anything to do with the MUW."

"Please don't call it *MUW*," she replies. "A) That sounds like some sort of noise a French cow would make. And b) you will. You will see exactly how climbing mountains has to do with the Master Universe Way." She retreats to the bathroom, the latch clicking.

I debate disobeying her and refusing to relinquish the comfort of the Egyptian cotton sheets, but there's no point in arguing with Vanessa. There never was, and to be honest, her hard lines and assuredness were a bit of a relief for someone like me, all grey, all middle ground, all soft edges.

As if she can discern my thoughts, she bellows from the bathroom:

"Listen, Willa! We have a contract with Random House and the *Dare You!* team, and I have a plan. This is my job, and frankly, you could use the distraction, not to mention the free therapy that this project is providing, so get your ass in gear."

She's not wrong, so I do.

The rush-hour traffic is grueling. For a city so intent on clean living, you'd think more people would walk the walk (figuratively) and carpool. A few really determined bikers whiz by, all spandex and neon and wind, but mostly it's just a crush of cars, everyone staring down at their phones, texting or tweeting or emailing, as we crawl forward.

"I really don't want to do this," I grumble as we accelerate through the sloth and turn south on the bend in the highway.

"What would you rather be doing?"

"I don't know."

"That's the entire point," she answers, and then we both fall silent as Mount Rainier unfolds in front of us, its majesty demanding silence, its expansiveness — the crystal blue sky, the white-capped peak, the wisp of clouds floating atop — demanding respect. For a moment, we just absorb and acknowledge its beauty, accepting the fact that this world is pretty damn magical, that its magnificence can still surprise us. It's easy to forget that. Especially when you've had a few weeks like mine.

"I still don't get what climbing a mountain has to do with proving my dad wrong," I say about thirty minutes later when the radio signals have faltered and we only have AM news to keep us company. "I hate hiking. I've told you that a thousand times. I hate mountains too. They're cold, and they are not meant to be scaled. Do you know how many people die every year mountain climbing?"

"Do you?"

"Well, no. But that's not the point."

"The Master Universe Way is, as your dad calls it, 'God's Plan.' Has it ever occurred to you that the fear that was planted in you at eight — the fear of mountains — is a fear of much more than that? That it's a metaphor? And that you've allowed this fear to become, well, your own Master Universe Way for your life?"

"Whoa." I flex both hands in the air. "That's too much for this hour. I was only eight. It was just a mountain."

We pull alongside a minivan with the bumper sticker MOMS FOR MARI-JUANA.

"And yet you've never gone back up one." She clicks down the blinker to shift lanes. "And I'm not a shrink, but I think that this could be a pretty good metaphor."

"So you think I'm unconsciously blaming my entire life on my eight-year-old self?"

Rather than answer, she accelerates, changes lanes, and gives marijuana mom the finger as we fly by.

It's nearly ten when we finally pull into the state park. There are trailers and caravans in the parking lot, hikers and families and more than a few leftover hippies who look very much in need of a shower. They're all consulting their maps, packing up their GORP. One particularly beleaguered mom is wiping down her son's face with a Wet-Nap while he tries to shimmy away and yells, "Gross! Stop! Disgusting!"

Vanessa eases the car to a halt, and I snap off my seat belt. She refused to stop along the way, insisting that we be here by ten to get in the full hike. My brow and palms are already sweaty with nerves, my stomach is flip-flopping with disgust. *Why did I let her talk me into this? Who cares if I undo my Master Universe Way/Plan? The MUW is a stupid fucking premise to begin with! Who doesn't know that?* If I didn't have to pee so badly, I'd never leave the car.

But nature calls. "I have to find a bathroom. Back in five."

I slam the door and run, and if Vanessa answers, I don't hear her. I find a fairly horrifying bathroom just left of the ranger's station. It has no soap, a shred of toilet paper, and a foggy mirror, in which I make out an exhausted, disheveled version of my face. I can't believe I look like this. Have I always looked like this? Why hasn't Vanessa said something? *I dare you to use better moisturizer!*

I pull my hair back into a braid but mostly decide to forgo vanity because we're just hiking, and it's not as if I'll run into Shawn. Or anything. I dare myself not to care, which, if I really considered it, wasn't too much of a dare because I'm not sure how much I cared in the first place. My ragged face in the mirror serves as exhibit A.

And exhibit A is exactly why my heart stops — literally stops — when I stumble out of the bathroom and I see him standing by the car, talking to Vanessa as if nothing has happened, nothing has changed.

Not Shawn, of course. He's too busy listening to indie bands with Erica Stoppard and breaking bread with the Zuckerbergs.

No, it's Theodore.

He was supposed to be in New Orleans! I never would have agreed to Seattle if he hadn't been in New Orleans!

He turns and sees me, and my instinct is to run. But the adrenaline is too much in my legs, too much for my brain, so instead, I am stuck, paralyzed, too shell-shocked to do anything. He waves, and I must wave back. Because then Vanessa shouts:

"See? This is what I mean. The theory of opposites! Reorganizing the Master Universe Way! You couldn't do it, so I did."

Finally, I start breathing again. And then my brain starts working again. And next, naturally, the first thing I do is flee. Straight up the hill, straight past the ranger's station, straight by a family with four kids who are in better shape than I am. I can hear Vanessa yelling:

"Wait! Stop!"

And then one of the kids from the family in my wake starts yelling over and over again: "Wait! Stop!"

And then everyone on the trail turns to look at me.

But no matter. I keep hauling uphill for a good two minutes more until I am certain I'm going to puke. There's a reason that Shawn and I quit jogging on Sundays.

I stick my hands on my knees, my head between my thighs. *At least I got a jump on them, at least I'll have a few minutes to formulate a plan,* I think. To tell Vanessa that she had *no right!* to meddle like this, even if I did agree to let her meddle but not *with this!*; to tell Theo that maybe he should take a goddamn hint and that when someone doesn't accept your friend request, maybe it's because she doesn't want to be *friends.*

But before I can figure out a way to resolve any of these questions, a pair of orange Nikes present themselves on the ground in front of me.

"Hey," he says from above.

I gnaw on my lip and wish that I'd gotten more sleep, taken the time to maybe brush my hair, adjust my braid so it wasn't tilted to the left side of my head.

"I thought I had at least five minutes on you."

"I'm used to you running," Theo offers. "So I was ready."

"You're supposed to be in New Orleans," I say, once I have wearily made my way upright.

"Vanessa called, so I came home."

"Just like that."

"Why should it be any more complicated?" he says.

"Things usually are." *Why is my life so*

goddamn complicated?

"Only if you make them more complicated," he says. "At least, that's what I've
found."

"Well . . . emailing your ex-girlfriend on
Facebook to tell her about your revelation
due to your testicular diagnosis tends to
complicate things."

"Touché." He smiles.

"Whatever."

"Vanessa said you wouldn't write me back
but that you wanted to." He gazes across
the landscape for a beat, then half-laughs.
"God, that sounds so trite now that I say it
out loud. I'd never tell my clients to hedge
their bets on advice like that."

"So I'm a bet?"

He waits a long time to answer. Then,
finally, he shrugs and responds:

"No. But I think we'd both agree that
you're a bit of a gamble."

Mount Rainier is an active volcano, though
it hasn't exploded in over 150 years. There
are over twenty-six glaciers and thirty-six
square miles of permanent snowfields, and
on clear days, the mountain can be seen
from as far away as Portland.

I learn all of this when I get stuck behind
the family of six again; after my initial explo-

sion of adrenaline that allowed me to flee and gave me the courage to forge small talk with Theo, I've gone soft and have slowed to what can only be described as an embarrassment of a tortoise's pace, red-faced, huffy, sweat dripping down the backs of my ears. I'm too angry to speak with Vanessa, and too discombobulated to speak further with Theodore, so I've let them set the pace in front of me as we ascend a 7.2-mile trail on which I have at least a 50-50 chance of dying from cardiac arrest.

The mom of the family is cute, perky, and has more patience with the four children than I ever had with Alan Alverson, much less my own (imaginary) offspring. We reach a plateau on the peak, and the mom tucks the brochure from which she was reading into her fanny pack, which I very much covet right now. Blisters have formed on both of my big toes, and I might slay a man on the mountain for some moleskin. Why hadn't I thought to bring a fanny pack? Be prepared! Why wasn't I ever a Girl Scout? Why hadn't my parents made me be a Girl Scout? Add that to my list of grievances: *Girl Scouts. Things could have all been so different.*

"Come on, family picture!" the dad of the family booms, and then looks around to find

188

a passerby to snap it. I avert my eyes, but he must not intuit that I am in the middle of a life crisis, and he beckons me over.

"Sure," I beam. "Happy to! Everyone smile!"

The kids fidget and make weird faces, but the parents manage perfect grins, even while clenching their cheeks and imploring the children to *please just hold still for one moment! Owen, I swear, if you don't smile normally, you will not get that Tootsie Pop I promised!*

I take two pictures just to be nice.

"I bet this thing is going to explode any day now," Owen says to me afterward, gesturing to the mountain, apropos of nothing, as if we're old friends, like he should talk to strangers.

"Oh, I doubt that."

"Doubt it all you want. But you can't keep something in forever. Like, eventually — *BOOM!* — it has to erupt."

"Oh, I don't know," I deflect, trying to make my exit, though I'm really in no rush to catch Theo and Vanessa.

"Please, lady, this thing is going to kaboom. Everything does eventually. The only thing you can do is hope that when it does, you're no place near it."

I nod my head and start running again.

He may actually be right — what do I know? — and I've never been one to place myself in the eye of disaster.

A good hour later, Owen passes me for the second or third time. I'm hunched against the railing, willing my insides to calm the hell down, the cramp in my side having evolved into a tornado of spasms. My lungs are on fire, my cheeks are sunburned and my big toes would be less painful if they were actually surgically removed. Right at the moment when I am thinking that death would be a more welcome reprieve than hiking the remaining two miles, Owen rolls past and yells:

"Come on, lady! You can't be that old!"

But I am that old. I'm thirty-two years old! And my husband no longer loves me! And I am barren and childless! And I lost my job because I can't think of a decent campaign for adult diapers. And my father has taken a lover.

So that's it. I quit.

"Tell my friends they can find my rotting carcass here on this rock!" I yell back to him. There's a rather pitiful-looking boulder to my left, and I pitifully join it.

"Suit yourself!" he shouts over his shoulder, already around the bend.

I will suit myself, I think, though I have no idea what this means. That's the sticky part about the weight of my dad's psychology: what's the point of suiting yourself, of being yourself, of honoring what you want out of life when it's all leading to a certain inevitability that's entirely out of your control? The Master Universe Way! You can't outrun God's plan because . . . it's God's plan, for God's sake! So why not embrace it? Love it? Enjoy it?

I stare out onto the horizon. Shawn is out there somewhere, and he's suiting himself.

I nudge the dirt with my toe and check my phone, like maybe Shawn's reconsidered and has emailed, but I don't have cell service up here in the thin air, which figures. I start typing a note to Nicky anyway — maybe he'll tell Shawn that I'm in Seattle, and Shawn will remember that Theo lives here and be driven mad with jealousy — but then I realize that Shawn has never been jealous of anyone because why would he be, and besides, I don't think he even remembers that I dated Theo. I once saw an article in the Sunday *Times* about him, and I casually slid it over to Shawn's side of the table while we were eating our eggs. Shawn scanned the piece and bounced his shoulders and said, "Eh, I sort of think that guy's thing is a gimmick. Like, if you need someone to tell you how to say yes or no to something, how smart could you be?"

I just slid the paper right back next to my placemat, and didn't say: *he used to tell me how to say yes or no to everything all the time.*

The sun is so goddamn bright up here on this godforsaken mountain. I thought it always rained in Seattle. *Why isn't it raining today in Seattle?*

I shield my face with my hand as Owen's mom makes her way into my sight line, then kneels down and offers me some GORP.

I wave her off. "I'm okay."

"Are you sure? You don't look so great."

I nod, so she stands and takes in the view, which I'd like to appreciate if I weren't in such agony.

"Well, this gives you perspective," she says, exhaling. Then she adds, "I'm sorry Owen has such a smart mouth."

"No worries."

She hands me some Wet-Naps, as if this is an apology for her nine-year-old's rebellion, and zips up her fanny pack.

"You know how kids are," she says, starting on her way.

Why does everyone keep saying that? Like I should know how kids are?

"Sure," I say because that's what you reply

to statements like this.

I don't know how kids are! I know how Nicky is, I guess. But he never really had a chance at normal. So I only know how *he* is, which is decidedly screwed because that's what happens when your dad is obliterated into dust in a terrorist attack while you're still gestating in the safety of your mother's womb.

I stretch my neck to the side and wonder if maybe all of my negative pregnancy tests were actually the universe's way of telling me that my husband was going to leave me, and that being a parent (now? ever?) really wasn't the best idea in the world. Maybe this was God's plan, the Master Universe Way. I close my eyes and wish that I had the muscle strength to catch up to Vanessa who would tell me that I'm an idiot for thinking this.

I check my phone again, but it's working no better than it was thirty seconds earlier, so I tuck it into my back pocket and chew on some almonds and yogurt-covered raisins, which have partially melted and aren't as good as I anticipated. I spit one out and think about Nicky. I wonder how he is staying busy with Shawn, hoping that Shawn has some downtime to nurture him, though I know that for all of Shawn's faults, his loyalty toward his nephew should never be questioned. And then I realize that I've never really thought of Shawn's faults. That until recently — with his stupid leather jacket and his rediscovered use of mousse and his oppressive need to "find himself" — I never found much fault in him at all. He was loving (if recently distant), he was sexy (though lately has been too tired for sex), he was cerebral (if bordering on snobby).

I slip my phone back into my palm and start typing:

SHAWN'S FAULTS:
1. Bedroom could use spicing up.
2. Not spontaneous. (See: eggs every Sunday.)
3. Loves coding more than he loves humans.
4. Newly-discovered sense of terrible fashion. (Leather jacket???)

It wasn't much, but it was something. A slow chip into Shilla. He was a good man, my husband — this short list of faults was proof. Most wives could offer a list of twenty things that annoyed them about their husbands. But I had only four. Five if you counted the mousse. Six if you counted his new use of "dude."

My back starts to ache from sitting on the boulder, so I ease to the ground, which really doesn't help. I pull off my sneaker, then my sock, and examine the gargantuan blister that appears to have eaten the entirety of my big toe. *A metaphor,* I think, though I know I'm being dramatic. One minute your toe is perfectly fine, the next, it's drowning in anguish. All because of a little friction. Shawn and I never had friction. Obvious case in point: I'd never even considered his list of faults until stranded on the middle of Mount Rainier with my best friend and ex-boyfriend two miles ahead of me, with only Wet-Naps and GORP for survival.

Raina once told me that she thought there was something seriously wrong with us because Shawn and I never argued.

"You're avoiding something," she said over sushi one night two years ago. "Healthy couples disagree on things."

"Says your therapist?" I reached over and took one of her spicy tuna rolls.

"Well. . . . yes! Says my therapist. But that doesn't make it less true. And PS, I don't think it's the worst idea in the world if you make an appointment too."

I lean forward and try to pop the blister

with my fingernail. It just puffs up like a balloon and then throbs more painfully to let me know that it's angry. I rest my head back against the boulder, the sun charring my cheeks. I should have worn a hat. I should have remembered sunscreen. I should have invested in better sneakers. I should have joined the Girl Scouts. I should have told Vanessa that no good can come from climbing a stupid mountain. I should have fought harder for Shawn. Or Theo.

This last thought startles me. But before I can consider it, he's there, standing above me.

I see his shadow first, then squint upward.

"That kid told us we'd find you here. You okay?"

He offers a hand to help me up.

"I'm okay," I say, remaining planted to the ground.

I hear Vanessa before I see her:

"So you quit? You didn't even try to make it to the top?"

"I tried. I just didn't."

"Uh-huh," she says.

Theodore's hand is still outstretched. He wiggles it and says softly, "Come on."

So I reach for it and feel the weight of him pull me up.

He steps toward me and folds his body

over mine into an embrace. Theo was always a good hugger, never afraid to lean in, let you feel it. I linger for a beat, then place my palms on his chest, pushing him away.

"So were you trying to kill me?" I turn to Vanessa.

"No," she says. "Don't be overdramatic. That would make it a pretty short book."

15

Missed Calls: 17
Voicemails: 3

Voicemail from Raina Chandler-Farley
Willa? Where are you? I've been calling you for the past hour! Do you not check your phone now? Is this part of your thing? Listen, call me. There's been a . . . setback.

Voicemail from Raina Chandler-Farley
Seriously, Willa, where are you? It's imperative that I reach you. I realize that you are off, like, finding yourself or whatever, but we've run into a situation here, and I need to know what to do. If you get this, call my cell. Um, or . . . shit. If I don't answer, try Jeremy. He'll be able to reach me.

Voicemail from Raina Chandler-Farley

Well, I don't know where the fuck you are, but your brother has been indicted. I hope that you are off enjoying yourself in la-la land or wherever you are because God forbid you leave me with an itinerary, but whatever. So, I've been calling you because the FBI arrested Oliver this morning, and they took him from your apartment. (Big sigh.) And maybe you're too busy at, like, a day spa, but when they came in, he was smoking pot (did you know that he planned to smoke pot in your apartment?), which means they also seized your apartment because our genius idiot brother had moved three pot plants into your closet. Evidently, this is the purest form of marijuana, so it is all he smokes. You know. Because that sort of shit is important when you're Oliver Chandler and a cosmic guru.

So if you would please take a goddamn moment to call me back, I would like very much to know what you want me to do now. (Big sigh.) Oh, PS, I have tried to reach your husband, but his assistant — no, I'm sorry, his "tech lady in waiting" because that is evidently what those losers are told to call themselves — said that

199

he was scaling a rock wall and couldn't be reached. Jesus Christ.

Page Six: iPhone Breaking News Alert!

Yogi-to-the-stars Oliver Chandler was arrested today on counts of money fraud. Chandler is alleged to have participated in a Ponzi scheme that raised over $1 million for the famous Kalumdrali Retreat in Mumbai. Celebrities such as Jennifer Aniston, Lady Gaga, Demi Moore and Halle Berry are said to worship at the ashram that promises "peaceful inner Zen to light and caress your very best and karmic soul." We at Page Six think a cool million bucks will sure help.

When asked to comment, Chandler's lawyer, Raina Chandler-Farley, said, "Ollie is innocent on all counts. He has devoted his life to nurturing his students' spirituality and has never cared at all about materialism." When pressed about the allegations of marijuana farming, Chandler-Farley said tersely, "No comment." (Page Six knows that this means: "guilty mother-effers!") Both Chandlers are offspring of the much-revered author Richard Chandler, who made headlines with his own Nobel scandal last year. We can't help but wonder if the elder Chandler sees this latest development as divined by the universe or if he's making calls to bring in the big boys and help save his youngest, the prodigal son. Calls to his publisher went unreturned.

"I need to know what you want me to do about your apartment," Raina says when I reach her.

"What do you mean? Can't they just take the pot plants out?"

"Yes," she replies, like this is the dumbest question in the world. "They are obviously not leaving the pot plants in your closet to get your winter boots high."

"Great then."

"Not 'great then.' *Because* Ollie is the subject of an FBI investigation and *because* they indicted him today and *because* he is such a moron that he had illegal drugs on the premises, they consider your apartment a crime scene."

"A crime scene for romance," Vanessa says because we're in the car on the way home from the mountain, and I'm on speakerphone.

"What?" Raina barks. "Who is this?"

"I don't understand what's going on," I say.

"This family is a goddamn mess, that's

what's going on. And naturally, I'm handling it." Raina's phone beeps twice, and she mutters, "Hold on," and then it's silent.

"Man," Vanessa sighs. We're stuck in the snarled traffic again on the commute back to the hotel. "You can't make this stuff up."

I don't answer because I'm still pissed off.

"Listen. I know you're mad about Theodore. But that's the point of this trip. Of the book. Of the dare. You have to leave your comfort zone if you're ever going to rejigger your own master plan."

I stare out the window and try to look angrier.

"Come on, Willa. I'm your best friend. You need to trust me."

I clench my jaw, and then Raina is back.

"Sorry. Grey has a stomach bug. Of course. Of course he does." She inhales. "Here are your options. One: come home and deal with this."

"We just got here!" Vanessa says too loudly, then adds: "Hey Raina, it's Vanessa."

"Well, your landlord is saying you've defaulted on your lease."

"What?" I say. "How?"

"Yeah, um, illegal growth of marijuana plants pretty much gives him an out."

I rub my face. "So then what?"

"Option two: move your stuff to storage.

Option three: pray that your brother didn't actually do any of the crap they're saying." Her other line beeps again. "God! Hang on."

She clicks over, but the line mistakenly goes dead.

"Hey look," Vanessa points to the car a lane over. "It's marijuana mom! Now *she'd* support Ollie."

Indeed it is. The MOMS FOR MARIJUANA minivan is just ahead. We inch up, trying to catch a glimpse.

"Ugh. I should probably go back to New York and help."

"Hold up. What's the easiest thing to do?" Vanessa asks.

"Go back to New York and avoid Theo."

"Interesting," she says. Then, after a pause: "So what would your revised master plan tell you to do, the opposite of what is easy?"

I sigh. I hate this stupid exercise. It runs counter to every instinct that I've spent my life adhering to: the instincts that tell me to tuck my head, make no sudden movements, linger in the shadows. Though admittedly, I have terrible instincts for just about everything.

"The opposite of what is easy would be to stay."

"So?"

I know what I have to do.

"My new Master Universe Way will be to stay."

I feel sick just saying it out loud.

Vanessa laughs and reaches over to squeeze my hand.

"See, just like that, we've changed your destiny."

16

Though Seattle natives swear that it doesn't rain in the summer, it is, in fact, damp and drizzly the entire next day, which is just as well because I'm too sore to move. Vanessa decamps to the hotel lobby to start writing, and I loiter in bed, mostly dodging Raina's phone calls but also dodging life

I have gotten what I know about Oliver's situation from TMZ and Page Six, and I can't tell if it's because he's my brother and I trust him or if it's because he pulls off doe-eyed innocence so well ("Namaste, my friends") or if it's just because my dad has brainwashed me to conclude that what is meant to be will be, but I believe Oliver's claim of naiveté. I believe him when he stands next to Raina and a publicist I didn't even realize he had ("Ollie has a publicist?" I text Raina), as they hold court outside Yogiholics, and Ollie rubs his prayer beads and says in a very calm but totally unpatronizing voice that *he doesn't believe in capitalism and if anyone is the victim here, it is him, his practitioners and the other devoted few who were also duped by Yogi Master Dari when he asked them to donate to his cause.*

It's true that the right thing, not just the *easy* thing, would be to go back to New York. Yes, to fly back immediately, even though I can offer no real counsel. Maybe I could offer my siblings some comfort, but truth told, they hadn't exactly enveloped me with sympathy when my own life fell apart. Raina slipped me a bottle of Xanax while I was packing, and Oliver stuffed a "healing necklace," whatever that is, in my toilet kit. But those aren't exactly the pillars of support that one's looking for when one finds herself at rock bottom.

There's a knock on the hotel room door and a muffled voice calls out:

"Room service."

Vanessa had mentioned that she'd send up breakfast, so I limp my way out of bed, my hamstrings creaking, my lower back explosive, the space between my shoulder blades a minefield. I try to pull on my sweats but it just isn't worth the agony of bending over, so I wrap the hotel robe around me in a loose knot and shuffle to the door.

I shouldn't have quit those Sunday runs with Shawn, I think. *Maybe I can start running again. Email him and tell him we should start running again. Rewrite our Master Universe Way together. Program our* Together To-Do! *app for tri-weekly runs. That seems nice. That seems lovely.*

I know that I claimed that we mutually decided running wasn't worth it. But really, it was me. We were married now, who needed to stay in shape? Wasn't it so much better to honor Sunday as God intended? As a day of rest? Shawn pointed out here that he didn't realize I actually believed in God, and that he couldn't help but wonder if I wasn't religious only when convenient. And I sat on the couch and thought about the fact that maybe he was right. But I still didn't want to go running.

Later that afternoon, when he went out to Hop Lee for Chinese food, it occurred to me that I had my own religion: that everyone in my family had been indoctrinated into the cult of Richard Chandler, and believing in that (or disbelieving, if you were Raina) was enough. It was already exhausting to spend your days rationalizing and theorizing and putting everything in its logical place, so if I didn't believe in God, actual God, well, who could blame me? My dad was God. That's what everyone had told me, anyway.

"Room service!" the man echoes again.

"Coming," I say, hoping for greasy eggs, which remind me of Shawn, so I reconsider and pray for Belgian waffles.

I unlatch the lock.

I look for the food cart, but there's no food cart.

It's Theodore. (Of course.)

"Sorry," he says. "I had to."

"You really didn't," I say. "You really shouldn't have."

He takes an arm out from behind his back and holds out a plate of waffles.

I shake my head. (He's the founder of Y.E.S., for God's sake.)

So he smiles. "Come on. Give a guy a break."

So I smile back. "Fine. Only because I'm starving."

One night, early in our relationship, Shawn and I were waiting on the popcorn line for the new *Batman.* He knew the guy who had done some of the special effects, so he was talking quickly, excitedly, about what we were about to witness. Two girls in line behind us overheard and interjected and said:

"Like, that's so awesome! You know some-one who worked on this movie?"

And as the line crept forward, Shawn beckoned them into the conversation, still spilling his secrets, and the two girls inched closer to him, and I was pushed ever so slightly further away.

Eventually, we bought our popcorn and sodas, and they bought their Red Vines and whatever, and on the way back to the theater, the prettier girl said to Shawn when she thought that I was out of earshot, "I don't see a ring, so you should call me sometime."

I turned around just as she handed him her card.

Shawn stood there shell-shocked for a moment, and then he got this loopy grin on his face, and then he noticed me watching, so he gave me this endearing look, like *what the hell was that about?* — and then he balled up her card and tossed it in the trash.

He had been a late bloomer, all pimples and bones and awkwardness in high school. His college girlfriend had been cute enough — she was from Missoula and was sort of boring, a little dull, and she liked reading *Popular Science* as much as he did. She broke up with him when she moved to St. Louis after graduation. So at *Batman,* he hadn't yet adjusted to his handsomeness or the fact that coders and Internet geeks ruled the world. He was still a kid who played Dungeons and Dragons with the neighbors in his parents' basement.

Later, back at his apartment, I asked him why he chose me, though I felt really presumptuous because it wasn't like we were engaged or anything. It wasn't like I had a ring.

"I don't know, we fit," he said. "You're Switzerland. I am too."

And we were. So I didn't dispute him. (Switzerland doesn't dispute anything.)

Now, I guess I hadn't seen it, that we no longer fit, that he outgrew me. That the gawky high school kid eventually discovers that he can go back to his reunions and make the prom queens jealous with regret.

But what's regret anyway?

Regret, I am learning these days, is a lot of things. But mostly, it's a slippery seed of longing, of looking back and asking yourself why you didn't know better when the answers were so obvious all along.

Theodore sits in the hotel room desk chair while I awkwardly position myself on the bed, clutching the robe shut so a boob doesn't fall out. He sets the plate of waffles in front of me, balancing them on a pillow, and then returns to his chair, a safe distance away so I don't feel threatened. I can tell that he does all of this unintentionally, even though with Theo, it's second nature. That's what he does: he reads your instincts and responds accordingly, before you're even aware of your own instincts yourself.

"I can go at any time," he says, once he's settled in.

I laugh. "You're such a bullshitter."

He laughs too because he's really not, but he also sort of is. Then he says, "I just wanted to see you. Talk to you. But I don't want to, like, make you uncomfortable."

I pick up a waffle and take a bite, buying my time, assessing him, how much the past eight years have changed him, or how they really haven't. He is still boyishly handsome; he still wears black-rimmed glasses that add to his allure; he is still skinny but strong enough for that twenty-mile bike ride. He's grown more confident, though that was a trait he never lacked, and he wears this certainty with ease, like he has all the answers. Which a lot of times, he does. He swipes his brown hair off his forehead and nudges his glasses up his nose, and I feel a tug of something inside of me, something familiar, something like what it felt like at twenty-one when I fell in love with him.

I push it all away and offer:

"I kind of have a lot going on right now. That's all."

"That's all?"

I chew for a few seconds. "Okay. That's not all."

"But you got my email. On Facebook."

"Did you know that Mark Zuckerberg's wife made him sign a contract before she moved in with him?" I grab the little bottle of syrup and try to wrestle it open.

"I did," he says.

"You did?" I say.

He reaches for the syrup and swivels it open, then hands it back to me. I dip the corner of waffle into the tiny mouth of the jar.

"I couldn't even get my husband to let me visit him in Palo Alto, much less have him sign a contract."

"Vanessa told me," he says. "And I'm sorry."

I stop chewing and stare at him. Theo was never that easy to read, mostly because he was so good at telling people what they wanted to hear, even if they didn't realize they wanted to hear it.

"You don't have to assess me," he says, and I feel my ears burn. "I mean it —

there's no double-speak here. It's a crappy thing he did. That's not marriage, that's not better or worse, thick or thin."

I shrug.

"Don't do that. Don't shrug. It *is.* It's a really terrible, selfish thing, to up and leave."

(LIST OF SHAWN'S FAULTS #5: It turns out that he really is an asshole!)

Then Theo adds, less forcefully: "It's why I ended my own engagement. I didn't know if I could be there forever. I mean, I thought I could. And then I got sick. And everything changed. And I didn't want to be the one to break that promise that I made to her."

"I'm sorry you got sick." I touch his knee. "I should have at least written to tell you how sorry I was for that."

He bites the inside of his cheek. "I found myself wishing I could talk to you then, have you there to help me."

"I don't think I could have helped much." I say, sliding my hand back to the safety of my side of the room.

"Why do you do that? Why do you say things like that?"

There's no answer for this, so I say instead, "I don't know how you handled it. The diagnosis. I don't think I could have."

"You handle it because you have to. And you could have. Everyone can. Everyone

213

does. Life sucks sometimes, but you handle it. Don't keep selling yourself down the river."

I try to think of something to deflect the conversation from me and my shortcomings. Because that conversation could last a lifetime.

"How'd your fiancée take it?" I ask.

"The cancer?" he asks.

"Your broken engagement," I say.

"Oh, less well than she took the cancer. So about as well as you'd think."

"So . . . well?" I smile.

"Depends on your definition of 'well,'" he says, grinning back. Then more seriously: "But it was the right thing to do. Ending it. Short-term happiness isn't worth a long-term disaster. I . . . have an entire business model built on it."

"I bet my dad would say that it was inevitable."

"My breakup or you and me in a hotel room in Seattle after my breakup?"

"Theo . . ." But I have nothing else to add, so drop it. I rip a waffle in half and offer it to him. He takes it but doesn't eat.

"So you got my email." It's a question phrased as a statement.

"You know I did," I sigh. "Vanessa told you. I told you on the mountain that I did."

"Should I not have sent it?"

"No . . . yes . . . I mean . . ."

"Because I'm usually pretty decent at reading the room."

"So I read in *Time* magazine."

"So you're reading up on me in *Time* magazine?" He sinks back into the chair and splays his hands behind his head and winks, and I hate him (love him) because he is so goddamn irresistible. He always was.

"I have a subscription."

"There is no chance you have a subscription," he says, laughing. "Zero."

So I laugh too because he's right: I am not the type of woman who subscribes to *Time* magazine. I make a mental note to at least download the app later, once Theo has gone.

"I'm glad you wrote," I say finally. "And I know I said it before, but Theo, it's true: I'm sorry about the cancer. I . . . I should have tried to find the words to write you back."

"Be sorry for my testicle," he says. "Otherwise, I'm fine."

"He was a good testicle," I say.

"That he was. And I miss him dearly."

"Ah well," I shrug, my eyes bright.

"Sucks to be me," he shrugs back, his eyes brighter.

"Oh please, your life rules."

"Oh please, m'dear. My life can always be better."

My phone vibrates on the duvet, breaking the spell.

"I should get that," I say. "Family disaster."

"With yours, it always is."

17

That Theo and I broke up is entirely my fault. I don't know if he would see it that way, but it's true. Maybe "fault" isn't the right way to phrase it. Relationships end. People fall away. That's life. That's, not to quote my dad or anything, inevitable. And so when Theo and I split, I did indeed chalk it up to inevitability, to the fact that fate must have had something else in store. And then when fate delivered Shawn, that was how I embraced what happened with Theo: he wasn't here, Shawn was. It absolved any personal responsibility in the way that placing all your faith in the universe does.

But eventually, exes are supposed to make sense. You're supposed to be able to see their name pop up in an old correspondence and think, "Oh my God, I'm so glad I dodged that bullet," or "He's not such a bad guy, but he wasn't the right guy for me." But I never really found that sense of logic with Theo. We were together, and then we weren't anymore. And I could attribute all of that to inevitability as much as I wanted to, but when I was really being honest with myself, when my brain and memory and nostalgia compelled me to google him and wonder *What if?* . . . I knew that really, inevitability wasn't the only explanation. I had ruined things, and it was as simple as that.

Shawn and Theo; Theo and Shawn. Is it possible to love two people at once? Vanessa has said, because we've discussed this ad nauseam, that she doesn't believe that you can truly *love* two people at once, but that doesn't mean you can't have two great loves. She has had three, actually, and always managed to both break their hearts but still have them, in some weird way, covet her. She was still Facebook friends with them; she still slept with the second one (Ryan) every now and then when they both happened to be drunk at the same time (and he invariably texted her for days after the hook-up, hoping they could reconcile); and I always wondered if maybe, because they were all so kind and well-mannered and friendly post-split, this wasn't actually love. That their feelings for Vanessa were something that they mistook for love, because how could you keep someone in your orbit when she was unwilling to move the earth for you to begin with?

But anyway.

Theo and I were together for three years before I blew it. The easy version of our breakup is that he asked me to move to Seattle, and I said no. But that's the version you believe because if you remember what really happened, you wonder if you'll ever forgive yourself for such a giant fuck-up. Isn't it funny how that happens? The cognitive dissonance that time provides? My father built an entire multi-national conglomerate around this cognitive dissonance, though he'd claim that it's just the opposite. That the Master Universe Way isn't about reflecting on our past and trying to rationalize our choices and shortcomings, rather accepting those choices and rephrasing "shortcomings" as "life-comings." I suppose that when I ruined things with Theo, I chalked it up to my own Master Universe Way: that what would be would be, and that if I screwed things up with Theo, well, you get what you deserve, as my dad would say. This was my own "life-coming," though that didn't really make me feel any better.

But my cognitive dissonance and my stupid Master Universe Way didn't change the truth of what happened: the years and time that slide one memory into a different one don't alter the honest events one bit.

About two years into dating, Theo decided that he wasn't sure that he believed in marriage. It wasn't a particularly revelatory announcement; he was an only child from parents who stayed together for "his best interest," which of course, wasn't his best interest at all. He channeled this loneliness into an incessant need to be sure that everything in life *added up,* and it was this obsessive need for order and logic that eventually made him such a success, turned him into the great mind of the future. He was, in many ways, the opposite of my father: rationality ruled, proof of something made it real. And though he had met my dad on occasion and had nodded politely when my dad marveled over the randomness and thus the inevitability of our meet-cute, Theo really thought that he was a quack.

But Theo wasn't sure that marriage added up, and when he made this decision, he told me about it quickly, honestly, lovingly. We had just gotten home from Raina's wedding to Jeremy at the Central Park Boathouse. It was a grand affair of 500 of my parents' closest friends, with a big brass band and more tiger lily centerpieces than you could ever dream of. Though Raina doesn't seem to remember it now, she looked so very, very happy. When the rabbi announced that Jeremy could kiss the bride, she literally jumped up, straddled him and knocked him to the ground. And when they emerged from their kiss, she held up her bouquet triumphantly and shouted, "I'm Raina Farley now!"

I had thought the wedding was pretty fun, as far as weddings go, but Theo evidently felt otherwise. And since Theo felt otherwise, I started to reconsider too. After all, Theo was a decision-maker, an expert at knowing exactly what to do. Whenever I was unsure about something (which was pretty much always), he would be sure for me. He urged me to accept my first job as a copywriter; he helped guide me away from a toxic college roommate; he encouraged me to be closer to Raina, to read more, to find one thing in life that I loved doing and do it. (I never got around to that.)

So when Theo and I sprawled on the couch after Raina's wedding and he declared that he didn't think marriage "added up," I didn't argue. He said that his parents stayed together out of obligation, not out of love. That he's never been one to follow the straight and narrow, and so why should he now? That he loved me more than anyone he'd ever loved but he'd been round and round and run the figures and the facts and the economics (evidently there were economics of marriage), and a legal union didn't "add up."

I nodded my head while he rubbed my feet, and said, "I understand. I can totally see why marriage doesn't add up." What the hell did I know? Maybe it didn't.

And then there was the opportunity in Seattle, and he wanted me to come. We were driving home from a weekend in Sag Harbor when he asked. And I loved him more than anyone, and yet, I immediately said no.

Even today, the same impulse rises up in my throat when I recall the memory. *No.* It sprang up quickly, unexpectedly, and I think neither of us knew how to react. It wasn't as if I was known for my strident opinions.

He turned off the radio and swallowed my answer for twenty miles. I figured he was concocting his plan to get me to reconsider. He always had a plan to get anyone to reconsider. I eased my head into the headrest and let my hair fly against the breeze of the open window and waited for him to tell me why I had to reconsider.

Finally, he just said, simply, succinctly,

without argument: "Why?"

And I said, much to my own surprise: "Because I believe in marriage."

So he said: "But marriage doesn't add up."

And I didn't answer because I didn't have any reason to insist that marriage added up, at least to me. Not with my own parents as examples, not with anything sturdy to support me. And yet, still, some part of me believed that it was too soon to abandon the notion of happily ever after, the sort of happily ever after that came with vows and a three-tiered cake and the people most important to you as witnesses to your union.

He said: "Why didn't you tell me you felt this way? Why wait until now?"

And I said: "I don't know." And then I paused and added: "But aren't you going to figure out how to get me to say yes?"

But he shook his head, and there were tears in his eyes.

"Not this time. No, I am not."

18

Email from: Willa Chandler-Golden
To: Minnie Chandler
Subject: Are you there?

Hi Mom,

No one has heard from you in a week since you went to Palm Beach. Are you okay? I know that Raina was in touch when Oliver was indicted, and she is grateful that you posted bail, but we are all a little concerned that no one has heard from you since. As you know, I'm in Seattle researching a book project (looks like dad might not be the only published author in the family!), and it is going . . . well. I think. I don't really know. I just do what Vanessa says, which is weird things like go up to 20 strangers and tell them they look beautiful, or learn how to ride a mountain bike (I think I broke my pinky yesterday, but

I'm okay — I put it in a splint I made with Q-tips), and she even forced me to hike up Mt. Rainier. Do you know Mt. Rainier? It's hell. It's hell on earth, Mom. It's raining again today, so I had some time to email.

Anyway, please either get in touch with me or Raina to let us know that you haven't set sail for Bali with a retired billionaire. If you have, please at least consider writing me into the will.

Also, before you ask, I haven't spoken to Shawn, though I'm hoping to see Nicky soon. We lost our apartment, and all of our stuff is in storage, and I think that's a pretty good metaphor for my life right now.

xoxo
Willa

PS — as you may know, Ollie is on house arrest and staying at Raina's. If you are back in town, I'm sure she'd appreciate it if you stopped in and checked on him.

Email from: Minnie Chandler
To: Willa Chandler-Golden
Subject: Re: Are you there?

Hi darling William!

I am so sorry that I have been remiss in staying in touch for a week. This time away from your father and the family has been so nourishing for my soul, and while I provided Ollie with his bail money (a sentence every mother can only dream of typing!), I had a spiritual awakening three days ago. And that is this: I love my family like all get out, but I have had enough. This is my time, my darling! I am sixty-six, and I am going to enjoy my sunset years without getting dragged into the horseshit that this family always manages to step into! It is so liberating! Try it, darling: just say FUCK IT! Go on, try it! You have been so like me your whole life, and damn your father, I am certain that he would tell you that shouting FUCK IT to the world wouldn't mean anything, wouldn't change anything, but dammit, it feels wonderful!!!!

I came to this spiritual awakening with the help of my new friend, Nancy Barnes. Do you remember Nancy? You met her so many years ago — twenty, perhaps — when we all vacationed at the Breakers. Well, we haven't seen each other since, but we ran into one another at this new meditation hut that is just soooo relaxing, and we reacquainted ourselves rather quickly. Nancy has opened new pathways in my mind and my emotions, and if I'm speaking freely, my sexual well-being, and I have never felt so nourished in my life.

I am not going back to New York for now. But please continue to email me, my darling. I know that this thing with Shawn is a mess, but I can only hope that one day soon you find the fulfillment that I am finding with Nancy.

xoxo

Your mother, Minnie

PS — while I am no longer on speaking terms with your father, he continues to email me incessantly. He is quite angry with you. I'll forward along his notes shortly. Nancy and I are off for sunset massages.

Email from: Raina Chandler-Farley
To: Willa Chandler-Golden
Subject: What's your plan?

Willa,

Your brother is driving me nuts. Not just me, but Gloria too. Jeremy is in Berlin, so he hasn't been here to deal with the madness, and for once, I'm not pissed at all of his travel because he would just be one more person around for me to deal with. Ollie has started holding yoga classes in my living room. Yes, really. Jennifer Aniston asked Gloria for a towel and some lemon tea this morning. All while I sit here and diligently work on his behalf. I'm not saying that you should come home because I can't blame you for running, but still. I do wish that you would stop running. We go before the judge in three weeks. I hope you can at least be back for that.

RAINA CHANDLER-FARLEY, ESQ
PARTNER
WILLIAMS, RUSSELL AND CHANCE, LLP
EMAIL: RCF@WRC.COM

Email from: Willa Chandler-Golden
To: Nicholas Abrams
Subject: How r u?

Nicky — it's been a few days since I've heard from you. Can you let me know if you're okay? I drafted an email to your Uncle Shawn (okay, I've drafted three) but am too chicken to send them. Do you think I should send them? Is he dating? Do you know a woman named Erica Stoppard? Is she prettier than me? Can you tell me why I am writing a twelve-year-old and asking his advice? Wait . . . have you ever had a girlfriend? This might be helpful for me to know before I ask for further advice. You know what? On second thought, please ignore this entire email. I should really hate your uncle right now, so let's pretend that I actually do.

Email from: Nicholas Abrams
To: Willa Chandler-Golden
Subject: re: How r u?

Dear Aunt Willa:
I might be 12, but I know a cry for help when I read one. I told Uncle Shawn he's an asshole and should send

you a note. Also, I have had a girlfriend named Mara Goldstein, who just got braces and changed her French kissing style, so I broke up with her. Speaking of Goldsteins, I am exploring Judaism. What do you know about being a MOT? (That's member-of-the-tribe, in case you didn't know.)

Email from: Willa Chandler-Golden
To: Raina Chandler-Farley
Subject: Our mother

Raina — I'm 99% sure that mom is now a lesbian. We should probably talk.

19

DARING YOURSELF TO A BETTER LIFE!
By Vanessa Pines and Willa Chandler
STEP TWO: RESIST INERTIA

Summary: This might be the scariest dare of all: to refuse to let life carry you along in its stream, to plant an anchor in that stream and say, "enough." "Enough" of letting life whiz by, "enough" of accepting just okay for yourself, "enough" of refusing to be bigger than you think you can be. Giving in to inertia is the most natural, most innate human tendency, so we cannot promise that this second step will come easily. But when it does, you'll feel it, deep in your soul, deep inside of your heart, that you — little old you — might just have the ability to change everything.

I immediately regret emailing Nicky, but Vanessa had urged me to, or at least sort of. It's part two of the book. *Dare Yourself!*

231

"Dare yourself to resist inertia!" she implored tonight, as we headed to Safeco Field to watch the Mariners play the A's. She didn't specifically say to email Nicky (or indirectly Shawn), but if she scoffed (or caught wind of the email, which I actually really hoped she wouldn't), I had an answer: I haven't exactly fought for anything in my life before, so if I'm going to fight for something, maybe it should be my husband. *That's* resisting inertia. *That's* rewriting my master plan: after all, the first time, I just let Shawn walk away. I let him draft the stupid rules of our intermission, and I didn't make a peep, didn't put up an argument, didn't throw a fucking pan at his head and tell him that we'd taken vows and this was the stupidest goddamn idea I'd ever heard. We were Shilla, for Christ's sake! Maybe now, my version of resisting inertia was fighting to get my husband back. So when Vanessa made a bathroom stop at a bar in Pioneer Square, I pressed "send" to Nicky.

Take that, inertia!

Vanessa got us tickets when our concierge mentioned a singles mixer at the stadium in section 210. Evidently, every single person in our near vicinity would be available and looking. I protested my involvement but Vanessa said: "Dare yourself, Willa! Jesus, if you end up sharing Cracker Jacks with a hot guy for a few hours, will you actually die of cardiac arrest?"

And I sucked on my cheeks and said, "No, I actually won't."

"Great, because I wasn't sure."

"But I haven't been on the singles scene in half a decade."

So she snapped, "Which is entirely the point. Maybe you'll actually have fun."

Now, in the bleachers at the ballpark, Vanessa says, "Damn, I love a baseball game on a perfect summer evening. The peanuts, and the buzz of the crowd, and the beer. And the men. Have you looked at all of the men?"

I dig my hand into my solo box of Cracker Jacks and I unobtrusively check my phone with my other hand, but less unobtrusively than I thought, because Vanessa says, "Yo, what the hell, William? Can you not put down your phone for a second? What are you waiting for? Your knight in shining armor?"

And something must give me away (okay, my face gives me away because my face always gives me away), so she says:

"Please tell me you didn't email Shawn."

And I say (without lying):

"I did not email Shawn."

And on home plate, a Mariner cracks his bat and the ball soars toward the stands, and the crowd is on its feet cheering, so we are on our feet too but not really sure why because we weren't paying attention, until the same crowd falls to a hush and sits back down when the ball lands foul.

Vanessa sinks into her plastic seat and says, "I didn't just fall off the dumb truck, you know. Why are you emailing him to get him back? The guy who *made a list of rules* of your break!"

At this, the very cute guy next to me turns. "I don't mean to eavesdrop, but what a dick."

"I know, right?" Vanessa extends her right hand and says, "I'm Vanessa. This is Willa. We're from New York."

And he says: "New York girls scare me."

So she says: "We don't bite."

And he leans over me and says: "Well, I don't mind a little nibble."

And I roll my eyes and stare up at the dusk sky and realize I'll never have to dare Vanessa to do anything because there's nothing she's afraid of.

I offer to swap seats with cute guy, and we do this awkward thing of pressing our bodies against each other while trying very much not to press our bodies against each other on the way to the other's seat. Cute guy's friend leans over, close enough so I can smell the beer on his breath, and says, "Hey, I'm Bill." Before I can answer, there's another loud pop from home plate.

The crowd is on its feet again, this time cheering louder, then louder still, and the wave of energy is pulsing right through section 210. I look up and I see it, the white flash of lighting, the ball coming right toward me. I don't have a glove, and though I know it is stupid, I know it is so moronic to reach up with my bare, open palms, I do so anyway. I resist inertia, resist the urge to let cute guy leap in front of me, to let anyone else stake his claim. I outstretch my hands, and I feel it, the hot leather ball land smack against my palm.

"Holy shit!" Vanessa yells.

"That was awesome!" the cute guy shouts.

Bill picks me up and pulls me into a bear hug, and then, much to both of our surprise — caught up in the euphoria of the moment — I lean down and kiss him.

Everyone in section 210 starts pointing and screaming, and I unclamp my lips from Bill's and peer across the field to see me, my face, 100 feet wide, up on the Jumbotron. It's a face that looks happy, a face that looks brave. A face that didn't duck when the smarter thing would have been to take cover. I offer a little wave, and the stadium cheers back.

"Sorry about the kiss," I say to Bill, once we're seated.

"I didn't mind," he replies, laughing.

"It was a one-time thing."

"One time is better than never."

I nod and suppose that he is right. *One time really is better than never.*

It's only about fifteen minutes later when the throbbing sets in.

I gaze down and realize that my fingers have swelled to hot dogs, that my palm is purple and bruised.

I knew it, I think, as I try to make a fist but fail. *Nothing good ever comes from reaching for the stars.*

Theo meets me at the emergency room of Harborview Hospital.

"First dates in ERs seem to be our specialty," he says.

"I told Vanessa not to call. I could come alone," I say.

In fact, I'd begged Vanessa not to call Theo, all the while insisting that she go share a drink with Cute Guy. I had grown weary of being her pet project, and I craved a break from her psycho-scrutiny, even if it meant trudging to the ER solo.

"Also, this isn't a date. Unless, like, you're a masochist," I add.

"Duly noted," he says, holding out his arm to steady the door, though the door was automatic and would have steadied itself. "And to the second part, I'm pretty sure you know that I'm not."

I do know that he's not. I know that he is a pretty good cook and always willing to bring home fresh flowers and the type of guy who will give you the covers if he notices that you're cold and also tell you (lightly, with enough humor so you don't want to kill yourself) when you need to go brush your teeth. He's not a masochist. But he didn't want to marry me. So I'm trying not to be a masochist and entertain the notion that this could be a date.

My face crumbles from the pain, and Theo notices the wince.

"Come on, I know the head of the ER. We'll get you to the front of the line." He takes my good hand, without even thinking about it, like he doesn't even consider the intimacy of intertwining his fingers in mine, and leads me down the hallway.

The doctor comes immediately and gives Theo a bear hug, slapping him on the back, and says: "Man, what can I do for you? I came as soon as I got your text."

And then he takes one look at my egg-plant, mangled fingers.

"Did you really try to catch a homer with your bare hands?"

"I can be an idiot. I was trying to resist inertia. It didn't work."

"Like hell it didn't," Theo says. He digs into my purse to get the ball. "Your fingers will heal but you'll always have this. A memento of the night you weren't afraid to reach up and catch what was coming for you."

By now, the Vicodin that the doctor has given me has kicked in, so I can easily read his metaphor, and I know that he's referring to more than just the ball. I sweep my good palm up to his cheek and say:

"You're sweet." Though I also want to say: *You're the one who didn't want to reach out and catch me. You're the one who didn't believe in marriage.*

Theo whispers: "Uh-oh. I think you're high."

And he and the doctor chuckle, and since I am indeed high, I chuckle too.

A kind nurse sets my hand in a cast, and I sit beside a six-year-old whose cheeks are tear-streaked and whose pigtails hang limply against her shoulders.

"What happened, sweetie?" Theo asks.

Her chin quivers, so her mom states:

"We've told her a million times not to climb on the bookshelf to get the remote. This time, the entire thing fell on top of her."

Silent tears tumble out of the girl's eyes.

"It's okay, honey," I say. "I'm a terrible listener too."

"Really?" Her voice is so very small.

"Really. You wouldn't believe how many times someone has to tell me something before I finally believe it."

I feel Theo's hand against my shoulder, and he gives me a squeeze.

"I'm getting a rainbow cast," the little girl says. "They said they could give me a rainbow."

"Then I'll get a rainbow cast too. That sounds nice. I will take the rainbow." I close my eyes and the room sways. I open them again and don't dare turn to look back toward Theo, though I know he's there, right behind me, holding me up.

"Do you believe in pots of gold?" she asks. "And leprechauns?"

"I believe in everything."

Though I also believe that when the Vicodin wears off, this will no longer be true.

■ ■ ■ ■

Vanessa insists that I accept a date with Theo.

"I dare you," she says, as we stroll through the Pike Place Market, sampling fresh nectarines.

"I'm starting to find that annoying," I say back. "You only dare me to do things that I don't want to do."

"Precisely. And it's not as if I've been wrong. It's not as if you're having the worst time of your life."

"Well, the hike up the mountain was the worst time of my life. But I'll concede that the baseball game was not horrid." I wave my rainbow cast in her face. "Of course, this happened."

"Hmmm," she demurs. "I guess perhaps we've tweaked your master plan."

"I'm not moving here. I'm not, like, getting dreadlocks and joining a drum circle."

"That's not a bad idea." She types "drum circle" into her phone. "No one said you had to move here, but you've had a glimpse of what your life could have been. What else your life could be. You open up your landscape."

"With Theo. You want me to open up my

240

landscape with Theo."

"Not with Theo! Or maybe with Theo! Theo isn't the point here. Finding out what else is out there for you *is*! Stop being scared of the unknown."

"You're forgetting that Theo didn't want to marry me. And I've resolved to fight for Shawn."

"Hmmm," she says in reply.

"Hmmm," I mock her back.

"Just go," she finally sighs. "What's the worst that can happen?"

Theo is waiting for me when I meet him on The University of Washington campus the next evening. I didn't agree to dinner. He asked for dinner, he wanted me to say Y.E.S. to dinner — but dinner felt too risky. Risky because though I have told Vanessa that my version of resisting inertia is to try to win Shawn back, the other version is me resisting thinking about Theo every last second. Because since the emergency room visit, I have spent an awful lot of time thinking about Theo, about the squeeze of his hand on my shoulder, about his easy laugh at my lack of lucidness, about the way he comes to my rescue when I don't realize that I need saving. I don't want to think about Theo — *resist inertia and think about Shawn!*

— and certainly, with my current state of affairs, there are plenty of things to consider other than Theo.

THINGS TO THINK OF OTHER THAN THEO:
1. My mom is a late-in-life lesbian.
2. Raina's reaction to mom's self-discovery. (That we should fly to Palm Beach immediately and bring her home.)
3. Oliver's headline news on *Access Hollywood:* celebrity yogi-types have started wearing taupe ribbons ("Because taupe is the color of peace," Halle Berry explained to Billy Bush last night) as a public display of Ollie's defense.
4. Shawn's Facebook page, which I checked again last night after taking half a Vicodin for my broken hand. I am 99% certain that he must be unaware that JDate posts a live update every time Shawn logs in (which is strange for several reasons — one, that Shawn isn't aware because he is nothing if not tech-savvy, and two, that JDate would think that this is a good idea because it's sort of embarrassing to

have this in your feed but maybe they think that it lets single people know that there are other normal single people out there, and they are on JDate. Which raises the whole question of if Shawn is single, and surely, that is something I should be contemplating more than my ex-boyfriend. I do give it some thought, but not as much as you'd think.) I bet Cilla Zuckerberg would never check Mark's page if he dumped her. I bet she would basically implode Facebook at its very core, like, literally go in and set their server on fire. I thought of this last night and eventually logged off, but not before trying to break into Erica Stoppard's profile and see all of her pictures. (She has hers set to private, which really sucked.)

5. Nicky, who took a right turn two days ago while in Palo Alto, likely in response to what he calls Shallow Alto, has definitely discovered God. Or his Jewish roots. He starts and ends his emails with "Shalom," and I don't think he's being ironic. I should devote more time assessing the mental health of 12-year-

olds and if this sort of thing is normal. (Also, I should email his mom, but I'm hoping Shawn has already done so. But of course, I can't ask Shawn and don't want to be an alarmist. What do I email Amanda? "Dear Amanda, your son has found God. Should we stage an intervention?" No. That seems odd.)

Theo is standing in front of the library checking his phone when I see him. He's in skinny khakis and a blue button-down, because he was giving a guest lecture called *The Art of Persuasion* to a grad-school summer class, but he's rolled the sleeves up to the elbows and looks more like a student than a professor.

Early July in Seattle is perfection. The sky is crisp and clear and blue and makes you forget that summer doesn't go on forever. It is not too hot, not too cold, and the air is clean and optimistic. The trees are cut from a storybook, and on campus, they burst with life, towering over you, ahead of you, offering insulation from the world outside.

I watch him for a moment as he pounds something into his phone, solving some sort of crisis for someone much more important than me, and I try to consider what would have happened if I'd just said "yes," back in the car when he asked me. At the time, I spoke impulsively, but once I did, I couldn't take it back. And when he didn't try to convince me — I had expected him to convince me, and then of course I would change my mind and go with him — I couldn't exactly beg.

He sees me now and smiles. "I was sure you were going to bail."

I walk toward him. "I'll be honest, I considered it."

Though I hadn't. I hadn't considered bailing for a moment. That was the unfiltered truth, the one I'd share with him if I had the guts to. But I never had the guts, so I just step closer and then kiss him on the cheek.

He pulls me in for a hug. "You look nice."

"You've only seen me hiking up a mountain and in a bathrobe the next day. Oh, and doped up at the ER."

"True."

"So I could only go up from there."

"You looked great before." He grins and nudges up his glasses.

"You are such a bullshit artist," I reply, and he grins bigger.

"Nice cast."

"It's rainbow!" I wiggle my hand in front

of his nose.

"Come on," he says. "Let's walk."

"Where to?" I say. "I've never been here."

"Let's go anywhere." He loops his elbow in mine. "Let's get lost."

There's a secret passage on the UW campus, or so Theo tells me. This might just be how he woos me, how he charms me, and leads me down the figurative path again so quickly. Because it's not really a passage, not really all that secret. We wind through the deserted back roads of the campus, past the administration buildings, past the intricate gothic halls of learning, until it is just the two of us, everyone else having faded away. Occasionally, a student or a TA walks by and nods, but mostly, it's just us. He tells me how he discovered his cancer ("one morning while washing myself in the shower"), and I tell him about how I don't really know what I'm doing with my life ("I don't really know what I'm doing with my life"). How much has changed for him, and how little has actually changed for me.

We don't speak of Shawn, and I don't dare ask him how he came to propose to his now ex-fiancée when he wasn't supposed to ever believe in marriage.

I want to ask:

Is it because you loved her so much more than you loved me?

Is it because it wasn't marriage that you didn't want — it was me?

Is it because you didn't think you could love someone forever but it turned out that if it were someone less needy, less uncertain, you could?

But I say none of this because for now, it's so much easier not to. I'm still married, after all, and we're only taking a walk. We wander until we find ourselves down on the waters of Lake Washington.

It's dusk now, the sun illuminating the water in ways that transcend the imagination: pinks and reds and blues and greens, all blended together, all magic. Two scullers row past, and then behind them, the UW crew. The coxswain's voice booms out, too large for her body, the oars and arms synchronized following suit. We linger on the railing overlooking the water, not saying much, just taking in the perfect moment of bright air and sunny heat and optimistic uncertainty.

A motorboat cruises in through the passageway leading to the open channel that lies ahead — three guys drinking beers, enjoying the evening. One of them looks up, spies us and shouts:

"Hey dude! Don't just stand there! Kiss her."

"Naw," Theo yells.

"Definitely!" he hollers.

"You think?" Theo responds.

"Go for it!" another one of them bellows.

"I'm okay!" I shout. "I'm fine!"

"But you could be better!" the second one roars as they cruise by.

"No, really, I'm good!" I yell. But I can feel my cheeks redden, my heart race ahead.

"Do it, do it, do it!" the three of them chant in unison.

And so Theo leans in and shrugs. And then he grins. And then he kisses me. And because he does so, and because I am resisting inertia, and because if I'm really being honest with myself, I want him to — I let him.

Later, he takes me to Husky stadium, to which he has private entry ("I worked with the football team on a situation," he says) and we sit on the fifty-yard line just because we can. The lights are on and the sky is dark, and I feel like I'm back in high school, though in high school, no one ever did this for me. I stare up at the sky and think of Shawn every once in a while, but then I remember the rules of our break: that there *are* no rules, and that I'm free to act on impulse, to act on whatever I damn please. Then I think of Vanessa's theory of opposites, and how impulse is exactly what we're aiming for, that our instincts — my father's philosophies be damned — are really all that we have to change our fate.

So I sit on the fifty-yard line, and I try not to do anything to ruin it.

Eventually, we run out of small talk, so Theo examines his hands, and I examine his hands too, which are slim and somehow beautiful. Then he takes my chin in his palm and says:

"I don't know if I've ever been happier."

And I deflect: "Don't say that. I don't know what I'm doing."

He drops his palm. "Who does?"

"You. You always know what you're doing, which is why you're so good at it."

"Good at what?"

And I say: "Life. You're good at life."

And he says: "I wasn't always good at life."

I know him well enough to know that he means his complicated childhood with his miserable parents and their frigid home and the endless afternoons he was left to closed doors and quiet space. Eventually, he filled that space himself, by helping his elderly neighbor with her errands, by single-handedly implementing a neighborhood ice cream truck. By now, Theodore's left his childhood so far behind that it's not even a glimpse in his rearview mirror anymore. It's another time, he's another person. I'm surprised he even remembers it, much less references it. But I suppose our childhoods are seeds inside of us that plant roots forever, even when we're certain their life cycles have long since been extinguished. How long will it take for my own roots to loosen their grip?

"Besides," Theo continues, "I'm better at life with you in it."

And I can't think of anything to say to that, so I just sort of crunch up my shoulders, but he doesn't accept that because he's Theo. Instead, he weaves his fingers into mine, pulls me up, and says: "Follow me."

And because it is what I do best, I do.

Theo lives on a houseboat on Lake Union. It takes a moment to adjust to the ever-so-slight sense of motion, the rocking back and forth, like you're ready to set sail. He brings us both beers, and we sit on his deck and watch the motorboats lazily glide across the water, moving onward to wherever they call home.

I try not to look at him because if I look

at him, I'll betray myself. I'll spit out everything that I am thinking, things like:

This is where I would have lived with you?

This could have been our home?

I can see how much I could have liked it here.

So this is the road not taken.

Why didn't I say Y.E.S.?

Eventually, he sets his beer down on the patio table, and he reaches for my good hand. So I take one more swig of my bottle, and clasp his hand and let him lead me wherever he wants to. That's what Theo always did. He stood in front of me, so I never had to face the wind. Shawn does that too, I presume, though not as well and not really any longer. Or maybe Shawn and I together turned our backs on the wind and walked in the opposite direction. We spent so much time moving away from whatever challenged us that life, for him at least, grew dim, too calm to be a life worth taking interest in.

Theo kisses me in the living room and my knees hinge just a little bit. I'd forgotten how he kisses. How slowly, how intimately, like he could read your mind and move to wherever you wanted him to move next.

"Is this okay?" he asks.

"It's okay," I say. Then worry that he's

251

misunderstood. "I mean, it's better than *o-kay.*"

He laughs and kisses me again. "Willa, you don't have to keep explaining yourself to me. I know you. I get it."

"You don't know the new me." I'm not sure why I say this.

He pulls back and studies me, then smile lines appear around his eyes, then his grin catches up to them.

"God, I'd love to meet her though. The new you. Rainbow cast and all."

We sink into his sofa and he kisses me for the third time, and I'm so lost in the moment that I think I'm imagining the buzzing in the background. It's endless, continual, like a hive of angry bees swarming his kitchen. Finally, he stops and says:

"Your phone has rung about twenty times. Maybe you should get it?"

His lips are swollen from moving against mine, and I can feel the stubble burn on my cheeks. I don't want to stop. Resisting inertia means that I shouldn't stop.

But then the angry hive buzzes again, so I reluctantly push myself up from the couch and dig into my purse.

Yes indeed. I reach right into the hornets' nest.

Family.

20

I steady myself against the counter in Theo's kitchen and dare myself to listen to my messages though I don't know if I have the stomach to. Something is wrong. Something has gone cataclysmically wrong. Good news never comes like this, in a wave. Maybe, I guess, if you got an Oscar nomination or something. But not for lay folk. Not for me.

No, this rush to find me could only mean one thing: disaster.

I inhale and find my guts and click on my voicemail as steadily as my shaking hands will allow. I think of so many people whom I love, so many people who could be felled in a quick swoop. No one is immune after all to life's unpredictable and dangerous whimsy.

Shawn. Nicky. Vanessa. Raina. Ollie. Grey. Bobby. My mom.

It's none of the first few who spring to mind, however. But it's the one I should have thought right off the bat. Because he would have told me as much. He practically predicted it.

My dad. It's my dad. The one who has succumbed to the very thing he always predicted he would: inevitability.

Voicemail from Raina Chandler-Farley

Willa! Where the eff are you??? Honestly, this is getting ridiculous! You're in god-damn Seattle! Not on the fricking moon! Have you not seen any of our texts? Jeremy and I have been trying to reach you for the past three goddamn hours! What time is it there now? It's, like, nine o'clock at night! Are you out clubbing or something? Is this part of your experiment to find the new you? Please call me. *(Rustling of something and then a large boom.)* Jesus, Grey! I told you not to throw the football in the apartment! Where is Gloria? GO GET HER. Willa? Are you there? Anyway, please call me as soon as you get this! It's about dad. *(Silence.)* Well, I may as well just come out and say it since by the time you actually decide to pick up the phone and get this, he might be dead. But . . . shit . . . Jesus . . . *(quieter now),* dad's had a heart attack. A bad one. Something about a ventricle failure . . . blocked arteries. I don't know. I don't really understand it. Please. Just . . . come home.

Vanessa meets us at Boeing Field. Y.E.S. has a corporate jet, so Theo makes some calls and within an hour, the three of us are waiting to board.

"This isn't resisting inertia," I say to Vanessa. "Please don't be disappointed." My voice breaks. "I have to go."

"Sweetie, you're my best friend. I'm never disappointed." She hugs me. "Besides, this is the hard stuff. This is life. This isn't about a self-help book."

I hold her tighter and feel my tears fall. I didn't expect to mourn him like this. Not that he's died, but he might. I didn't antici-pate the agony or the empty pit or the blank moments of wondering what life means when your parents start to die. I bat my hand in front of my face and try to compose myself. My dad is okay with dying! It's part of his life's plan! Why am I not okay with it too?

Vanessa hands me a Kleenex. "Theo's

coming with us?"

"Only because it's his plane. He has clients he needs to see in New York."

"Uh-huh," she says.

"It's not really anything." I'm already diminishing whatever it was because it's too difficult to consider what it really could be. It was just one night. On a football field. With some kissing. High schoolers have nights like that every weekend. I blow my nose and hand the Kleenex back to Vanessa, who pops her eyes and says:

"Willa, come on now. I know that we're best friends and you're really upset, but I don't do snot."

I laugh, though it's more of a sputter, so she laughs alongside me, and I try to go still and absorb the enormity of leaving Seattle and jetting back to disaster and how very grateful I am that she dared me to betray my comfort zone. That she dared me to step outside of myself, even if it lasted only ten days, even if I'll be home in six hours and everything will go back to how it once was.

When we board, Theo turns on the satellite TV and flips it to CNN. My dad is all over the screen.

NEWS ANCHOR #1: "We are devastated to report that our colleague here, Richard Chandler, whom many of us have come to

256

think of as a mentor . . .

NEWS ANCHOR #2 (interrupting): "As a bit of a God in these parts . . ."

NEWS ANCHOR #1: "Richard Chandler has had a heart attack. The details are still coming in but our source on the scene tells us that Chandler was on his way for an early swim at the New York Athletic Club when he suddenly collapsed in the middle of 60th Street."

NEWS ANCHOR #2: "Yes, Tim, evidently, a passerby recognized his famous face and leapt in to perform CPR, which may have saved Richard's life. As our viewers know, Richard is the author of *Is It Really Your Choice? How Your Entire Life May Be Out of Your Control* . . ."

NEWS ANCHOR #1: "Great book, Audrey. Just great. It changed my entire life."

NEWS ANCHOR #2: "I couldn't agree more, Tim. And to Richard's point, emergency personnel are claiming that if this fan hadn't stopped to perform CPR, that, in fact, Chandler would have died on the street. Everything happens for a reason, indeed."

NEWS ANCHOR #1: "Remarkable, Audrey. Just remarkable. Richard Chandler. He has never been more of a God of Wisdom than today."

NEWS ANCHOR #2: "Chandler is currently in doctors' care at Mt. Sinai Hospital. There are conflicting reports as to his condition, but we trust that he is at peace with whatever happens. That is what he would have wanted."

NEWS ANCHOR #1: "Let's take a moment here and say a prayer for our colleague."

NEWS ANCHOR #2: "I think we should pray for his family. Richard wouldn't want our prayers."

NEWS ANCHOR #1 (choking up): "Audrey, how right you are. We will pray for his family. They'll need it."

21

Raina and Jeremy are seated in the emergency room, clutching coffee and staring at their phones. I can see them from down the hallway: the fluorescent lights, the harsh shadows, the bleakness of it all. Raina sighs and rests her head on Jeremy's shoulder, and he reaches up and touches her cheek, then kisses her forehead.

"Oh, thank God." Raina spies me and hops up, spilling Jeremy's coffee on his pants.

"I came as soon as I could, straight from the airport. How is he?"

"He's probably going to live," she says.

She leans in and hugs me — clutches me really.

"Oh my God." I purge my relief through my tears.

"They're going to have to operate again, and then they'll know for sure, but the doctors said the odds of success are high." She pulls back and straightens her blouse, tucking the hem into her waistband. Zippering right back into pre-crisis Raina.

"I'm sorry you had to deal with all of this on your own."

"Ollie's here," she says. "I mean, he can't leave the apartment, but he's calmed me down."

"Are you wearing a taupe ribbon?" I ask, angling closer and staring at her collar.

"Ollie made me." She sits, so I do too.

"It's the color of peace," Jeremy says, angling over and kissing me.

"Have you reached Mom?"

"I reached Nancy, her 'partner.' " Raina holds up air quotes. "Mom was on a twenty-four-hour solo spiritual retreat —"

"They have those in Palm Beach?" I interrupt.

"Evidently. But Nancy said she would try to get in touch with her."

"You know that mom is just finding herself," I say gently. "Forty years with dad and his philosophies, and this is the first time she's been allowed outside those bounds."

"I know," Raina says. "And it's not because it's 'Nancy.' You know that. I mean, we donate every year to support gay marriage."

"We do?" Jeremy asks.

"We do a lot of things you don't know about," Raina says.

"That's probably true," Jeremy says to me.

"You're not great with change," I say to Raina. "That's all. I get it."

"Well, I believe in marriage. They've been together forty years. I think that's worth something."

I believe in marriage, too, I want to say. *Though I'm starting to wonder about mine.*

Raina pulls out a prescription bottle from her bag — Bobby's backpack. She unscrews the lid and shakes out a pill, then offers me one. I pinch it up and drop it on the back of my tongue.

"You guys realize that's not candy, right?" Jeremy says.

Raina ignores him. "I'm just saying . . . Dad just had a heart attack. I think Mom should be here."

"Dad's sort of the one who told her to get lost in the first place," I counter. "Which is sort of exactly what Shawn told me."

Yes, maybe I should refocus on Fault #5: he's a total asshole!

"Well, maybe you and Shawn should also try to make it work," Raina says. "You did take vows."

"It's not up to me." The bitterness of the pill is etched onto the back of my throat.

261

"He established the rules. No contact, sex with other people —"

Jeremy cuts me off: "Sex with other people? Wow."

"Don't be jealous." Raina smacks his arm.

"Not jealous," he answers, though he looks a little jealous. "Impressed though."

"I actually resolved in Seattle to fight for him, to get him back, but now . . ." I trail off.

"But now what?" Raina asks.

But now a million things! I think. *But now Theo! But now Dad! But now I've seen that baseball games can kind of be fun and that a drum circle might be cool and that hiking is still the worst thing in the world, but eventually, your blisters heal.*

"But now, I don't know. But . . . I guess . . . if he comes back for Dad, if he's there for me during this, I'll try."

"Okay." Raina eases her head back, the Xanax sinking in. It doesn't really seem like she cares too much either way.

Jeremy says, "I texted him to let him know what was going on."

And I want to shout: have you seen his Facebook page? Do you know that he is compulsively JDating? Are you aware that he appears to be wooing Erica Stoppard? And while we're discussing it, can you run a background check on her because she is the sole person in the history of the world who leaves no Google footprint?

But instead I mutter: "Cool. Well, we'll see what happens."

And he says, pointing to my rainbow: "Nice cast."

So I say: "Long story."

And then Raina opens her eyes and focuses them on my hand and says: "What the hell happened to you?"

But before I can launch into my long story, before I can tell them about the dares and the master plan and inertia and Cracker Jacks and the Jumbotron and Bill and maybe even Theo, I hear a voice behind me.

"Hey," it says.

And my insides buckle.

I know it's him without even turning around. But then I do, just to confirm that I'm not totally losing my mind.

I see Nicky first. He's wearing a yarmulke and greets us by pressing his hands together in prayer and bowing his head. And then, behind him, with his leather jacket and moussed-up hair and Wired2Go graphic tee, he's there.

My husband.

Shawn came.

"How'd you get that?" Shawn asks, nudging his chin toward my cast, while we're on line at the hospital cafeteria.

I think: *Where'd you meet Erica Stoppard?* but say, because I am trying to win him back: "At Safeco."

"Safeco Field?" He turns and looks at me.

"Yes, at Safeco Field," I say, mostly because I know that he'll find this intriguing. "I went to a Mariners game." I slap my tray down and reach for a fruit cocktail. "It was singles night. I made it onto the Jumbotron."

"You made it onto the Jumbotron?" He freezes, lost in what this might mean, until he realizes that he's holding up the people behind us. When he catches up to me, he says, "Since when do you like baseball?"

I shrug and try to look coy because I can't exactly say: *I don't like baseball! I just went because Vanessa dared me!* I eyeball something that looks like baked ziti but might also be chicken Parmesan or possibly some sort of congealed eggplant and say:

"Anyway, I caught a home run. But I broke my hand."

He echoes, like he's in a daze: "You caught

a home run. But you broke your hand."

And I just want to laugh and laugh and laugh, but I do it on the inside, resisting what would be easy, what would be obvious, because I don't want him to recognize that two can play at this game. Two can come up with a plan. Two can make their own rules and live by them, even without the consent of the other.

I try not to think of that night in the ER when Theo dashed to my rescue, when I promised that six-year-old that I believed in everything, when Theo kissed me on the bridge, and then kissed me again on the houseboat and then assured my safe passage all the way back to New York. No, I stare at the waxy cafeteria selections, and I do the opposite of what my mind wants to do, though sometimes, the mind wants what the mind wants. Even my dad would agree with that.

I settle on the "baked ziti" (?) and shuffle down the line toward the cashier.

Shawn touches my arm.

"Hey," he says. "You seem happy. I'm glad. I'm happy too."

My stomach tumbles as I sense my brilliant plan faltering already.

"I didn't realize that you really meant it . . . to not talk to me at all," I say. "I mean,

I've been emailing with Nicky."

He bobs his head and grabs a chocolate pudding, peeling off the lid and licking it, then licking it again, which I find a little repulsive.

"It's . . . I mean . . . you're happy, I'm happy. It's working."

I turn away from him without answering and tell the cashier to ring us up separately.

"Willa, come on," he says. "Does it help if I tell you that I missed you?" He looks at me like he means it, like maybe he's happy, but maybe this has been hard on him as well.

"It helps," I say. Then: "I missed you too."

He rests the chocolate pudding on his tray and winces. "This is so complicated."

"Why does it have to be?" I ask. Not because I haven't found some sense of happiness during our break, but because I'll take uncomplicated over happy. I am Switzerland, for God's sake! Didn't he and I agree to that on our Match.com profile way back when? That complication and conflict weren't in our nature? We like easy people! We like things to be gentle and calm and soft as a bunny rabbit's ears! Why is this suddenly so hard?

"I don't know why it has to be so complicated," he sighs, then unconsciously touches my hair. "It just is."

Cilla Zuckerberg has a dog named Beast. Did you know that? I googled her again last night and joined her Facebook fan page. If I had a dog, I'd never have the guts to get an animal that lived up to the name "Beast." I'd have, like, a Teacup or a Princess or maybe Max if I got crazy. But *Beast* implies ferocity, and I've never been ferocious. I wish I were. I wish I could be.

For all the reasons my future dog would be named Cinderella, I don't say any more to Shawn now. I don't say: *we're married, for God's sake! You don't take breaks from that!* Or: *Whatever happened to Shilla? To Sundays on the couch? To foot massages? To Chinese food? To baby-making? To our plan?*

I should have said these things four weeks ago, and I should say them now. I vowed to myself that I would. But I am so damn tired, and Shawn seems uncertain, and besides (and Vanessa would be so mad at me for this, but no one is perfect, and I'm still a work in progress), it's easier to just say: "Well, even if we stick to your rules, maybe we could go to a baseball game sometime."

And he considers it. He takes forever to consider it. And I think: *do you not see the leap I just took? It might not be exactly what I need to say but it is something! It is more than*

I ever could have said before!

Finally, he says, "Sure. I'm leaving town again, but maybe when I'm back. We'll see. Let's not promise."

And I think: *what are promises anyway? Just another thing, in a world full of broken things, to be broken.*

Because Shawn and I are now homeless — a side effect of your superstar yogi master brother who also grows his own pot in your closet — I decamp to Raina's apartment on the Upper East Side. Shawn tells me that Wired2Go is putting him up at some super-hip hotel in the Meatpacking District that I pretend to have heard of. Nicky comes with me because kids under sixteen aren't allowed.

"Don't worry," Nicky says to me in the cab from the hospital. "The Jews have been tested for millions of years. This is just but another test."

I screw up my face like he's a lunatic.

"What? Haven't you read the story of Passover? Of the Dead Sea parting?"

"I think you mean the Red Sea," I say.

"Hmmm," he considers. "Whatever."

We fall silent.

"Has Uncle Shawn been in touch with your mom?"

"Why? Because it's such a sin to have found God? I'm a *Jew,* Aunt Willa, and I won't be shamed for it." He wiggles his finger at me, and I wonder if he's been watching the *700 Club.* Or something. The *700 Club* for Jews. Do they have that?

"No. Not because you are a Jew." I sigh. "Because I thought someone should let her know what's going on with Shawn and me. And with my dad. This wasn't exactly the plan when she left you with us for the summer."

"Oh," he says, with that perfectly pubescent realization that the world does not at all times revolve around his problems.

"Though it might not be a bad idea to tell her that you've found God, too," I add.

He takes my good hand and gazes soulfully into my eyes.

"It's not too late for you, Aunt Willa. It's never too late to find your calling."

The cab whizzes forward toward Raina's, toward the epicenter of the Chandler family dysfunction. He's not exactly right. But he's not wrong either.

My mom and Nancy make a grand entrance a few hours later when we've all retreated home for dinner and showers before heading back to sit vigil (is it a vigil if you know

269

that he'll live?) for my dad. Oliver has just wrapped a guided meditation in Raina's library — ("I don't know why my students should suffer just because the government has launched this oppressive witch hunt! Also, after all of this stress with Dad, I really needed some inner-Zen time," he declares, right before powering up the blender for a wheatgrass smoothie), and his fresh-faced, uber-calm, Lululemon-wearing flock is filing out the door when I see my mother waiting in the foyer.

"Mom!" I cry, grateful for her presence.

"Mama Bear!" Oliver says.

"Hello, Mother," Raina states.

We move single-file to hug her, and we're all a little surprised when I tear up. I flap my hand in front of my nose, willing myself to stop.

"I don't know what's wrong with me," I say. "You know I'm not a crier."

"Oh, honey," my mom answers. "You're like a butterfly getting her wings."

And I'm not really sure how to reply to that, since I sort of feel like it's something I'd write for a tampon client back at the ad agency. So my mom wipes away my leaky eyes and says, "I get it, sweetheart. Your father's in the hospital and your husband turned out to be a dick."

Before I can protest, she steps past me, tugging her companion alongside. My mom flourishes her arm and says, "This is *Nancy!*"

Nancy blushes and bows her head, as if she doesn't deserve such adulation, though she strikes me as the type of woman who knows exactly what she deserves. She looks vaguely familiar, like perhaps I do remember her from my childhood, from that vacation at The Breakers. Or it could simply be that I just recognize her from the society pages. She is pretty, with luminescent skin that is well taken care of, and a chestnut bob that is entirely appropriate for her age. She's wearing chic white capris, and a scarf fancifully wrapped around her neck, and frankly, I can see why she's a bit of a catch. She's not the type of woman who seems like she needs to rewrite her master plan or find a way to swim upstream. She just knows her Point North and doesn't misjudge it as disastrously as I seem to have and moves toward it with certainty.

"Nancy!" I say, clapping my hands together.

"Fancy Nancy!" Oliver says.

"Hello, Nancy," Raina offers, then says to our mom: "I didn't know if you were coming up. It was hard to reach you."

271

"I've been living a life that doesn't revolve around your father." Mom sets down her bag on a console table and fluffs her hair. She looks healthy, vibrant, pink and shiny. "Forgive me if I wasn't on speed dial."

"Mom," Raina says. "It's complicated. We know. But . . . he almost died."

"Your dad is well aware that death is part of life. He wouldn't want us to make a big to-do. It's part of 'God's plan'." Now she's the one to hold up air quotes, and in that moment, she looks so very much like Raina.

"Did someone mention God?" Nicky says, wandering in eating a Go-Gurt.

"Are you wearing a yarmulke?" Nancy asks, speaking for the first time.

"I am, ma'am."

She lifts her eyebrows like she's impressed, and since no one has anything much more to say, we head to the kitchen where Gloria is preparing pork chops, which Nicky has renounced eating because they are trayf.

"I heard about your marital troubles," Nancy says to me later as we gather around the kitchen island and fill our plates. Raina leans over and slices my pork chop since I can't maneuver a knife and a fork.

I check the clock on the microwave and wonder when the doctors will call to implore us to come back, to tell us that he is awake.

They shooed us out tonight, saying he was resting, saying nothing more could be done until the surgery to repair the damage, but . . . it didn't feel right not to be there. I look around the kitchen. Why am I the only one who thinks it doesn't feel right not to be there?

"Shawn's having a bit of an early mid-life crisis," I say to Nancy. "It's complicated."

"Marriage always is," she replies.

Raina snorts but then says, "Sorry. You're right. Marriage is."

I eye Jeremy to see if he's giving her some sort of look, but he's not. He just sips his wine and accepts the fact that it's public knowledge that marriage is complicated, even if he should be offended that his wife is the one announcing it.

"Well, you're not married," I say to Nancy. *I mean, obviously. You're a single, gorgeous lesbian!*

"I was once. A great, great man. Not like your dad." She catches herself. "That came out wrong. I only know about your dad through your mom."

"He can be a real a-hole," my mom offers, still nibbling on her pork chop bone.

"Mom! He's at death's door!" I bark. "Can you stop?" I glance to Oliver for backup, but he just gives me this weird look like *whaddya gonna do,* or *namaste!* Or something. Who the hell knows? No one in my family was ever good at backup, I realize, and spear the meat with my fork.

"I was widowed at fifty-seven," Nancy says. "Pancreatic cancer."

"That's terrible," I say.

"We loved each other well for a very long time. That he died was terrible. But when he was alive, it was wonderful. So I have that."

"I admire that attitude so very much." Ollie's speaking in this weird, soothing tone. "It's what my students are searching for. Perhaps you'll speak at one of my classes."

"Mom," Raina interrupts. "You know I'm the first one in the family to come down hard on Dad, but . . . I mean . . . he's . . ."

"He's fine!" my mom states succinctly. "He is going to be fine. Do you really think that a little ventricle trouble will take out your father?"

"I don't think that ventricle trouble is something that you can really control," Raina says.

"Well, if anyone can, it's your dad. And the doctors said that he's stable! And besides, you know what he says: everybody dies sometime."

And Nicky chimes in: "Does this mean I

can stop researching how to properly sit shiva?"

And we all say: "Yes."

So he says: "Okay." And then, "L'chaim." And then excuses himself from the table.

"Frankly, nobody's stable in this family," Raina says, and everyone laughs a little to diffuse the tension, but we also take deep gulps of our wine. I can't help but look at the clock again and wonder when they will call with good news.

"Stability is where you choose to plant your roots, where you find your foundation," Ollie says.

Nancy looks at him sideways but says nothing. The rest of us just ignore him.

"I think it's lovely that you loved your husband so much," I say to her. "In light of . . . the complications."

"Oh, you mean that I'm with your mom now?" She laughs and reaches for my mom's hand. Raina pales. "Listen, life is short. Be happy. That's all I know."

Ollie exhales like this is the most brilliant thing he has ever heard.

Raina refills her glass, and Jeremy rubs the back of his neck.

I lean back and think: *Life is short. Be happy.*

That shouldn't be so hard.

■ ■ ■ ■

Text from: Theodore Brackton
To: Willa Chandler-Golden

I'm sticking around for a while. Can we grab a drink?

Text from: Willa Chandler-Golden
To: Shawn Golden

Know I'm not supposed to text u, but I thought mayB we cld get a drink? Or take in a game? Yankees? They're baseball, right? (Har, har, har.)

Text from: Vanessa Pines
To: Willa Chandler-Golden

I know you r mid-family crisis. Need a drink?

Text from: Shawn Golden
To: Willa Chandler-Golden

Jammed 4 the next day or so, working l8t. Talk Tues?

Text from: Theodore Brackton
To: Vanessa Pines

Really want to pursue this but I want to give her space. WDYT?

Text from: Vanessa Pines
To: Theodore Brackton

Since when do u ever need advice from any1? U founded Y.E.S. for God's sake. Here's advice frm r nxt book chapter: open ur eyes & life follows.

Text from: Theodore Brackton
To: Vanessa Pines

So you say Y.E.S.?

Text from: Vanessa Pines
To: Theodore Brackton

Honey, I say Y.E.S. to everything. I'm not the 1 u shld be asking.

22

DARING YOURSELF TO A BETTER LIFE!
By Vanessa Pines and Willa Chandler
PART THREE: OPEN YOUR EYES AND
WRITE YOUR OWN MAP

Summary: It sounds so easy, doesn't it? Open your eyes, look all around you, breathe it in and follow that breath toward wherever it takes you! Richard Chandler advises you to do the opposite. To *close* your eyes. When has anything good ever come from closing yourself off to anything? (Well, sure, there was that lousy ex-boyfriend who kept texting you for sex, but readers, we know that you're smart enough to deduce the difference between closing yourself off to a douche bag and closing yourself off to life.) Try it. Try it now. (After you've read this paragraph.) Close your eyes. Focus on your other senses. You hear more, yes. You might smell more. You might be more aware of the goings-on around you. But then pop open your eyes and see, really see, the beauty and the colors and the brightness and the contrast and the faces and the smiles and the triumph and the grief and the wisdom that is all around you. *See it all and learn from it and then be big and brave and chart your course.* Write your own map. Get lost. Then get found. Closing your eyes really just means closing a door. Never close a door when you have the chance to leave it open.

My dad wakes up two days later, on Tuesday. Vanessa is taking the day to write, and since I don't have anything better to do, I tell her I'll just peek over her shoulder and won't bother her at all. But she says, "Seriously, go to the hospital, Willa, even if you don't want to. Don't close yourself off because you're scared. Open your eyes. *Write your map.*"

I didn't want to go, it's true. Hospitals remind me of Theo, and I don't want to think of Theo, and also, all I do now is weep when I think of my dad and what life would mean without him.

Raina has gone into the office for the day to prepare for Ollie's arraignment, and my mom and Nancy are taking a Skyline Harbor Cruise ("It's a lesbian thing," she says to me before kissing me on the way out the door), so I'm the only one sitting at his bedside today. I'm passing the time figuring out how to join Twitter when he comes to; he must watch me for a good minute before he makes re-entry into the world of the conscious.

Finally, he clears his throat, and I shriek and bolt upward, dropping my phone as I do.

"William," he says weakly. "I'm so thirsty. What happened?"

I surge to be next to him and clutch his hand, but it's limp against mine, flaccid, near dead.

"You had a heart attack, Dad," I say, my cheeks already damp, my nose so quickly running down my chin. "But you're going to be okay. We thought we might have lost you. But we didn't."

He bobs his head almost imperceptibly, as if any movement at all is asking too much of him. His skin is waxy and wan, his hair looks thinner, his lips like sandpaper.

"I'm so glad you're awake," I say. Maybe I should have resented him more, for my lost childhood, for my wandering ambition, for my incomplete sense of self. But here, on his near-literal deathbed, I can't be angry. Anger would be the hard choice, the one that requires more effort, and this time, I don't have the guts for it.

The doctor rushes in with his team of nurses, and as quickly as my dad was awake, I am ushered out of the room, like I'm disposable, like I can so easily be cast off. I know that I'm taking it too personally, that they're just trying to do their job, but I wish that my dad had asked them to let me stay. I peer through the tiny window in the door and wonder why he didn't ask to let me stay.

The nurses move all sorts of tubes around, and the doctor speaks to my father with words that I cannot hear. But then one of the nurses exits, and for a sliver of space and time, the air between my dad and me is connected. I press myself forward to hear: I want to hear them telling him that everything is going to be okay. That they will perform his surgery now, and he'll be as good as new. And then maybe my dad will reply that he *has* to be good as new because he doesn't want to leave us, to leave *me,* because he and I have so much unfinished business to muddle through.

Instead what I hear is the most crushing blow of all.

My dad says weakly, "You know that I signed a DNR, right? I don't want to be resuscitated if I go. I'm not afraid to die.

Everybody dies, after all."

The doctor answers, "Everyone does, sir. But not today."

My eyes are swollen and achy from crying, but I have been locked inside a stall in the ladies' room in my dad's ward for over an hour, and I know that if I stay much longer, one of the nurses will suspect I have, like, Ebola and take me away on a gurney. I want to text Theo and ask him to come find me. To lead me out of here like he used to lead me out of everything. But I can't make this about Theo, and though I shouldn't make this about Shawn, I text him instead. Through better or worse. Sickness and health.

This is sickness. And he should be here.

I press send and sigh a deep sigh and push myself out of the bathroom stall onto my wobbly legs and go in search of daylight.

On my way past the gift shop that's stuffed with cutesy teddy bears and withered flowers, I do a double-take. She does too. She looks so different now. Skinnier. Healthier, but pale. Still though, shinier, with clean hair and a decent night's sleep. She almost looks pretty.

"Hannah?" I say. "Oh my God. Hi!" It's my old boss, Hannah. The cocaine-addicted, recently rehabbed Hannah.

"Willa Chandler-Golden! Get out."

"You look amazing," I say. "I heard . . ."

"Oh, you can say it. You heard I went to rehab."

"Yes," I concede because there's no less awkward way to come out with it. "I heard you went to rehab."

"And I heard your husband left you, your brother got arrested, and your dad almost died." She pauses. "I read the *Post.*"

"When you put it that way, you got the better end of our unemployment tenure."

She laughs, and I muster something close to a laugh, too. I wonder if she ever replaced her Live Free or Die poster, and lose myself for a moment in the memory of that last day, when she unceremoniously fired me, when my life tipped off its balance.

"I'm here getting some tests, picking up some meds." She falters for a breath. "Trying to pick up the pieces."

"Good for you," I say.

"It's not like I had much of a choice," she says. "Are you keeping busy?"

I shrug. "I'm working on this book project. It's kind of fun."

"That's cool," she replies. "What's the book?"

"You know that show *Dare You!*? My

283

friend and I are writing their book. And it's sort of about my dad's book. I don't know."

"I love that show!" she squeals. "That show totally kicks ass!"

"Yeah," I say, wondering why I never knew that about her before. "It's okay."

"Oh, Willa Chandler-Golden. That's the thing about you. You're always, *'I don't know'* and *'it's okay'* when you should fucking know and it's pretty fucking awesome! That's what you should be dared to do: accept that your life is so goddamn great!"

"Besides my brother and my husband and my dad," I say, but I'm in on the joke, and she laughs so hard her face turns tomato-red and she shouts, "Oh em gee, I'm gonna pee in my pants!"

Then we hug goodbye like she never balled up her Live Free or Die poster and chucked it at my head.

"Well, don't be a stranger. Email me. Maybe you'll be a contestant! How fricking cool would that be?"

"Oh," I deflect, before meandering down the hall. "I doubt it. It's not that kind of book. And even if it were, it's not for me."

She shakes her head and chuckles.

"I get it," she says. "Some people watch, some people do. At least you know you'll never be eaten by a bear."

■ ■ ■ ■

Shawn meets me on the 96th Street entrance to Central Park. He's waiting when I get there, though his downtown commute was much further than my walk across the street from the hospital. He's on a bench, eating an ice cream sandwich, and I stare while the light changes from red to green, wondering if he thought to buy me one too. When we first started dating, back when we went to Hop Lee and made out for free egg rolls, he always would have thought to buy me one too.

He looks up, so I wave and take an awkward quick step as if to feign that I was in motion the whole time and not just standing there spying.

"Hey." He kisses my cheek, as I sit. "I actually happened to be in the neighborhood, so I was right around the corner."

"Oh. Aren't you working downtown?"

He bounces his head up and down. "Yup. But I had a thing."

I want to ask: *what sort of thing? A thing with Erica Stoppard? The old Shilla wouldn't have a "thing" without the other. Any sort of "thing" would be programmed in our* Together To-Do! *app, for God's sake.*

285

Instead I manage, "Thanks for coming. I know it's breaking the rules. Or whatever. But . . . I don't know if I can do this alone."

"Is your dad worse?"

"No. He's better."

His brow wrinkles and he seems a little confused by this, that I need him now, when maybe everything is going to be okay.

Finally he says: "So that's good news, right?"

And I say: "It seems that way, but it's really not."

His phone beeps a double-beep, and he tries not to look at the incoming text, holding his eyes to mine, but eventually, he gives in to his weakness and holds up a quick finger to me and types quickly with his other hand. Before I can think it through, I fold my good hand over his BlackBerry and say:

"Please. Don't. Just give me you for ten minutes."

And he looks sad, weary really. "Willa, we can't figure this out in ten minutes."

So I plead: "I get why you were bored. I get golf and *Grape!* and the mousse and the leather jacket." He looks perplexed, so I clarify: "Like that ridiculous Varvatos leather jacket that's meant for an Italian male model?"

And he says: "You don't like the jacket?"

And I exhale: "I think we're not com-municating."

And he nods: "That was sort of the point. Of the break. To start fresh."

"Well, my dad almost died, Shawn!" I'm on my feet, angry now, that I can't rely on him like I used to be able to, that he has the audacity to make this about him when it is about a million other things, not just him.

"Willa . . ." he starts, then drifts off because he doesn't know what to interject to change anything. He squeezes his eyes shut like he has a migraine.

I sit back next to him. Then I say:

"Open your eyes, Shawn. Look at me."

He doesn't. So I say it again.

"Open your eyes, Shawn. *Look at me.*"

He complies this time, and I can see that they are lost, so much like mine.

Neither of us has a map.

23

I am drowning my sorrows in one of Raina's Xanax when the doorman buzzes up. Raina and Jeremy have one of those massive, winding, jealousy-inducing apartments that you see in *Architectural Digest* thanks to one very wise investment that Jeremy made in a company that created the GPS in the iPhone. (These days, Jeremy is a "documentary filmmaker," though I've never been totally clear on what this means exactly. Raina demurs whenever I ask.) Vera Wang lives two floors up; Donald Trump is rumored to have the penthouse for his mistress.

Tonight I've taken to her fainting couch in her living room, though the room is only for show and not for the children under any circumstances. (Raina to the kids: *"DO NOT PLAY IN THE LIVING ROOM UNDER ANY CIRCUMSTANCES! UNDERSTOOD?"*)

Nicky walks in reading the current issue

of *Jewish Living* and says, "Doorman called up. Some guy is here for you."

I sit up suddenly, and the walls morph to and fro before they steady themselves, the wonderful, glorious side effect of this mind-numbing pill.

"Is it Shawn?"

"Uncle Shawn?" he asks.

"Do you know any other Shawn?" I say.

"Actually, I do. A kid in my grade whose dad is like, the CEO of the Yankees, and he always has this really cool autographed shit that he brings in and sells under the table. I tried to pinch a Jeter ball off of him . . ."

"Well, obviously, it's not *that* Shawn," I interrupt.

"*Obviously.* But you asked. Hey, speaking of nothing of the sort, do you think you could take me to Jerusalem?"

"In Israel?"

"You and I really aren't in sync today." He walks off.

To his back, I yell: "Hey, that is not the behavior of a good Jew!"

He doesn't answer, and I hear a door slam somewhere down the hall. I remind myself that I should really write Amanda, because I'm a poor substitute for a mother, but then I hear the doorbell and forget everything.

Theo offers me gardenias when I let him in.

"You remembered," I say.

"Why wouldn't I?" he answers.

When Theo and I first met, I was earning $22,000 at my crappy assistant to the assistant executive job. In New York City, this basically rents you a bathtub to sleep in and pizza slices for sustenance. My parents helped, but not much. My dad, no surprise, thought that I'd find a way to work it out, to work myself up, and actually, I did.

I couldn't afford that much back then, for the first year that we were dating. But my one indulgence was gardenias. I bought a bouquet once a month, even when I should have been more prudent. But they were so luscious, and their scent reminded me of my mother. I'd keep them in their vase for three days after they'd wilted, unwilling to toss something that had such beauty in the garbage, until Theo would inevitably do it for me.

Tonight, I take the gardenias from him and set them on the coffee table.

"Raina invited me for the fireworks," he explains, like he needs an excuse to be here. Then, gesturing to the flowers: "They need water."

"I know." I rest back on the couch.

He fiddles with his hands until he shoves them in his pockets and sits too.

Ollie wanders out, barefoot and wearing a hemp tank top and shorts.

"Oh hey, Theo! Wow, man. Hey."

They clasp wrists, like some sort of man-shake, and then pull into a hug. Ollie looks at me, and then looks at Theo, then back at me.

"So hey. I was just wandering through. Off to the kitchen for a smoothie."

"Good seeing you, Ollie. Let me know . . . if I can help in any way."

"No worries, man. No worries. But I'd love for you to have a taupe ribbon. I'll get one for you from my room."

Theo narrows his eyes at him as Ollie walks off, then shakes his head and chuckles.

"Some things never change. Remember when he visited from Wesleyan? Talking about . . . what was it back then?"

I think about it, try to conjure it back up in my mind. Either it's been too long or things are too fuzzy from the Xanax. Then it comes to me:

"Chinese medicine. He wanted to major in Chinese medicine."

Theo laughs out loud now. "Right. And I couldn't believe that Wesleyan actually offered that as a major."

"Kids these days," I laugh, but then run out of things to say. I glance at him, then away.

He's better looking now than eight years ago. He was always cute, attractive in a way that made you look twice, with cheekbones that thrilled the *Time* editors. But now, the years have sunk in, the fine lines around his eyes have lent him a gravitas. He wasn't just boyishly cute anymore in a way that you didn't have to necessarily take seriously. I wish I didn't notice the shift.

"I can't remember the last time I was nervous," he says.

"Why are you nervous?" I'm sure I'm nervous too but the Xanax doesn't let it register.

"Well, for one, I've texted you. Twice."

I sigh. It wasn't that I didn't want to write him back, it's that I had no idea what I should say. There's too much. Or maybe not enough. I don't know. For the same reasons I didn't write him back on Facebook.

Accept.

Deny.

Ignore.

(Damn you, Mark Zuckerberg! How have you discovered the meaning of life??)

"Look, Willa, you turned me down once way back when, and if you don't want me in your life, just turn me down again. Put me out to pasture."

"I . . ." I start to say something but either my senses are too dulled to put together a coherent sentence or I just don't know what to say.

"I came here to find out something . . . I have something I need to ask. And if after telling me the answer, you want me out of your life, then I will be. Forever."

"No one knows what forever is." I lean back and shutter my eyes. "Forever is just a thing my dad says."

"Is something else wrong with your dad?"

I wave my broken hand and accidentally swipe my eyebrow with the back of my cast. "Ow! No. The surgery went well yesterday. Practically as good as new. If you consider 'new' to mean that he doesn't give one respectable turd about dying and leaving us all behind."

"Sorry? I don't follow."

"Open your eyes and write your map, Theo!"

"Are you okay?"

I roll my head up and meet his concerned gaze.

"Sorry," I say. "I took a Xanax. I didn't know you were coming. It's been a bad couple of days."

"Oh," he says, with a friendly smirk. "Well, let's talk later. When you're . . . less stoned."

"Why would anyone ever be less stoned?" I say, as I press back against the sofa pillows and let the warmth of the Xanax envelop me. "Life is so much better when nothing matters."

"Don't say that."

"Okay."

"Everything matters," he insists. "I thought that was what you were trying to prove."

The fireworks begin their dance around nine o'clock. Raina lets the kids stay up late, even though they'll be disasters tomorrow. Theo lingers, thanks to Jeremy, who trespassed through the living room, didn't pick up on the enormous bubble of awkward tension, and instead poured Theo a Scotch and invited him to stay. And also because he wanted to "pick Theo's brain on this new film investment he's considering."

We gather on Raina's building's rooftop deck. It's a perfect Manhattan evening: warm enough to feel it under your skin, not hot enough to make you curdle. The sky is clear, a few stars poking their way through despite the bright lights of the NYC skyline. Raina and Jeremy mingle with their neighbors, who have popped champagne and are passing stuffed olives and prosciutto melon skewers and other Upper East Side-ish finger foods. I lean against the balcony and feel the breeze against my cheeks, and I gape at the big bad world, wondering how everything ever became such a mess. I was always sort of a mess, even at five when I became Willa, not William; even at twelve, when my dad bought me a skateboard. I'm thirty-two now. How much longer could I go?

I feel Theo's hand against the small of my back, and then he's next to me, staring out, waiting for the spectacle of explosions to begin.

And then they do.

BOOM.

BOOM. BOOM. BOOM. BOOM. BOOM.

BOOM. BOOM. BOOM. BOOM. BOOM. BOOM. BOOM.

There are yellows and pinks and purples. And stars and flowers and at the end, an American flag up in lights.

"I've never quite understood how they do that," Theo says, his neck craned up at the sky. "Those shapes, the images."

"I stopped trying to figure it out," I answer.

He floats his gaze down toward me, and for a moment, his face is awash in something that I never see on him: sadness.

"Don't stop trying," he says, his eyes back on the sky. "There's always an answer, even when you're sure that there's not."

Later, once the fireworks have subsided and Theo has said polite goodnights to all, I realize that he never told me what his question was. I consider texting him to ask — I *want* to text him to ask.

What was your question to me and how will it change things?

I start typing with my good hand but my bravado fades. There are some things that are better left unsaid, and besides, now that I'm sober, I suspect I wouldn't have an answer for him anyway.

24

My dad holds a press conference the next day. He sits at the podium and sips slowly from his water glass, looking a dozen years older than he did when all of us gathered at the Four Seasons and he announced that he was taking a lover. The cameras snap his photo for the front page of their websites, of their newspapers. The reporters, and there are many of them, hold their recorders in the air, as if my father has something so important to declare that it cannot be missed.

My dad leans into the microphone and starts talking about fate, about death, about embracing both. He gazes into the CNN camera and says that he hopes that he can offer comfort to those who are dying or those who are losing loved ones or those who simply fear the inevitable.

"It *is* inevitable!" His voice rises. "But let us all know that what will be will be. This was not my time. But if it had been . . . I would have been at peace with that too." Then he shifts back into his wheelchair with a contented smirk, as if this is the most brilliant thing that has ever been said. I want to raise my hand and say, "Hey dumbass, you wouldn't have been at peace with it, because, you know, you'd have been, like, dead." But that's not the part I play today. That's not the part I play in the family. That would be something Raina would say, but she is simply focused resolutely ahead, staring at nothing, her eyes glazed over.

The nurse wheels my father out a back door, and the reporters holler more questions to his doctors. I watch him go and realize that the one thing my dad didn't mention is family: how he was thinking of us, how we got him through. Nearly everyone says that on their deathbed, don't they? *When I saw that white light off in the distance, I was thinking of my dear wife, Rose, and how I couldn't leave her just yet!* But not my dad.

"Do you think your dad believes in God?" Nicky asks me after we usher out of the press room and down the hall. He drops quarters into the soda machine.

"I really don't know." *I really don't know him at all.* "I think . . . he believes in something though." *His theories. His sci-*

298

ence. That's what he believes in.

"So you think that he actually believes all this bullshit?"

The machine spits out a Dr Pepper, and he pops the lid.

"Nicky, it's ten in the morning. Should you be drinking that?" I feign an attempt at step-parenting.

"Probably not." He slurps from the top.

I sigh.

"How can he not see that it's all bullshit?" he asks again. "Like with my dad."

"He doesn't think that any of it is bullshit," my mom says from behind us. She pecks my cheek. "And thank God that pomp and circumstance of a press conference is over. Speaking of bullshit."

"Did you know that he has a DNR?" I ask her.

"Of course he has a DNR, sweetie. Who wants to be a vegetable?"

I exhale again. "That's not what I meant. I just . . ."

She squeezes my shoulder.

"He believes what he believes. Nothing's going to change that."

"So that means that he knows about you and Nancy? And that he trusts that it will all work out?" I plunk in my change and aim the back of my cast at the Dr Pepper button. Then I remember that yesterday Vanessa dared me to get in shape, so I opt for a water.

"He does not know about Nancy, no." My mom grows quiet.

"Do you think he believes in God, Minnie?" Nicky asks.

"Do you believe in God?" she asks back.

"As a Jew, I must." Nicky puts on a solemn face.

"That's not really an answer."

"It's an answer."

"Not really," my mom says.

"You asked, I answered." He takes a long sip of his Dr Pepper and swallows down a burp.

"That's a rote answer. There's no critical thinking involved."

I squint at my mother. This is new territory for her, for me. Before she had Raina, she'd been a high school math teacher. I'd forgotten that somewhere in her, she'd once been pinned to logic, to $10+10=20$ because you can *prove* it. I watch her now and wonder if maybe she hadn't forgotten too. Maybe she can explain to me why $1+1$ no longer equals Shilla.

"I don't get it," Nicky says.

"You're accepting that there's a God because you're a Jew. That's wonderful. But you're not asking yourself why you accept it so easily, when there are plenty of reasons not to. Sure, that's why people call it 'faith.' But I'm not exactly getting the faithful vibe from you." She reaches over and takes the Dr Pepper from his hand. "And you shouldn't drink that crap. It will kill you."

She aims the can into the garbage, and it hits the bottom with a clang.

"Wow," Nicky says, as my mom heads down the hall. "What was that about?"

I smile and am surprised to feel a twinge in my nose, tears ready behind my eyes.

"That's about being a mom. I didn't know she had it in her."

"Huh," he says. "I don't really get it."

"Yeah," I say. "Some of us are slow learners."

Email From: Shawn Golden
To: Willa Chandler-Golden
Subject: Your dad

W—

Saw your dad's press conference and thought I should reach out and let you know I'm glad he's going to be okay. All's well that ends well. I have to go back to Palo Alto tomorrow. I know that you want to talk and that our August

301

deadline is just a few weeks away . . . how about if I call you when I'm back? Nicky wants to stay here with you. Guess he got bored of the zipline. I still think it's awesome. That kid. Who knows what goes through his brain?

-S

Email from: Theodore Brackton
To: Willa Chandler-Golden
Subject: Hi

So hey. I can't stop thinking about you. And what's going on. I've been asked to consult on a project for Goldman Sachs for the rest of the summer (insider trading, but you didn't hear it from me), but I'm not going to accept if you don't want me here. I'm trying to do the right thing, Willa. I know what that means for me. I have no clue what it means for you.

Email from: Raina Chandler-Farley
To: Willa Chandler-Golden
Subject: Theo

W— don't kill me but I just called Theo to ask for his advice on Ollie's case. The govt wants some heads to roll, and Ollie's a high-profile head to axe.

Theo said he might be staying in the city for the summer, so I figured it was cool to bring him on. Just wanted to ask you if that's okay?

Email from: Willa Chandler-Golden
To: Raina Chandler-Farley
Subject: re: Theo

Please, you already called him so why are you asking me for my permission now?

Email from: Raina Chandler-Farley
To: Willa Chandler-Golden
Subject: re: re: Theo

I was trying to be polite.

Email from: Minnie Chandler
To: Raina Chandler-Farley; Willa
  Chandler-Golden
Subject: Your father

Girls —
Willa (I'm cc-ing you Raina because you should know this but keeping your brother out of it because lord knows he has enough problems), I wanted you to be aware of the fact that when I stopped

by the hospital today, your father inquired as to the current standing with your book with Vanessa. He is and continues to be quite worked up over the thought that his own kin is publicly contradicting him — I believe that's an exact quote — and he sat up in his flimsy hospital gown and with his thinning hair flopping every which way and with his teeth unbrushed and his rage turning his cheeks nearly purple and spit out: "I cannot believe that our daughter is publicly contradicting me!" and I must say, girls, I have never been less attracted to a human being in my life. Anyway, I think he may be struggling with facing his own mortality (despite what he says) or perhaps just getting old (it's really no fun, though better when you're a lesbian!) or maybe I just caught him at a bad moment. But . . . it is something to be aware of. His displeasure. Do with it what you want. Lord knows I have spent too much of my own life nurturing his pleasures and displeasures and now, I frankly don't give much of a fuck.

Can we get lunch tomorrow? Nancy and I will be at the opera tonight.

xoxo
Your mother, Minnie

Email from: Willa Chandler-Golden
To: Theodore Brackton
Subject re: Hi

It's okay if you stay. I actually think it's kind of sweet.

Sleep refuses me that night. Raina's out of Xanax, and the Ambien I found in her medicine cabinet while stealing some of her eye cream does nothing to help. I flop to one side, then I flop to the other, my mind like a million electrical wires, all interconnecting, all flipped on high. Shawn. Theo. My dad. The book. Good lord, wasn't it all so much simpler way back when there was just Shilla and our plan and the notion of a baby? Even if I wasn't sure that it's what I wanted — motherhood and its complications and the guilt and the fear and the worry that comes with ten tiny fingers and ten tiny toes. Still, it was *easier.* It was inertia. It was what should have been my master plan. It's what should have been my fate. Fate doesn't have to equal happiness, you know. Fate just has to be. Fate just is.

My mind drifts to Theo and my new fate and his question. What was it that he needed to ask me? What was it that he needed to know?

I start a list:

THINGS THEO WAS GOING TO ASK ME:

1. Do I still want to sleep with him after so many years? (Yes.)
2. Did I think about him even when I shouldn't, even when I was married? (Yes.)
3. Do I understand what exactly this means? (No.)
4. Am I willing to throw caution in the wind and give him a chance? (Caution into the wind is not my strong suit.)
5. Do I still love Shawn? (Yes.)
6. Do I still love him? (Yes.)
7. Is that enough? (How do I know?)

Ollie shifts in the bed next to me, and then the nightstand light goes on, and he says:

"So I take it you're going to keep me up all night?"

"I'm sorry. Insomnia."

"Have you tried melatonin? It's nature's cure."

"Shut up, Ollie."

"Sorry." He does sound truly sorry. "I can't help it. It's instinct."

"Dad doesn't believe in instincts, you know."

We fall quiet, though he doesn't turn off the light. I make bunny ears with my fingers, and the little rabbits hop along the wall.

Then he says: "I'm not trying to be annoying when I say this but you should exercise more. It would help with your stress."

"I know. Vanessa said the same thing. She dared me to be able to run five miles. I think she's, like, angling to make me enter a marathon or something. It's a little preposterous that she doesn't have to do any of this crap that I do."

"She was born brave," Ollie says.

And I can't dispute that because she seemingly was. Which also made her too independent and maybe meant that she'd never settle down, settle in, but courage wasn't the problem.

"Still, she could maybe start running with me."

"Run alone. It's quiet time. I work out a lot of my mental crap when I work out."

"But I hate it."

He says: "That's a dumb excuse, Willa. You know that. You sound like you're eight."

"Neither of us is exactly an expert at taking responsibility."

"Hey," he says. "I'm employed! That's responsibility."

I tut: "You're running celebrity yoga classes from Raina's living room. And . . . that wasn't what I mean. I meant *responsibility.*"

He doesn't say anything for a while, so I waggle the bunny ears in the shadows. Quiet seeps into the room until he whispers:

"I really screwed the pooch."

"A Chandler family specialty."

"You're kind of in deep shit yourself," he says. "Falling for Theo when you're still married."

I sit up suddenly, the bunny ears no more.

"I'm not falling for Theo!"

"I read bodies for a living, Will. I know you think it's BS, but I'm good at it."

I flop back onto the pillow.

"I don't think it's crap. I just never had the same conviction."

"I can't disagree." He doesn't mean it rudely, I know.

"Does Raina know you did it?"

"More or less." He rolls over onto his elbow and looks toward me. "But I did it with the best of intentions."

"It was a shortcut." I mirror him, up on my elbow now too.

"I was never good at the long-cut," he states. "Responsibility was never either of our things."

"I'm sure they'll be more lenient for your good intentions."

There's not much more left to discuss after that, so eventually, we both lay back, and he flips off the light, though I know I'm no closer to dreaming than before. After a few minutes, I'm certain he's asleep, his breath slowed, his body still.

But then he says:

"Willa, you know, it's not too late."

"What do you mean?" I stare up to the blackness of the ceiling.

"For conviction. For you to find it. If I can find responsibility, maybe you can find conviction."

"Oh," I say. "I don't know."

"Well, that's your first problem," he says. "If you don't know something, ask."

Theo picks up on the third ring. He's groggy but I'm certain I didn't rouse him. Theo never sleeps. I used to wake up in the middle of the night and find his pillow cold, then I'd pad into his kitchen to discover him hovered over the computer, fixing whatever needed to be fixed in the world. I'd fold my hands over his shoulders and try to help him relax, and maybe I'd make him a cup of tea, but eventually, he'd implore me to go back to sleep, and I reluctantly would. Though I never felt great about leaving him alone in the kitchen, never felt great about slipping into bed without my other half. With Shawn, I never had to worry about that. He was always *there,* next to me. Until he wasn't. Until he was at *Grape!* or at golf or at God knows where now with Erica Stoppard. Theo welcomed space but never so much that he didn't know where to find me, couldn't make his way back to bed and vacuum up the distance. Shawn never needed space until suddenly, he needed an ocean.

"Hello?" Theo says tonight, his voice gravelly.

"Did I wake you?"

"No," he says. "You know that I never sleep."

"Can I come over?" I ask, tentatively, though I'm certain it's the question I want to pose.

He hesitates, then says: "Yeah, of course. Is . . . are you okay?"

"I am okay," I say just before hanging up. "I'm writing my map."

Later, we discuss that *this doesn't mean anything big* but also concede *that maybe it could mean something big.* But *that I'm dealing with a lot and right now, I just want to forget about it all for a little bit* and *that we both totally understand and agree on everything.*

I say that I'm not on the pill and I'm not very fertile anyway, and he says, well, I've been tested and am totally healthy and also, I only have one testicle, but we take no chances (because taking chances like this is really dumb and only proves my father's theories correct) and he wears a condom, which he has stowed in his wallet.

The sex is sweet and surreal and sticky and a little weird and more tender than I remember it ever being with Shawn. I close my eyes when we're done but then I remind myself to open them, that maybe I'll see something I didn't before. And I do: I see *him.* And I wonder why I didn't say Y.E.S. to Seattle. How my whole life might have been different. How I wouldn't have met Shawn, how I would have lived in Seattle and grilled fresh salmon for dinner and become an avid Mariners fan and driven a Prius to the co-op for organic fruit.

Theo rolls off me and kisses me on the forehead like he really means it.

"I'm so glad you called."

"Well," I say. "You did just get laid."

And we both laugh, and I feel like I'm in a romantic comedy, and the whole audience is cheering and weeping and rewinding their DVRs just to watch that amazing scene all over again.

And I am totally prepared to bask in that feeling forever, or at least until I wake up and realize that I just slept with my ex-boyfriend while I am still married (technically, but I'm following the "rules") when Theo jolts up on his forearms and says: "Shit!"

And that's when we both look down and realize that we really may be screwed.

Fate. Inevitability. Destiny. Meant to be.

The condom broke. (Of course.)

25

"I don't want to do this," I say to Vanessa.

"You never want to do anything," she replies. "That's the whole point."

I groan and look down. About half a mile below and to the left of the bridge, I spot the *Dare You!* crew, with their cameras pointed toward us like Uzis. The producers thought that a DVD companion video would be a smash, so they've ordered us back atop the Brooklyn Bridge (the second time for Vanessa; I'm the virgin) for a healthy dose of insanity in which we plunge ourselves off and pray that this ridiculous cord that is now attached to my waist somehow saves us.

I steady myself on the rail and tilt myself halfway over. If I hover my rainbow cast over the railing and Instagram it, I could write something really witty about, like, a rainbow over the Brooklyn Bridge! But my cast is sad-looking now. The rainbow is faded and greyish, and I'm certain there is mold curdling on the inside, and it itches me to the point of insanity. Even rainbows can't stay perfect forever.

"Remind me again why we're doing this?"

"Because we're contractually obligated. Also, it's goddamn awesome."

"You and I must have very different definitions of awesome," I say. Vertigo sets in and the world skews to the right, and I quickly jump back to the walkway. "I suppose this is a bad time to tell you that I think I may have caused my father's heart attack?"

"What?"

"My mom emailed me with the theory."

"Jesus Christ," she sighs.

"She wasn't blaming me. If it's any consolation, she thinks he's a jackass."

"So you're blaming you?"

I exhale and let the hot July breeze fall over me. Maybe it can lift me up and carry me into a different, less complicated life.

"I'm saying that I feel responsible."

An assistant comes over and tugs my harness so tight around my waist that I think I might lose consciousness.

"You're good to go." He pats me on the back, like this is totally normal. That sane people throw themselves off bridges every day without a care in the world. "Have fun!" he adds over his shoulder.

"Please," Vanessa says to me, and I can tell she's a little bit out of patience. "I love you, Willa, but I am getting a little sick of your orbit revolving around him. It's your life. Fucking live it."

"I *am* living it! Do you think I want to be up here on this bridge, basically doing the dumbest thing I've ever agreed to in my entire life? All because you dared me? All for some reality show?"

"This isn't even close to the dumbest thing you've ever done in your life," she says. And then the assistant is back, squeezing her harness, and we fall silent.

"Okay, cool," he says, and then looks from one of us to the other. "Hey, don't jump angry, man. It will kill the vibe."

He makes this hang-ten symbol with his hand, and I wonder if he's friends with Ollie, and then I spin quickly toward Vanessa.

"Well, if you're keeping track of the dumbest things I've ever done, then you should know that I slept with Theo two nights ago."

And her eyes bulge a little and she smirks just a touch, but before she can reply, another assistant pops in and screeches, "It's go time! Let's do this, ladies!!!!" And his enthusiasm makes me want to throttle him, but I have no choice. Because I am here, and I am under contract, and I am starting to think that I'm the worst daughter in the world, though my father is also the worst father in the world, but I think he'd agree (and probably write a chapter on it) that the apple doesn't fall far from the tree.

Vanessa goes first, because that's what she's always done in our friendship. Then it's my turn. I'm certain I'm going to puke. I can feel my insides rising up, and I see my life in front of me — the Alps and Disneyland and Doc Martens and Theo and Shawn and everything else, too. I know that I'm going to die now. This is what happens to people before they die. I wonder if my dad also saw his own life in front of him, like a spread of Polaroids, when he was splayed and catatonic on 60th Street.

And then assistant number one is back. "Smile if you can remember! They'll take a picture and send it to you!"

And then without warning, he yelps: "On your marks, get set, jump!"

And I murmur goodbye to this sweet life. But before I die, I try to muster the one thing that I would have done differently in this life if I had the chance. What's the one thing that could have made all the difference? I can rewrite my master plan, I can

316

resist inertia, I can open my eyes. But what I really need, what I'm so utterly lacking and what feels as critical to me now as oxygen, as blood flow, as air, is guts.

Guts.

If I can corral just a smidgeon of guts, then whatever this new path has in store will be okay.

So I breathe in and then I go deeper still, and beneath the panic and adrenaline and my ever-present instinct to flee, I find it.

Guts.

And so I jump.

Email from: Rick@dareyoushow.com
To: Willa Chandler-Golden
Subject: Rad!

Willa — Hey! I'm part of the *Dare You!* camera crew, and I snapped this pic today just as you caught air — it's attached. Well done, lady! I thought you might want it as a reminder of your leap. See you in a few weeks! (I dare you!) (Ha ha ha.) — Rick

Email from: Willa Chandler-Golden
To: Rick@dareyoushow.com
Subject: re: Rad!

Rick — Hello. This is Willa. What's in a few weeks?

My dad is released from the hospital the same day that my cast is due to come off. Vanessa tells me that this is a metaphor, and I can see what she means, but then they slice the plaster in two and my wrist and fingers emerge, dried up but also somehow moist (the worst word in the world), and truly, the smell is akin to death warmed over, so I discard the metaphor pretty quickly. Your cast is off, and your dad is free! By the transitive property, you should be free of him too!

I get it, I do. But there are still so many things to ask of him, so many questions unanswered. It's not as if he can just stop being my father. It's not as if I can just stop being his daughter.

"So ask him what you need to ask him," Vanessa said over the phone earlier this morning while I was getting ready to head to the hospital. She was still a little irritated, just like she was up on the bridge.

"I'm trying," I said. "It's not easy. It's not like I haven't had thirty-two years of programming."

"I know," she said before making an excuse to hang up.

We all show up for my dad's send-off from the cardiac ward, even my mom. The media is there too — partially because he called them. A statuesque brunette who can't be that much older than I am wheels him out the front doors, angling her chin toward the photographers, brushing her hair back, cocking her head.

"Who's that?" Nicky asks, with more than a little pubescent interest.

"A hospital admin?" I suggest.

My mom says: "Your father's girlfriend."

Raina says: "What?"

"That's what he told me. I think the girlfriend should perhaps be in quotations." My mother makes that air quotes gesture again.

I sputter: "You can't be serious."

My mom raises her eyebrows, and then smiles for the cameras because that's what she's always done when she trails my father anywhere. But then she stays true to her new master plan: she makes a sharp right and heads toward her own Town Car, the one waiting across the street.

I watch her go, and she must sense it, because she turns and says:

"Oh William, who cares who that girl is? Open your eyes and live your own life! Don't worry about it too much. Your dad is

always full of shit. I should have told you
earlier."

26

Facebook Profile: Willa Chandler-Golden
Hometown: New York
Friends: 261
Occupation: Fired
Religion: Looking
Relationship Status: Married to Shawn Golden
New Facebook Notifications: 2

From: Equinox Gym
Wall Post:

Dear new member, thanks so much for "liking" our page! Now that you've joined the club, we hope you'll swing by and use your free training session. There's no time like the present. Fitness is life. Life is fitness. *(1 hr ago)*

From: Minnie Chandler
Wall Post:

Willa! Look! Nancy taught me how to use the Facebook! Will you be my friend? (Is that how I say it?) *(5 hrs ago)*

Oh my God, I think, *I have no life.*
I download Rick's jpeg file to my hard drive.

Willa Chandler-Golden has updated her profile picture!

I can fly, I write as the caption.
I stare at my screen and wait for the little red indicator lights to blip at the top, blipping to show me how much my friends like me. *Like me, really, really like me!*
I busy myself scrolling through photos of other people's lives. People who never mattered much to me. Faces from high school, random acquaintances from college. They all seem so glittery. So content. So sure of their Points North. Their eyes are always open, and they're always bright and crystal-clear and wonderful. No one ever posts a shitty picture of her husband with his hands down his pants, passed out on the sofa with Cinemax on behind him. No one ever snaps

that just-so image of her toddler, right as he's on the cusp of a volcanic explosion, with grubby cheeks and a hateful scowl and fists so dirty that baths four days in a row won't do the trick.

What's illusion and what's not? Maybe Mandy from sophomore bio lab really does have *the best, sweetest, most awesome husband and partner in the world!!!!* Or maybe she'll be divorced by Christmas. No one really knows. Maybe not even Mandy. It's my dad who knows: he knows that fate will be what it is. Even if your husband is an asshole or if it turns out that your kid is, too. Mandy will find a lot of solace in that, my father's chapters, when her divorce papers come through.

The red indicator light flares atop my toolbar. I hurriedly aim my mouse toward it.

Shawn Golden likes your profile picture!

Shawn Golden commented on your profile picture!

Comment Shawn Golden:
That's pretty awesome. I never knew you had the guts.

When I return from my first stint at the gym, Raina, Theo and Ollie are huddled around the kitchen island snacking on a something that looks like kale chips but could also be some other sort of veggie "chip" that I'd never dream of eating.

"You went!" Ollie says.

"You look pink," Raina says.

"Very funny," I say. "I did three miles. I'm getting back in shape."

"Taking responsibility," Ollie chimes in, which I find really irritating. "I'm helping her."

I unpin my taupe ribbon and drop it on the counter. Ollie's insisted they be worn at all times while in public, just in case anyone knows who I am. I've tried telling him that no one knows who I am — I have seventeen Twitter followers and most of them are twelve-year-olds who live in India — but he's waved me off.

I unscrew the cap to a Diet Coke and drink deeply.

"That undoes all the healthy benefits of the gym," Ollie says.

I ignore him, and Theo stops chewing whatever it was he was chewing and says:

"Hey."

And though I have a million things to ask him, to share with him, instead I just say: "Hey." And then the blood rushes to my already fluorescent-pink cheeks, and I hope that he thinks I'm just warm from the exercise, not warm from him.

"Give me one hundred crunches right now," Ollie bellows, like he suddenly thinks we're in the middle of a military drill.

"What?"

"You heard me. One hundred crunches."

"In the kitchen?"

"Do you not see the floor?"

I gape at him slack-jawed until I realize that he's serious, so I crouch my way to the rug and curl myself into a ball and hope that he accepts this as a crunch.

"That's one," he says.

"Ugh," I say.

"Keep going. Only ninety-nine more."

"I hate you."

"You hate everything."

When I hit 56, and it's obvious that I do not have 44 left in me, Oliver flips a hand and says: "I don't want to kill you before we even get going, so you can be done."

I splay my limbs on the kitchen floor and shut my eyes and try to breathe.

From above me, Raina says:

"Ollie's going in front of the judge on Wednesday of next week. Can you be there?"

"Where else would I be? I mean, assuming I've made it off this floor."

"We're thinking of plea-bargaining," Raina

says. "I want the whole family there to demonstrate that we believe Ollie's a good citizen, that he got in over his head."

I prop up on my elbows and then say to Theo:

"You think he should plea-bargain?"

Theo was never the plea-bargain type.

"I'm just here to advise, as a friend. And I think it's a tough call. Ollie did it. There's documentation of it. But he didn't do it knowingly. He did it at the request of . . ." He consults the papers on the counter. "Yogi Master Dari."

"Where's Yogi Master Dari these days?" I find my way to my knees.

Ollie shrugs. "Kathmandu? Hong Kong? His Twitter feed has been quiet for weeks."

"Yogi Master Dari has a Twitter feed?"

"Of course! Gaga retweets him all the time."

I clutch the counter and pull myself up to standing.

"Anyway," Theo says, "sometimes you have to accept that you broke the rules, even with good intentions. So that's what I think we present to the judge." He reaches over and sips my Diet Coke thoughtfully. "Judges have to listen to the law, but they also respect the fact that people are human, that even the most well-intentioned screw up, and part of the time, they don't even know why."

"I like that," I say. "Even the most well-intentioned screw up."

"Well, it's true," Theo says. "We do." And then there's that awkward beat when everyone assumes he's talking about me, and I wonder, *Christ, is he actually talking about me?* And then Theo continues, filling the dead air: "I usually like to go for the big win, to go in for the kill, but sometimes you just have to accept that this is what the cards have dealt."

"Don't say that," Raina says. "You sound like our dad."

"No, I'm nothing like your dad."

He looks at me now straight on.

"It's a good plan," I offer, remembering how I screwed up everything by not saying Y.E.S. to Seattle. Of not asking what needed to be asked, saying whatever needed to be said. It was inertia and master plans and closed eyes and no guts. A life without a map. Then. Now. Always.

"It's just my instinct," he says. "It's sometimes wrong."

Raina and I check in on our father at the apartment, our childhood home, the next day.

"I'm fine!" he keeps saying, though he looks pale and shriveled and doesn't get up from his bed. Instead, he darts his eyes over news feeds and websites and sometimes mutters something to himself that I don't bother listening to. Aloud he offers: "It was just some blockage! I wish everyone would stop acting like it's the end of the world."

Raina orders Chinese food, despite the fact that my dad has been given a diet of bland and healthy foods. He insists on eating the potstickers and moo shu pork, and Raina looks at me when I ask if that's the best idea and says:

"What? If he doesn't care, how can I?"

Raina's too skinny now; I've told her as much every night when I try to tempt her with the ice cream sandwiches she keeps on hand for the kids. And her Botox is fading, even though it hasn't been that long. I caught her staring in the bathroom mirror the other day, squinting and tugging her hairline every which way. She saw me and said, "They said it would last four months! I blame this family and the stress it causes me for my cosmetic dermatology bill."

"What did you think of when your heart gave out, Dad?" I say, when I'm done chewing my own potstickers, and no one else has anything else to discuss.

"I thought that this might be my time. That I might keel over on 60th Street, and if it was, it was a hell of a way to go. I'm a New Yorker after all."

He misses my point entirely.

"You know that we were worried, right?" I press. "That you might be ready to die, but that doesn't mean we're ready for you to leave us."

"William!" he says. "I know it is difficult to accept, but *everybody dies*!"

"Jesus Christ, Dad!" I unintentionally knock my half-empty plate to the ground. "If this is your best advice as a parent, it's no wonder that I've spent my life convinced that I'd be a shitty one."

"Willa." Raina reaches for my hand, soothing me like I'm one of her kids.

"It's true, Raina! And you know it as much as I do."

"So it's your hatred for me that is driving you to write this ridiculous book about me," my father states flatly.

"I don't *hate* you. And it's not ridiculous. And it's not about *you.*"

"Of course it's about me!" His voice is rising. "How are you so naive as to think this is not about me?"

"Dad!" Raina cries. "You cannot get upset! You can't work up your heart!"

"If I die, I die!" he shouts. "And at the rate you're going, I'm pretty sure that you'll kill me soon enough!" He clutches his chest, and Raina's on her feet, but it's just for dramatics, just so he can yell: "You have broken my heart! Literally! You have broken my heart!"

"Your heart is broken because you ate too much crap for the past two decades!" I yell back. "And newsflash: my life is *not* about you!"

"Your life is about whatever your life is already about," he says calmly, turning on a dime, just like that, just like I fell into his trap.

And I swear to God, I rewrite my master plan right there and then. Because every instinct in my body tells me to throw my chopsticks firmly at his head. To take aim and put one straight through his pupil. But I breathe in and breathe out, and I open my eyes and I dig deep, and I find some guts. And even if it's only in my mind, even if I can only escape into the kitchen to be free of him for a few quiet minutes of peace, I start charting a new route somewhere as far away from here as possible.

We can't leave until the "nurse" arrives.

Raina is busy on her BlackBerry, so I slip

off to my old room, where I morphed from William to Willa and am now just me. After I moved out, my parents turned it into a study, even though the apartment already held an office, and even though I half-heartedly asked them not to.

The once-purple walls are now covered with deep plaid wallpaper. The corner where my bed once rested now houses a bookshelf. The shelves are adorned with photos of my dad with famous people whose lives he changed: George H. W. Bush, Bruce Springsteen, Liz Taylor. (!!) I sink into the desk chair and try to remember what it felt like to be five or eight or sixteen, kept between these walls, kept so much within myself. I lean back, close my eyes and listen to the legs of the chair squeak back and forth, back and forth, back and forth. Then I remember the closet off the bathroom. The door handle sticks for a minute, then gives way.

I find everything here, all the pieces of my old life, all the pieces of who I was and how I came to be. My Doc Martens are coupled together on the floor, like they're just waiting for a pair of feet to take them around the block. My BU sweatshirts are folded neatly in stacks.

My wedding dress is lovingly wrapped and hanging toward the back. I unzip the garment bag slowly, taking my time, savoring it, unsure if it will be as beautiful as I recall it to be, unsure if I was as beautiful as I remember myself to be on that day. Because I was. Despite what has happened and all of the stuff in between. Shawn and I got married under a huppah made of fresh bamboo and green vines and deep ivory roses and willow and hydrangeas and delphinium. Like Jewish women the world over, I circled Shawn seven times, which used to symbolize a wife's commitment to her husband, but which many people now assume to be a wife's commitment to *family*. And I understood this, my desire for a different family. For a new start. Even if I loved my own in profound, complicated ways. The rabbi pronounced us husband and wife, and Shawn raised his foot and smashed the wine glass, and all the guests shouted:

"Mazel tov!"

And we kissed under that huppah of bamboo and vines and roses and willow and hydrangeas and delphinium. And he dipped me a little and then swung me back up quickly. And I thought:

Finally.

And he said:

"I'm glad I didn't screw it up!"

And it really didn't occur to me that we

should have said: *I love you!* Or *Oh my God, this is the best day of my life!* Or something. Not *I'm glad I didn't screw it up.* Not: *Finally,* even if I only said that to myself.

I unzip my wedding gown bag and hold my breath. There it is — and it *is* still as beautiful as I remember. The lace is immaculate; the beading is hand-sewn with grace; the waistline swoops like the curve of a swan; the fabric is rich and sumptuous and a bit like heaven. I try to force myself to zip the bag back up, to put the memory in context, where it belongs, in the deep unknown of what's next for Shawn and me, what's next for merely . . . me. But my brain stumbles, and my fingers tremble. And I find that I simply can't do it. I can't close what I just opened.

So instead, I take a step backward, out toward the door from which I entered. But before I can find my escape, I stumble on something in my path, and I land on the floor. I look down and see it then: the skateboard my dad gave me at twelve. I didn't notice it before. Or maybe it snuck out as a reminder, with a mind all of its own.

Funny, I think, though it's not funny at all. I can pretend to be Willa all I want. But that may not be who I am at all. Never who I was to begin with.

27

DARING YOURSELF TO A BETTER LIFE!
By Vanessa Pines and Willa Chandler
PART FOUR: BE WHAT YOU ALREADY
ARE (BUT AIM BIGGER)

Summary: We would never tell you to be anything but you. There's only one you, so why even bother to be anyone else? But that doesn't mean you can't try to shine a little brighter, try to set your sights higher on the horizon, try to leap off the Brooklyn Bridge. (See our earlier chapters.) Chandler suggests that being you is enough. And of course (holla natural beauties!), it is. But that doesn't mean you can't strive to be your very best version. It's easier than you think, but harder, too. Up next: we'll share how we leapt toward our own best selves, all the while knowing that there's never a promise of a safety net, but that if we caught air, we might actually touch the stars.

■ ■ ■ ■

Bookmarked Favorites
Facebook/login
FEED:

Oliver Chandler invited you to join the group: "Say Om Innocent" *(3 hrs ago)*

Raina Chandler-Golden joined the group "Say Om Innocent" *(3 hrs ago)*

Hannah Burnett sent you a friend request! *(5 hrs ago)*

Cilla Zuckerberg liked "Chicks Who Mountain Climb" *(7 hrs ago)*

Shawn Golden has been tagged in two pictures *(12 hrs ago)*

(click)
The elusive Erica Stoppard has tagged Shawn in both photos, and I am grateful that she hasn't thought to change her "friends of friends" privacy settings. They are on a golf course, the blue sky behind them, the greens sprawling out in front of them. Shawn is tan and grinning, happy in the way that I used to make him, with one

hand tucked around her waist, and another on the shoulder of a guy I don't recognize but who is tagged as "Peter Chin." And Peter Chin slings his own arm around "Nabov Slotkin." I look at them, pull the screen close to my face and stare. Erica is striking, with long legs and rich almost-black hair, with dewy skin and straight, white teeth. She has dimples on both cheeks and smiles at the camera like she just knows that she can crush all the men in a round of eighteen holes. She looks confident. She looks assured. She looks nothing like me.

Right then, Nicky knocks on my door, and I snap my laptop shut quickly.

"Looking at porn?" He flops on my bed.

"What?"

"I'm twelve, Aunt Willa. I know what porn is." He rolls over and cradles his head in his hands, his elbows splaying to the sides.

"Okay . . . well . . . that's maybe something to discuss with your uncle."

"I don't need a porn expert," he says.

I turn magenta. "I didn't mean to intimate that your uncle is a porn expert."

He shrugs. "It's cool." But then he lingers. "Can I ask you a few things? About . . . what's been going on with me?"

"Anything." I'm surprised to find myself so open, and to find that the openness comes so easily to me with him. But to be sure, I amend: "I mean, not about porn. I don't want to discuss that with you."

"Are you and Uncle Shawn getting a divorce?"

I smile. "I thought you meant questions about . . . your life. Or . . . puberty." I sort of pray that he doesn't want to discuss puberty, but his mother is somewhere on the African continent, and if he needs to hear about a woman's menstrual cycle, I guess I can explain it to him without dying of embarrassment. Until I realize that I'm probably not the expert. I filter through my brain and try to track my own period, when it's next due, what it means in context of a broken condom. The dates are murky; the math not adding up. I file it away.

"It's just that everyone's wondering."

"How nice for them."

"Okay, how about: is Grammy Minnie a lesbian now? I think that's kind of awesome."

"Nicky," I chide.

"Okay, fine." He sits up and leans back against the headboard. "I guess I have some questions about my dad." He chews his lip, and for a moment, reminds me so much of the kid he was when I first met him seven years back when Shawn and I had just

started dating: more innocent, less complicated.

"I'll try to answer them," I say quietly. "I
know your mom's pretty far away. But
maybe the subject of your dad is better
meant for her?" Puberty I might be okay
with; I'm not sure if I'm emotionally profi-
cient enough for this.

"I dunno. My mom's sort of a mess
herself. Trying to save people all over the
world. I mean, *I'm* right here."

I push his bangs away. He looks at me
with those big eyes, just like he did back at
five.

"Okay then, ask away," I say, hoping I
don't totally screw this up, screw him up
forever.

"I guess . . . I just . . . I mean, I don't
really get why it happened. Why he had to
die. Then. Like that."

"Oh buddy." I reach for his hand.

"Do you believe in karma?"

"Hmmm," I demur. "That's hard. If
you're asking if I think your dad did something to deserve this terrible thing, then of
course not. He was a good man. Your Uncle
Shawn thought of him like, like a brother, I
guess. He told me this story about how your
dad once took Uncle Shawn camping . . .
and you know that Uncle Shawn is *not* a

camper . . ."

"We actually went camping overnight when we were in Palo Alto," Nicky interrupts.

And I say: "Really? Oh." I fall quiet but then resume the story because this is about helping Nicky, not about how wide the divide has grown between my husband and me. "Anyway . . . just before they got to the campsite, your dad swerved to avoid hitting a squirrel. Ran the car right off the road and flattened the front against a tree. And Uncle Shawn was freaking out, checking himself for broken bones and debating calling 911, and all of that. But your dad . . . the first thing your dad did was hop out of the car to check on the squirrel."

I pause. I hope this all doesn't sound dumb. I'm relaying it, and it sounds sort of dumb, even though Shawn marveled about it for weeks later. That Kyle was the type of guy who swerved for a squirrel. Shawn wanted to be that type of guy too, and when Nicky was born, he embraced it: swerving for the figurative squirrel whenever Nicky found himself about to be run over. Which, given this kid, was often.

Nicky is quiet for a moment, then whispers, "I didn't know that about him." He swallows the air, considering it. "I guess, like, I'm trying to figure it all out. Like, with God, and what it's supposed to mean . . ." He pauses. "I guess that's what the whole 'Jewish' thing was."

He runs his hands through his hair, and I realize he's no longer donning the yarmulke.

"These are pretty big questions," I say. "I guess I'm still sorting this out for myself, too."

"It's easier to think like your dad thinks," Nicky says. "Like, everything happens for a reason, and there must be some great meaning behind my dad dying. Like, maybe I'll grow up and be president because of it. But . . . I mean . . . I'm not gonna be president. That's bullshit. I'd rather he'd have gone into work five minutes later that day or missed the train than be, like, president."

He stares down at his lap, but I can still see the tears on his cheeks.

"I dunno. I'm just twelve." He shrugs, an apology.

"I think you're pretty smart."

"Not really," he says.

I sigh.

"It's a hard thing to accept: that you can't change what's happened. People spend their lives filled with regret over not doing things differently. Over not having those metaphorical extra five minutes."

"Do you regret a lot of things?"

I laugh and look at the floor. "Don't use me as an example. I'm totally fucked up."

"You said 'fuck.' " He grins.

"I guess you're growing up," I say. "I thought I could."

He nods his head like he's gotten a sliver of what he came for and slides off the bed, nearly out of the room. I'm about to reopen my laptop when he hesitates in the doorframe and chews his thumbnail.

"You know, Aunt Willa. You're a pretty good substitute mom."

"I'm not, really." I frown.

"You are. You're just too busy doubting everything to know it."

I lay in bed and revisit the math, and whether or not my period was late. I should have gotten a morning-after pill when the condom broke, should have gone to the doctor to ensure that, even with our low odds — one testicle, one faulty uterus — I couldn't be pregnant. It wasn't that I hadn't thought about it. It's that I wasn't certain what I wanted to do. Some things in life can't be undone; on that, both my father and I can agree. I wasn't sure if I believed in fate, but after months and months of negative EPT tests, I wasn't willing to prove that I didn't either. Not like this. Even if I didn't know what I wanted, with Theo, with Shawn, with a baby.

I'd lost track of my periods once Shawn and I stopped trying — when was that? Eight weeks ago? A lifetime ago? The day he told me he needed his space, the day he drafted our rules. I hadn't been particularly regular before the pill, so now . . . I don't know. *Why don't you ever know? Cilla Zuckerberg probably knows everything! Probably has an Excel spreadsheet on her period!* Maybe I should have gotten it yesterday. Or the day before. But it could be tomorrow, too.

I slip out early the next morning to the drugstore, after Nicky gives me the courage, unknowingly, but the courage all the same, to accept that maybe this time it would be different — the test, the results, my certainty, my conviction. I still didn't know what I wanted it to be — motherhood or . . . not. Everyone thinks that we grow up, we get married, we have babies. But what if we don't? What if we don't want to? How do we swallow the discomfort that comes with that acceptance? Because even if we ourselves accept it — *parenthood is not for me* — there are still so many questions from everyone around you: Why not? Is it medical? Is it physical? Is it psychological? Were her own parents monsters? Is she cold-hearted? Why wouldn't anyone want to be a parent, want to give life to something else? These are complicated questions, and I can't even bring myself to ask Theo — or anyone — the easy questions. How on earth am I supposed to know whether or not I want the pregnancy test to say Y.E.S.? But Ollie had urged me toward responsibility, toward conviction, and he wasn't wrong. So I got two tests at Duane Reade; in case I wimped out of the first one and tossed it, I'd have the second for backup. That felt like responsibility, even if it wasn't much.

Now, I sit on the toilet with my sweatpants around my ankles, and I contemplate fate, on how the universe works in ways that no one, not my dad, not Vanessa, not Punjab Sharma, my father's arch-rival and recipient of the Nobel Prize, can predict. There are some things that feel inevitable — the collision of egg and sperm, the randomness of it happening at all, the further unlikelihood that the couplet implants inside of me and forms a life. At here, now, with the utter nakedness of my fear and my listlessness, it's hard to doubt my dad, to question whether or not inevitability is, well, inevitable. The condom broke. He has one ball. My reproductive system has proven unreliable.

I stare at my toes and run them through Raina's plush bathmat and buy myself time. *No matter what the results,* I think, *I'll get a pedicure later.* After Ollie's arraignment. Treat myself to something nice.

And then, before I lose my nerve, before my guts give out on me entirely, I hover the stick between my legs and pee.

When I'm done, I set the test on the vanity counter, slide down the wall onto the floor, and then, just as I had for seven months, back when I was still one half of Shilla, back before everything changed, I wait.

Whatever happens next is no longer mine to control, no longer mine to own. So I close my eyes and I wait.

NEW YORK POST COVER STORY: HEADLINE: DOWN DOG!

Oliver Chandler, the son of the *New York Times* bestselling author Richard Chandler, found himself in court today over charges that he ran a pyramid scheme for his boss, Yogi Master Dari, to raise money for their celebrated yoga retreat in India. You would think this would be enough drama for one family, but the courtroom antics were so over-the-top that we hope Hollywood producers were listening in. Someone revive *L.A. Law* stat and rip this story from the headlines!

The younger Chandler was joined in court by his wide-reaching family, which included his counsel, his sister Raina Chandler-Farley, his mother (with an apparent lady friend, which set off gossip whispers throughout the Upper East Side . . . Page Six will have more tomorrow!), and his famous father, who was pushed in a wheelchair by a leggy nursemaid who sources are reporting is his mistress. Repeated requests to Chandler's agent as to the state of his marriage went unreturned.

Several famous faces were also on hand to lend their support: Halle Berry arrived wearing Versace; Jennifer Aniston rushed through the marbled halls in stilettos. There was a rumor that Lady Gaga slipped through the judge's chambers, but that is yet unconfirmed. Nearly 90 percent of the courtroom wore those ever-present taupe ribbons that have swarmed yoga studios ever since word of Chandler's arrest hit the spa circuit.

Once inside, we are told, Ms. Chandler-

Farley began to plead her case, entering in a plea of not guilty, when she was loudly interrupted by a man shouting for a one William Chandler-Golden. When Ms. Chandler-Farley's sister stood up and explained that she was William, the man brusquely approached her and stated, "You've been served!" Ms. Chandler-Golden then opened the paperwork, read it quickly, handed it to one Mr. Theodore Brackton — *Time* magazine's Face of Our Future — and then turned to her father, Mr. Richard Chandler, and said:

"A cease and desist? Are you kidding me? Here, now?"

And Mr. Chandler then rose quickly (a miraculous recovery in his wheelchair!) and shouted:

"What is here? What is now? It is all one big circle! It is karma, it is forever!"

At which point, Halle Berry started whooping and pumping her fist until the younger Mr. Chandler gave her the stink-eye.

To which the judge banged his gavel and said:

"Order! And what is going on? And Mr. Chandler, what on earth are you talking about?"

And Mr. Chandler said: "I have served

my daughter with papers."

And the judge said: "So I see. This isn't the time or place."

And Mr. Chandler said: "With all due respect, your Honor, because I do have the utmost respect for the judicial system, but time and place are irrelevant. My daughter, William, has betrayed me. And perhaps I should have seen it coming, because, after all, I am the one who has proven that all roads lead to here, but I did not! I did not see it coming! So I will serve her whenever the time approached, as it did now!"

Onlookers report that he then became ghastly pale, and one eyewitness added, "He sank into his wheelchair like he'd just had an exorcism or something!"

Mr. Chandler was quickly wheeled out of the courtroom by his nursemaid/mistress and two security guards.

After all of this pomp and circumstance (Hollywood, are you listening?), Ms. Chandler-Farley rose wearily to her feet and said:

"Not guilty, your Honor. Though please allow a little leniency. As you can see, the Chandler kids are working with a stacked deck."

Halle Berry applauded at this until her

bodyguard shushed her.

Later, I find Raina nursing a glass of wine and overseeing a 100-piece puzzle with Bobby and Grey in their playroom. She's tucked into one of those child-sized chairs, her knees folded into her chest, her back hunched over her knees.

She reaches over and rubs Bobby's back.

"B— no, no, look for a straight edge. Yes, right there. Try that one."

She doesn't see me for a moment, and I hover in the doorway, watching, learning, absorbing.

Bobby snaps two pieces together and grins triumphantly at his mom. She leans over and kisses the top of his head, then notices me there, an interloper.

"Hey," she smiles. "Let me guess. This is about Dad."

"Well, I also happen to be really excellent at puzzles."

Grey waves me in and stands so he can sit on my lap. I wedge myself into his mini-chair, and he plops down atop me.

"Is it legitimate? Like, can he order a cease-and-desist?" I ask.

Raina laughs, real laughter.

"Oh my God, no. Haven't you ever heard of the First Amendment? It's ridiculous.

Even with copyrighted material, you can work around it." She hands Bobby a corner piece. "Here, try this one."

He connects the corner and suddenly, a planet takes shape.

"Look, mommy! The earth!"

She runs a finger over his cheek.

"So why'd he do it then?" I say. "I mean, serve me?"

"Because he can. Because he figured it would work."

"Like how?" I spy the lower quadrant of the earth and set it into place.

"Because you always cease and desist. That's what you do. I mean, initially, you sometimes puke or maybe, like the other night, consider throwing your chopsticks . . . but then you cease and desist. I'm sure he figured it'd be the same thing this time."

"How'd you know I wanted to throw them?"

"You're my baby sister, Willa. I'm sure Dad knew too."

"Oh." I mull over her words. "So . . . I guess I need to aim higher?"

"With the chopsticks?"

"With everything."

"For sure," she replies. "But when you do, at least try to nick him in the ear."

28

It's pouring the next afternoon, and I almost use the monsoon as an excuse to back out, even though I'm the one who called Theo in the first place. The rain comes down by the bucketful, purging, heavy, impossible to avoid.

"So I took the test," I say, staring at my latte at Caffe Latte, which actually specializes in desserts. But it was two blocks from Raina's apartment, and I knew if I didn't meet him somewhere easy, somewhere close enough that I couldn't run, I would. I would run. I already vomited just before leaving her apartment.

"Okay." He waits.

"It's fine." I exhale. "It was negative."

Theo forks at his lemon pie. The barista recognized him from the *Time* cover and insisted on giving him something for free.

"Okay," he repeats.

"Did you not want it to be?" I break off a

piece of the crust.

"It's sort of irrelevant, isn't it? What I want? What I wanted it to be?" he says, pushing the plate away.

"I'm sorry?"

"I've texted you a million times, Willa."

"Not a million," I say, trying to make light.

"I'm not laughing. I know that things are complicated, and I don't have expectations . . ."

"I'm still married!" I cry. Like this is any sort of defense to an ex-boyfriend I just slept with.

"Well, you could've replied. To tell me that you were okay. Or to wonder if I was doing okay."

"Oh," I manage. I can't remember when I've ever seen him like this: deflated, dimmer, like his usual kilowattage isn't turned up on full dial. Then I do remember when I've seen him exactly like this: it was the day that I said no to Seattle.

"Why didn't you make me say yes?" I ask quickly, before I can think it over too much.

"To what? Texting?"

"To Seattle."

He lets out a long exhale now; it feels like it goes on forever. And then he focuses on the lemon pie, unwilling, unable to grant me comfort by meeting my eyes. He offers quietly:

"I didn't realize I was supposed to. To 'make you say yes.' "

"That's what you do. You get people to yes!"

"Because that's what a guy dreams of . . . talking his girlfriend into commitment?"

"I was committed! You can't say I wasn't committed!"

"You were committed in the way that you do commitment."

"Don't put this on me!" I nearly hiss. "You didn't believe in marriage."

"I didn't believe in marriage to someone who didn't trust herself because then how could you ever fully trust me?"

"So this is about me!" I'm shrill enough that the waitress does a double take.

He rubs his face.

"Willa, the condom broke, and you didn't trust me enough to help you through it. To talk about what it might mean, to talk about what we would do. Imagine a marriage like that."

I don't need to imagine it. I already have it with Shawn.

"So you're disappointed in me?"

He smiles at this, a sad smile, like I really don't get it at all.

"It's funny, we had the same question for each other: why you didn't say yes." He gestures to the waitress for the check. "But I think I always knew the answer anyway."

"And what was that?"

Because he didn't believe in marriage! I think. But then: *No. It was more than that. A lot more than that: fear and inertia and total lack of guts.* But I can't bring myself to acknowledge this all just yet, not with him, not even with myself. It would be so much easier if he just told me why I said no, and then we could let it be.

He shakes his head: "There you go again, hoping someone else will fill in your blanks." He looks at me now. "You can fill in your blanks, you know, Willa. You might not believe that, but it's true."

"Oh," I say. "All right."

Then he says: "Do you ever think about what would have happened if you hadn't been allergic to truffles?"

All the time, I think.

I glance away and say, "Yes."

Nothing else needs to be said, so we both stare out the window at the passersby scampering hurriedly underneath their umbrellas. I wonder about the lives they lead, if they're mostly happy, if they're mostly fulfilled, if they know how to get

353

themselves to Y.E.S. in ways that I do not and that Theo most certainly does. The waitress wordlessly slips the check next to him, and he digs into his back pocket for his wallet. Finally, he states:

"Look, Willa, I'm pretty sure I've made it clear how I feel, what I want. But . . . like . . . I don't want to be caught in the in-between. I'm not an in-between type of guy. That's just not who I am."

"Okay." I nod, like this is good news.

"You need to figure out who you are, too. What really *matters* to you. And when you do, and if it's me, you'll know how to find me."

"Facebook?" I try to play the joke again.

"Here," he replies back, touching his heart — the human heart that gives us life, and also so easily takes it away.

And then he stands. And then he's gone.

Text from: Shawn Golden
To: Willa Chandler-Golden

Almost done in Palo A. Back soon. Will b in touch.

I can't sleep again so Ollie kicks me out of the room. I make myself a cup of tea and then wander into the den, flipping on the

TV, pulling a blanket over my legs to ward off the chill of the air-conditioning.

At this time of night, the pickings are slim — bad infomercials for juicers and cellulite reducers and mouth guards that promise to put an end to your husband's snoring. There are old reruns of shows like *CHiPs!*, and *Law and Order*, and if you're lucky, maybe you'll catch a decent episode of *Seinfeld.* But I'm not that lucky.

I keep flipping until I land on the Game Show Network, and discover that *Dare You!* has made it into syndication. I cradle my tea in my palms and tug the blanket closer.

It's the episode that Shawn and I watched the very last time we watched: the one with the vipers and the woman who simply couldn't control her fear. Knowing what I know now — that she'll tremble until the snakes attack — I want to reach through the television and save her. Stick my hands straight in, throw my entire body through, and rescue her. But I can't. We all know that. There's nothing to be done for those who can't rescue themselves. So I sit, rapt, well aware of the doom that is careening toward her, and right at the point when Shawn let out a whoop and a "Holy shit!" I start crying.

Real, hard, purging, exhausting, swollen-eyed sort of tears.

By the time I'm done, the episode is over. The woman is off to the medic, her wounds being treated, an antidote being served.

I flip the television off and sit in the darkness, the silence cocooning me, offering peace.

Why is it so hard to save myself? It's not as if I couldn't see incoming disaster, it's not as if I didn't know better.

Some people, I think, *are probably just lost causes.* And then I have another thought too:

Maybe it's time to write my own map.

29

My key still works in our old apartment, which I almost wasn't expecting. The latch turns easily, and the door gives way, and then I'm inside. It looks different now, barren, with no furniture, no artwork, none of Shawn's computer crap or that looming TV in the living room or all of the egg splatter in the kitchen from when he made eggs all the time.

The landlord, Mr. Dubrovsky, has given us a day's notice. Eviction. Just like that, we're out. Raina texted me this morning to let me know.

When we moved in, I wasn't sure about renting the place. Shawn wanted to upgrade from our homey one-bedroom into something with a spare room for a home office and a space for Nicky, but I was content to stay just as we were. There were plenty of reasons to move, to be sure: the heaters in our old apartment had two modes — not working and a thousand degrees; the bathroom was so small that you had to turn sideways to sit on the toilet; the reverberation from the subway shook the living room pretty much continuously during rush hour. (Vanessa once remarked that it felt like "she was sitting on a couch atop the world's largest vibrator.") But still. We'd leased it shortly after we'd married, and I'd grown to love it, flaws and all.

Eventually, Shawn talked me into trading up, mostly by endlessly insisting that we trade up, so I said goodbye to our old home, and we packed up and left.

And here we were again: packed up and gone from this home, too.

Today, I step into the empty apartment, my flip-flops echoing and bouncing off the space. There are marks on the wall where we once hung paintings, faded planks on the floor around where rugs once lay. But mostly, it's been stripped bare of everything that made this plain old place our own, other than my memories, of course, which pile atop each other. I run my fingers over the windowsills and head to the bedroom, where I find two boxes stacked on top of each other, marked "Stuff."

Stuff.

That is so exactly Shawn and me. Nonspecific, middle-ground, no idea what's lurking below until you open it.

Accept.

Ignore.

Deny.

My phone buzzes just then.

Facebook: Nancy Thomasson (friends with Minnie Chandler) has added you as a friend!

I click onto my app but rather than accept Nancy's request, I find myself back on Shawn's page, lurking, trying to uncover the intricacies of my husband's life on Facebook.

I run my thumb over my screen, scrolling down, down, down. Then I quickly scroll up, up, up.

And I see that Shawn's no longer tagged in Erica Stoppard's photos.

I check his "Photos" folder to be sure.

Indeed, he has erased (or she has erased?) any sign of her on his page. My pulse accelerates, and my stomach churns with something that I think is excitement but I'm no longer really sure these days. Either way, I let out a triumphant "ha!" and tuck my phone into my back pocket and smile.

And then I remember the boxes.

Stuff.

Who knows what sort of *stuff* is shoved inside? It can't be important, I decide, if we'd simply named it *stuff.* So rather than open it, I bend at the knees, put my weight behind the box and heave it over to the front door. I'm crouched over, my arms curled underneath the bottom of the second box, when I hear the lock unlatch behind me.

"Hello?" I shout. "Mr. Dubrovsky? I'm here, taking the boxes. My sister texted me! I know that we have to be out today!"

There are footsteps, and then there are sneakers, and jeans, and his Wired2Go graphic tee.

"No, hey, it's me," he says. "Dubrovsky called me, too."

And then Shawn's in front of me. Standing in our old bedroom in our old life though everything's changed now.

It's me, he said. Like I should have been expecting him, like his text was warning enough that he'd be rewriting the rules all over again.

He extends his arms and relieves me of the weight of the box, lifting it easily into his own, carrying the burden for both of us.

"My flight was delayed," he offers. "I would have been here sooner to help out. I hope I'm not too late."

■ ■ ■ ■

We walk to Hop Lee, just like we used to, and we order too much Chinese food and egg rolls, just like we used to, though we don't kiss to get a freebie like we used to way back when. Instead, we sit in a booth by the window, and I try to think of how to start talking to my husband. Shawn fiddles with his phone and types something quickly, then deletes it, then types something else, then finally sets it aside and says:

"So."

"So." I laugh nervously, though it sounds more like a mule in labor. "I wasn't exactly expecting you. Your text wasn't exactly conclusive."

"No." He pauses, as if I have any idea what he's trying to convey. He opens up a pack of crispy noodles, the plastic crinkling to fill the dead air and dumps a mound in his hand. Finally: "I realized this is crazy. What we're doing."

"What are we doing?"

"I guess I don't know." He examines the noodles in his palm, not really eating them.

"I thought that is what you wanted."

"It was," he considers. "But I was being an idiot."

"Did Erica Stoppard dump you?" I say quickly, too quickly, until I realize what I've said and what it's betrayed.

"What?" He looks shocked, then kind of surprised, then delighted. "You kept tabs on me? On Facebook?"

"Well, I mean . . . you're still in my feed. I wasn't exactly *keeping tabs.*"

"It's fine." He waves his hand. "No biggie." I open my own set of soup noodles and think: *so he wasn't keeping tabs on me?* Then he notes: "No . . . Erica and I . . . we work together. It wasn't anything."

Which is just ambiguous enough for me to feel stupid for asking anything else and not ambiguous enough for me to have any clue what he's talking about. Erica Stoppard is exactly like our aforementioned box of *stuff.*

"So you came back," I say finally.

"Here I am," he says in response.

"Because you wanted to or because Dubrovsky called?"

He sighs. "Dubrovsky called, and I also wanted to. It was dumb what I suggested — this break."

Lucy brings over our egg rolls and some egg drop soup.

"You two. Why the sad faces? You two always so in love. I want to see in love!" She gestures like we should kiss, so we both smile awkwardly and then I blow Shawn an air kiss, and he does some extremely weird thing where he pretends to catch it, and Lucy gets this really odd look on her face and says:

"Moo shu coming in five minutes." And she walks off.

"So, what you're saying is that we're fine?" I ask when she leaves. "Because this seems very out-of-nowhere, and I'm a little caught off-guard."

"Look, Willa." He stares at his egg roll for a beat and then dunks it in the duck sauce. "I was being a dick. I don't know why I did what I did . . . but I did it. Sometimes, you do stupid things and you have no clue why, you know? Just that you wish that you hadn't done them."

I said no to Seattle.

"Anyway," Shawn continues. "I guess I needed to get something out of my system. Like, I wasn't sure if I was okay that 'this was it.' " He makes air quotes (why does everyone I know make air quotes?) with one of the egg rolls still in his hand. "Like, you know. How a guy in his forties dumps his wife and buys a Porsche? This was my mini-version of that . . . I don't know. I felt like I was suffocating."

"And you don't anymore?"

"I guess I just miss being married." He stuffs the egg roll in his mouth, making the chipmunk face that I used to love so very much.

I smile, though I can't force a laugh.

Wired2Go has put Shawn up in a suite at the Tribeca Grand. He invites me down to the hotel and up to his room for a drink, and since he's my husband, I say yes. His room is on the top floor and has views of the Hudson and the lights beyond. I stare out the picture window until I see his reflection behind me. He offers me a Reisling, which has always been my favorite.

"They're sending up some dessert," he says.

"So Wired2Go is treating you really well."

He pauses before answering. "They actually asked me to move there. To help launch their global initiative."

"Wow," I say. "That's amazing. You're rewriting your master plan."

He cocks his head like he doesn't get it, so I offer:

"It's the book we're writing. Like . . . changing your fate, shifting the pieces around so maybe your entire life will shift with it."

He smiles at me, breaking my heart just a

little, but opening it up a little, too. The familiarity of how his stubble hugs his jaw, of how his dimples pock his cheeks, of his genuine sense of absolution now. I can read it all over his face, and I wish that I didn't have the past two months reminding me that the pieces have indeed shifted for me too, and that perhaps that's not something you can shift back. In June, before his rules, before the implosion of everything, before the book and inertia and guts, and yes, also before Theo, this plain open plea of his face would have been enough.

"I thought you didn't believe in fate?" Shawn says now.

"I never knew what to believe in."

He nods. "I guess that's true. I guess maybe I didn't either."

He sits on the couch, and I follow his lead, sinking in, careful not to spill the wine.

"This is nice," he says. "I've missed it. I was thinking. . . . maybe I should do it." He catches himself. "I mean, what I'm trying to say is that maybe *we* should do it. It could be a fresh start."

"A fresh start for us?"

"Well, yeah," he says. "We don't have an apartment here, your family is a mess . . . why not leave? Why not make a break for it? Start over. It wouldn't be the worst idea in the world. We'd still be us. We'd still be together. I guess, like you just said, we could 'rewrite our master plan' together."

"We could," I say. And at that exact moment, though I'm not sure why, I think of Theo.

"I made a list," Shawn states, reaching for his laptop on the coffee table. "Of all the reasons you should come."

In the movies, you sometimes see the heroine press pause, freeze everyone around her, and break the third wall. This is what I do now in my mind. I press pause on Shawn and try to be still, try to talk to the camera and break my own third wall. I consider Vanessa's theory of opposites. That sometimes, you need to run in the other direction of what you think is meant to be. That running — jumping — flying — can change everything.

I slow my mental electricity, and I try to listen to what my inner heroine would tell me, but I can't resolve anything conclusive.

"It's okay," I say to Shawn, unpressing my pause button. "You don't have to read it to me. You don't need to give me a list."

He furrows his forehead. The old me, the old Shilla, would have very much preferred a list.

"I just wanted to be prepared. Do the

research. Convince you if you needed convincing."

Convince me to follow him. The opposite of Theo.

We fall asleep fully clothed in the king-sized bed with the 600-count Egyptian cotton sheets. He kisses my cheek goodnight, and I shift to the other side of the bed, already heavy, already dreaming.

When I wake the next morning, the sun is streaming through the slivers of the blackout shades, and it takes me a few seconds to orient myself, to remember that suddenly, Shawn is here, and maybe I'll still get everything I wanted.

I rise and splash water on my face and find him pacing in the living room of the suite. He holds up a finger and gestures to his earpiece, then mouths, "Conference call."

I nod, and he waves toward the cart of room service that he's ordered. He whispers, "Eat!"

I pull off the silver lid of the serving dish to discover eggs. Shawn has ordered me scrambled eggs while I was sleeping.

He covers the mouthpiece of his Bluetooth and kisses the top of my head.

"It's Sunday. We always have eggs on Sunday."

30

Text from: Vanessa Pines
To: Willa Chandler-Golden

Hey. Call me tmrw. Finishing up draft
of early chaps. Ready 4 final dare. R u?

Email from: Shawn Golden
To: Willa Chandler-Golden
Subject: List

W— I know you didn't need to see
this, but just in case. I've attached the
list of reasons. I don't want you to think
I'm not serious about this. Working all
night but talk tomorrow?
(1 attachment)

Voicemail from: Minnie Golden
Willa, sweetheart, I must have missed you
at Raina's earlier. Nancy and I are heading back to Palm Beach today. Please

check in on your father. I believe that his "nurse" may be "on vacation." I am concerned for his well-being but am done checking in on him. Raina is so busy, and Ollie can't leave the house — ooh, did I tell you that I met Jennifer Aniston this morning, and now she is following me on Tweeter? — oh, that was exciting. Anyway. I love you, sweetheart. I know this is a growing period for you. I understand more than you know. You have such a full heart. Just make sure that it's shining brightly.

My father is smoking a cigarette on his balcony when I arrive. The doorman has buzzed me up, but I use my key anyway, the same one I've had since childhood, to let myself in.

"If your mother sent you to ensure that I haven't keeled over just yet, you can go home," he says, without even turning around, the smoke billowing around him on an exhale.

"Smoking will kill you."

He flails his arm rather than state the obvious: *everyone dies. Get with the program, Willa.*

I coax the sliding glass door over a few inches and join him on his post.

"Mom did send me," I say, batting my hand in front of my face, diffusing the smoke, suddenly feeling queasy at the thought of more confrontation. I swallow hard on my gag reflex, and mostly, it passes for now. "Can you put that out?"

A muscle in his jaw flickers, but he stubs out the remaining nub and tosses it over the ledge, which I believe is technically littering, but you have to pick your battles.

"Your mother has a new life now. With her lesbian friend. What's her name, Nanette?"

"Nancy. I'm pretty sure you know that her name is Nancy." And then, because I'm my father's daughter and feel just a twinge of pity for him, I add: "I think it's just a phase."

"It's *her* life." He crams his hands into the pockets of his robe and shuffles back inside the apartment. "I just thought she could give me the common courtesy that forty years of marriage bring, that one expects when *one's heart fails*! That she would *show up*. And *help*."

He lifts a bottle of Scotch from the bar, but struggles to open it, so just plunks it back down.

"You told her to go."

"Well, taking a lover and ending a marriage are two different things!" he says.

Then: "I am not sure you should be here. With the papers I have served."

"We should talk about those. I'm not sure the papers have much legal merit. Also, Dad, we're family." I am trying to be kind now, though I don't know why. But he is so frail and so pathetic, and he is my *father.*

"Well, how about the merit that I deserve?" he says. "Can you imagine what people are saying? That Richard Chandler's own middle child is making a mockery of his life's work? You don't have a life's work yet, William! You can't know how it feels!" He wrestles with the Scotch bottle again and this time, comes out victorious. "Did I do something wrong with you, William? Did I not love you enough? Is this about that ridiculous skateboard that you always held against me?"

I didn't even realize he remembered the skateboard. I don't say anything in response, and instead, focus on my breath, focus on not puking.

"Well, William? What is it? Do you have no answer? What could possibly have gone so wrong in your terrible childhood with two parents who loved you, and two siblings who loved you, and the finest education and books and toys and everything else?"

My tears come before anything else.

Then quickly after that: *"Why wasn't I your life's work?"*

Finally, posing the question that needs to be asked.

He looks at me like he's never considered this before, like of all his theories and philosophies and musings, this one somehow slipped through. Or maybe he just thinks I'm insane, to hold such expectations of a parent to his child.

He sits now, slowly, as if sudden movements might literally stop his heart.

"You think that I failed you. I'm not so thick-headed that I can't see that you think I've failed you."

"You would say you didn't?"

"I would say that it doesn't matter," he says flatly. "But you already know that. What I would say. So what I don't understand is this: if you are so intent on humiliating me . . ."

"That is not my . . ."

He flashes his hand — *don't* — and I fall silent.

"I will rephrase, because you are. You *are* humiliating me. If this is your path, then stop seeking my approval. You're not going to get it. You will never have my blessing on this. In fact, just the opposite."

Now it's my own heart that's shattered. I

understand the weight of his words, what they really mean to say, even if he — just like his daughter — isn't so good at saying them. After so many years, I should be furious, not crushed, at how easily he caves, how quickly he abandons unconditional love. I consider my own parenting instincts and wonder how I can ever be sure that I won't do the same. But rage doesn't come at the realization of the extent of his selfishness. Only devastation. I stand there in my childhood home, and I'm gutted all the way through. Heartbroken. I read about it way back when, back at the *Bodies* exhibit. The human heart. There are so many ways to destroy it.

After what feels like an eternity, I stutter: "So if I do the book . . . you and I . . . am I understanding correctly that writing this book will mean . . ."

I cannot even manage the words. To have spent a lifetime in his shadow, only to be proven disposable when I'm finally trying to step into the sun.

He eases back in his armchair and gazes, unblinking, at the ceiling for so long that I start to worry that he's gone into cardiac arrest again. But then he says, "I don't know what will become of you and me, William. You're my daughter, and that's blood. But this is something different. This is fate. And that's not up to me."

I linger in my father's vestibule until I have no more tears to shed. Until I've thrown up all of my guts right there in the hallway. And then, I take one step away from him, then another, because it's not like I have any other choice. If the map you've been given suddenly proves unreliable, you have to write your own. Even if you're lost in the nothingness of dead space, even if you're sure there's not really a way out.

Shawn is lurking in the lobby when the elevator delivers me to the bottom floor.

"Hey," I croak. "What are you doing here?"

"Raina said you'd be here."

"Oh," I say. Then: "Is everything okay?" Then, "I really need some fresh air." I walk through the revolving door and out into the night without looking back to see if he's following.

He is there though, right by me.

"I . . . well . . . I guess the thing is . . ."

"What?" I snap, exhausted.

"I don't really know how to say this . . ."

"Oh my God!" I bark. "Are you here to break up with me after already breaking up with me? Will it never end?"

A woman strides by walking her poodle and meets my eyes, and then, as she passes, says over her shoulder: "Asshole. Don't let him give you shit! Men are pricks!"

Shawn watches her head down the street and round the corner, then turns back to me and says:

"Anyhoo . . ."

"Anyhoo?"

He drops his chin. "Sorry. Nicky taught me that. I'm just nervous."

"Look," I say. "I'm having a pretty terrible evening, so if you're here to tell me that you're, like, getting back together with Erica Stoppard because she's, like, way more spontaneous than I am or, like, does triathlons on Sundays, then please, just. . . . just do it. I can't take another incoming disaster."

He tilts his head and furrows his brow, like he didn't know I had that in me. Then he says: "Wow, I didn't know you had that in you."

And I exhale because I guess it's nice to know that I can still read my husband, even if he's about to massacre me right outside my father's Park Avenue apartment building.

His face softens. "I broke up with Erica, for the record. She was too . . . I don't know. Like, we always had to be doing something — golfing, happy hour, fricking bowling. Bowling happy hour. It was exhausting. Like, what's wrong with a Saturday night on the couch watching Starz?"

In my old life, a Saturday night on the couch watching Starz was my idea of heaven. Now, I wasn't so sure. I'd caught a ball at Safeco Field. I'd leapt off the Brooklyn Bridge and felt a little bit like I could fly. But still, I purse my lips and say: "I guess nothing. Nothing is wrong with Starz on Saturday. Though I'm pretty sure that's exactly what you went looking for, isn't it? All excitement and fireworks and jazz hands?"

"I don't really know what jazz hands are. But anyway. I actually came here to ask you out on a date."

"A date?"

"Yes . . . the type of thing that two people go on when they like each other and maybe have a few drinks and if they mutually agree upon their attraction, they might hook up at the end of the night."

"Oh," I say, forgetting all about my dad. I burp into the back of my hand. "Sorry. It's my stomach."

He shrugs like he's seen it before. Which, of course, he has.

I mull it over. "Okay. I guess we can go on a date."

"I was hoping for a little more enthusiasm," he says.

"Well, Shawn. That's life. Sometimes, you take what you can get."

He squints. "Is that, like, a quote from your dad's book?"

"No," I say, already on my way. "But it might be one from mine."

31

In yesterday's text, Vanessa said to call, but it's 94 degrees out now, and I might actually die of heat stroke if I don't seek shelter after a four-mile run.

"Are you kidding me? What's with that?" She gestures to the taupe ribbon pinned to my tank top when I let myself in. "You're doing that now too?"

I situate myself in front of her air conditioner, my shirt billowing in the artificial breeze.

"It's a thing. About responsibility. Or conviction. Whatever," I mutter. "Besides, Ollie's helping me get in shape . . . you're the one who told me to do it in the first place."

"I did. Because you're going to need it."

"If it's a marathon, I'm out."

"It's not a marathon." She opens a box of chocolate chip cookies and offers me one, which turns out to be more of a bribe. Or maybe a peace offering for what comes next. "The producers want you for *Dare You!*"

I emit sharp staccato laughter until I realize she's not kidding.

"No way."

"It's part of the contract."

"I can't do it."

"You won't do it."

And I think of a million reasons why this is true: death, public embarrassment, broken limbs, further humiliation (a reality show!) of my father.

"I think my dad will cut me out if I do it," I say quietly, shifting from the air conditioner to her couch.

"Out of his will?"

"Out of his life."

"Oh please." Vanessa rolls her eyes.

"Stop belittling me!"

"Stop belittling yourself!" she snaps.

"It's fucking hard." My tears mount without warning like they do nearly all the time now. "My life! It's fucking hard! Why don't you get that?"

"You're life's not so hard," she says simply before she exits to her bedroom. "But until *you* get that, it always will be."

I let myself out of Vanessa's and jog back to Raina's apartment, though it's foolish in the suffocating late-July air. But I need to indulge my urge to flee, to race as far away from whatever wreckage I have made, and on to whatever new wreckage awaits.

Maybe that's my master plan, I think, as I turn north up Fifth Avenue, my feet pounding, my thighs on fire, a cramp needling my belly. Maybe these tables of contents, these self-help books filled with ideas and advice and what-have-you can't do anything to throw me off course. (Which would mean my dad was right.) Maybe I'm just a tornado moving from one disaster site to the next. Wreckage. My life's plan is wreckage.

I'm drenched all over again by the time I throw myself into Raina's elevator. The fabric of my top sticks to my skin, my hair is matted with sweat, my cheeks are the color of a fire engine. Frankie, the doorman, just points at my taupe ribbon and says:

"You tell your brother that the government can't bring him down! Rise up!" He pumps his fist like Halle Berry did.

"Rise up," I say weakly and move both hands to my heart in prayer.

Theo is sitting in the kitchen reading something on his iPad. I hesitate in the flicker of a moment and debate running the other way, making a getaway before he even realizes that I'm there, but instead, I exhale and steel my nerve. And then I say:

"Do you plan to just randomly show up when I'm looking my worst? Though to be fair, I managed almost four miles. And it *is* 94 degrees out. So I'm sort of kicking ass."

He glances up and gives me a tight grin and says:

"Hey. I didn't think you'd be here. Sorry. I'll go." He stands abruptly.

"You don't have to go."

"I'm not here for you, in case you were worried. Raina's on her way, Ollie's in the shower. Gloria let me in."

I say: "It's really not a problem." (It seems to be some sort of problem!)

He says: "I heard Shawn's back in town. I mean, I figured because you didn't answer my texts."

I say: "Oh." Then: "He is." Then: "I don't know."

Theo's phone vibrates in his pocket, and he snaps it to his ear and wanders into the living room, discussing deal points and strategy and angles and persuasiveness. I eavesdrop for a minute and hope that he'll return, but then I hear Ollie's voice somewhere else in the apartment and a door closes, and then it's just me.

I tilt my torso ninety degrees and rest my

head on the cool granite counter and look at everything from a new perspective. Life looks different from down here. The lights force you into a squint, the angles are more jarring. This is what everything looks like as a kid, I suppose. But this is also a little bit how the world still looks to me. Some people never get over their childhood. I think of Nicky and say a quiet prayer that he's not one of them. Why can't I wish that very same thing for myself?

I right myself and listen for Theo's footsteps, in case he comes back to me, but there's just Gloria's voice filling the air, calling to the boys to get into the shower.

It hurts more than I expected. Theo's distance. His detachment. Though who can blame him? I haven't exactly proven my devotion. I've doled it out in dribbles — the flirty evening in Seattle, the phone call and sex a few weeks back. If I really considered it, I'm not so different from my dad — giving love, taking it away, expecting it to be there when I'm ready. And Shawn isn't any different from me: working through his own bullshit on my psychological dime.

I never even accepted Theo's friend request. I couldn't even do that.

But Theo's not like me. We both know that. He's always aimed high, and he's never stooped low. He draws his lines firmly, and mine — with him, with Shawn, with my dad — are always blurry.

I flatten my head back onto the cold counter, and it's like a balm for my soul.

Even Vanessa can't dare me to do whatever comes next.

Text from: Willa Chandler-Golden
To: Vanessa Pines

Ok. I'm in. My eyes r open & I'm aiming high. I think I have the guts. Let's fly. (I don't mean that literally if u talk to the producers.)

Later, Nicky and I lay in bed together watching *Iron Man 2* and eating popcorn. Ollie strolls in, falls at the foot of the bed and says,

"Oh, I love this movie. I used to train Robbie. He's very spiritual." Then to me: "You look horrible. No offense."

"I never sleep. And I just agreed to go back to Seattle on Thursday."

"Seattle?" Nicky angles his head up at me. "Can I come?"

"Probably not, buddy. Uncle Shawn will hang with you. Text him. He's gonna plan some fun stuff." I burp up some of my dinner and know that it's my nerves.

"Uncle Shawn works too much. And I like hanging with you. But whatever. I know I'm a drag to have along."

"You're not a drag to have along! You've actually grown on me."

"Ha ha," he says. "Well, my mom never takes me anywhere."

I pause the movie and sit up straighter.

"Well, okay, this is sort of confidential but . . . I can't take you because . . . I'm going on . . . drumroll please . . . *Dare You!*" I can't help it; I squeal. "I don't think you're eligible at twelve."

"Shut the front door!" Ollie jolts upright.

"Shut the fuck up!" Nicky knocks over the popcorn bowl.

"It's my last dare of the book. They've been holding the spot as a 'surprise.' " I make stupid air quotes though I immediately regret it. (They're an epidemic.) "Also, another contestant got malaria and had to back out."

"Jesus!" Ollie says.

"No, he didn't get malaria on the show," I reply, scooping up popcorn kernels from the sheets, dropping them back in the bowl. "Bad coincidence."

"You *have* to let me come," Nicky begs. "Remember that episode, with the ten-year-old who had to choose between poisonous and non-poisonous berries?"

"Vaguely," I say. Then it comes back to me. "Oh yeah, but he was a prodigy. He'd memorized every possible variation of berry in the world."

"Are you implying that I'm not a prodigy?"

"In your own special way," I laugh.

"Pleeeeeease?" Nicky bows in front of me, his hands folded in prayer.

"I'll ask," I concede. "And you'll need to speak with your mom. You've forgotten I'm not actually responsible for you."

"Yesssssssssss!!!!!"

"Well, I'm shocked that you have this in you," Ollie says to me. Then adds: "You know that Dad might kill you."

"What the hell," I grin back and say in my very best imitation of my father: "Everyone dies sometime."

He laughs so hard he falls off the bed.

Nicky falls asleep under my duvet, so I let him be. Ollie dims the light and settles into his nightly reading: *How the Gift of Daily Prayer Raised Me Up from the Ashes! (One Ex-NBA Star's Story from Heroin to Heroism!)*, and I just watch Nicky breathe. I want to trace the freckles that run from one cheek to the other, tuck his wayward hair behind his ears, wrap my arms around him and tell him that it will never be as bad as it was for him once. But I know that I can't promise this, that I can't ward off disaster any more than his father could, any more than his own mom could, so instead, I just perch on my elbow and watch his chest rise and fall.

It's amazing what the human spirit can endure. And maybe that's something on which my father and I can agree.

Shit happens, he would say. Your husband might decide one June afternoon that he wants a break from his life with you, or you might ask your girlfriend to move across the country with you, and she might say no. Or your dad might go to work one day and four planes may fall from the sky and two buildings may come tumbling down, and he might never come home.

Shit happens. Your wife leaves you for a woman. Your mentor sets you up as the fall guy when the Feds come calling. The question isn't, did this all happen for a reason? Because maybe that doesn't even matter. Maybe my dad is asking the wrong question, pinning his career on the wrong answers.

It occurs to me now, with Nicky's breath and spirit and ferocity as my guide, the questions, after all of this shit happens, are actually these:

So what? What's next? What now?

32

Dare You! Psychological Questionnaire
(To Be Filled Out Only By The Contestant)

1. Have You Ever Been Treated by a Licensed Therapist?
No. But I'm starting to think that wouldn't be the worst idea in the world. If you have a referral, I'm all ears.

2. What would you describe as your greatest strength?
That I am a work in progress.

3. What would you describe as your greatest weakness?
That I am a work in progress. (Also: I am not very good at being alone. Or making decisions on my own. Or making decisions at all. But back to the work in progress: I'm trying.)

4. What would you describe as your biggest fear?
Confrontation. Being alone. Confronting the fact that I may be alone because I've made the wrong decisions. (See above.) (Also, I really hate mountains. Something to do with my childhood.)

5. How do you cope with stress?
Usually by vomiting. Also, less disgusting: I suffer from acute emotional paralysis when stressed. Inertia is a great placator — no sudden movements, nothing too jarring, so you can pretend like nothing has happened, nothing will ever change. (But I'm also trying.)

6. How would you describe your life's philosophy?
Right now, I'd go with: So what? What now? What's next?

7. If you could be any animal, what would it be?
Oh God, really? Is this question actually the real psychological test? Like, if I answer a "bird," will you all roll your eyes? Or if I say a "butterfly," will you be like: that's such a cliché! I don't know. A bird would be nice, and a butterfly would, too. But sometimes, I think it might be nice to be a turtle. Slow,

steady, always safe in your shell. I know I should say a hawk, and maybe one day, I'll be ready to . . . but wouldn't it be nice to walk around with that armor, unable to be cracked?

8. Do you understand that certain "dares" are extremely dangerous, and if so, how do you feel about risking your life for a television show?
I understand. Everybody dies sometime.

9. Do you believe that your response to question number nine is normal?
What's normal? I was a girl named William born to a famous (slightly insane) father who didn't believe in free will. If you're looking for normal, you're probably not looking for me. Be what you already are. That's me.

33

DARING YOURSELF TO A BETTER LIFE!
By Vanessa Pines and Willa Chandler
PART FIVE: SET YOURSELF FREE

Summary: So here we are; we've nearly come to the end. You've pushed yourself into uncomfortable places, you've defied your own expectations, you've jumped when you wanted to keep your feet firmly on the ground. What is now left to do? *Reward yourself.* Stop thinking too much or agonizing too much or living in the shadow of those same new expectations. Be happy. You've tunneled through so much, why not see the light through the darkness, poke your head out and feel the sun, strong on your cheeks, and be grateful for all that you've accomplished, for your new life, for your new self. Then leap again and again and again. Go fly. Be free.

Shawn picks me up at Raina's on Monday night. I'm nervous, but maybe less nervous than I should be, given the weight of what this date means, given where it may propel us. Back to Shilla. Back to where we once were, who we once were. I dab my eyes with shadow and think about the Jumbotron and of that kiss at the stadium, and I consider how perhaps going back to who Shawn and I once were isn't exactly what I've aimed for, even if it's what I thought I wanted all along.

Shawn greets me with roses, which he used to buy me on important occasions, and I smile and say they are lovely. They are. Though they are *roses,* which aren't exactly the *Dare You!* equivalent of flowers. They aren't gardenias. But still, I press them up to my nose and inhale and appreciate their beauty, appreciate them for what they are: a gesture, a symbol of what we were.

Shawn's made reservations at this tiny Korean barbecue place in Koreatown that we went to all the time when we first got married. They greet us warmly and whisk us to a table in the corner, which has a circular grill in the middle, but also more roses and candles, which strike me as a fire hazard so close to the barbeque, but Shawn grins and says:

"I called ahead and asked them for the most romantic spot possible."

"That's really sweet."

"Remember how we got totally addicted and came back for the beef eight days in a row?"

I laugh because I do remember, and also, eight days of Korean beef now seems really gross, and further, because it feels like so very, very long ago.

Shawn clears his throat.

"I really screwed up. I'm sorry. I want to say that first, get it out of the way. I thought I needed something different. It was my early mid-life crisis, but it turns out, I'm not that guy. I don't need anything different. I like things exactly as they were."

And I consider this for a beat, and then I bob my head because what he's saying makes sense. It *adds up,* as Theo might say. The comfort in the familiar. The numbness this familiarity breeds. I can't blame him. Before all of this, I wasn't any different.

So I say: "Apology accepted."

The waiter brings over a plate of beef, along with some raw vegetables, dumplings, noodles, soups and crispy rice.

"I pre-ordered all your favorites."

"That's so nice. I'm touched."

He forks the raw beef slabs onto the grill.

"So I thought we should write some new rules."

"New rules," I echo.

He takes out his phone, clears his throat and says:

THE RULES FOR GETTING BACK TOGETHER

1. We never have to talk about the old rules.
2. We never have to talk about who we were with, what we did, whatever happened. What happened on "the break" stayed on "the break."
3. Delete all evidence of our break on Facebook.
4. Let's have a kid!
5. Let's do all of this in Palo Alto! But if you don't want to, we won't.
6. We both agree to resume life as if this never happened.

He sets his phone down and looks at me, eyes wide, face hopeful. Then he adds, "I mean, only if you agree to those rules, too. I don't get to unilaterally write the rules in our marriage."

I gaze at the open flame on the grill as it

shifts and moves and evolves right in front of me. *Resume life as if this never happened. That's not exactly what my book is about. That's not exactly resisting inertia, opening my eyes, finding my guts. Charting my own map.*

Here we are: Switzerland all over again. Switzerland stuck right in the middle of Koreatown. I consider everything that I've always considered because of my father and my history: fate and karma and destiny. That all roads lead to here, that our break was nothing more than a hiccup, that Theo was nothing more than a distraction.

And then I consider my guts.

And so I say: "I need some time."

And he reaches for my hand and says: "Willa, I really think we were meant to be. Like, this is what the universe had planned."

And I don't say anything at all.

Bookmarked Favorites
Facebook/login
FEED:

Say Om Innocent posted a link to the *New York Post* article: "Yoyo Yogi Found Hiding Out in Thailand" *(2 hrs ago)*

Shawn Golden changed his relationship

status from *It's Complicated* to *Married (3 hrs ago)*

Minnie Chandler posted a status update: *FW: FW: FW: If you can see this status update, it means that your computer has been hacked with the newest virus out of the Ukraine!!!! Please delete all of your cookies and reboot your computer four times to ensure that your hard drive is safe!!!! (5 hrs ago)*

   Reply from Raina Chandler-Farley: *Mom, click here on Snopes. This is a hoax.*

Ollie Chandler posted a status update: *"To live well is the best vindication of all." — My beloved mentor, Yogi Master Dari. However, learning that YMD's been caught in Phuket is pretty good vindication too!!!!!!! Phuket-you, YMD! (But really, Namaste. Grateful for all of your support over these two months!!!)*
721 likes

   Reply from Halle Berry: *You go, boy!!!! I knew it! xoxoxoxoxoxo*

Vanessa Pines tagged Willa Chandler-Golden in a post: Spoiler alert — my BFF and I are off to Seattle this week to finish

up our book! (And maybe join the ranks of the best reality TV contestants ever!! Not me, her. I don't do on-camera.) She's going under duress — everyone give her a metaphorical fist bump!
12 likes *(7 hrs ago)*

Comment from Hannah Burnett: *Hey! Willa, Willa-bee. It's me! Your old boss! I knew you could do it, you little ass-kicker!!!! Live free or die, bitches!! (Just don't get eaten by a bear.)*

New York Post:
Yoyo Yogi Found Hiding Out in Thailand
In a shocker to the federal agents who doggedly built a case implicating yogi-to-the-stars Oliver Chandler, the real enchilada in the case has been found holed up in a luxury resort at the ritzy beach locale of Phuket, Thailand. Government officials were given a tip-off when one of Chandler's celebrity clients, who has not yet been named, was also vacationing at the resort and recognized Yogi Master Dari (birth name: Stan Reynolds) and phoned the Feds.

What does this mean for Jennifer Aniston's favorite downward dog guy? He's not totally off the hook. Anonymous sources tell the *Post* that Chandler may still have participated in the pyramid scheme, which bilked investors out of over a million dollars, but to what extent is now unclear. Chandler's lawyer, Raina Chandler-Farley (also his sister), said to our reporters, "The FBI seized Mr. Reynolds' computer, and we are confident that all of the evidence retrieved will absolve Oliver of the charges. He just wants to get back to helping the world live calmer, more peaceful lives." Upon hearing the news, Lady Gaga tweeted to her over ten million followers: "Kick-ass day, monsters! My friend/pal/teacher is innocent!! F U, FBI!"

Chandler was not available for direct comment but also added to his Twitter feed: "Namaste," which was retweeted over four thousand times by his fans and supporters.

Of course, while this is all very good news for the Chandler clan, mum is the word on the broiling tensions between the patriarch of the family, Richard Chandler, and his other daughter, William. Last month, Chandler served his youngest child with a cease and desist that disrupted court proceedings. According to Facebook, William is set to be a contestant on *Dare You!,* about which she is writing a book.

One rumor we have confirmed to be true: Chandler's leggy "nursemaid" has dumped him and has been spotted at Nick and Toni's in East Hampton with none other than Donald Trump. (Donald, is there something you'd like to share with us?)

34

FAX FROM: LUSAKA ZAMBIA
   HILTON
FROM: AMANDA ABRAMS
TO: WILLA CHANDLER-GOLDEN

To Whom It May Concern at *Dare You!*

This fax serves as my permission for my son, Nicholas Abrams, to participate on the show *Dare You!*, with the understanding that he is a minor and may not be placed in any life-threatening circumstances. And if he is, I will pursue a 20-million-dollar lawsuit against the production company.

However, I have come to learn that life is short and meant to be lived, and when my son called me with an impassioned plea to have his chance to participate on his favorite show and to perhaps figure out a bit of who he is, I understood that it wasn't my place to tell him no. We can only protect our children from so much.

(And to reiterate: if you put him in harm's way, I will ruin you.)

Please find my attached notarized release form. It is not easy to find a notary public in the brush of Zambia, so I hope that you appreciate the lengths to which I have gone to ensure that a "minor," who will certainly draw huge ratings (I worked in TV ad sales before I devoted my life to charity, so don't think I'm naïve), can participate on your show.

All the best,
Amanda Abrams

"Shawn wants to get back together," I say to Raina and Jeremy on Tuesday night, once the kids are down and Oliver is out for freedom drinks with his publicist and various celebrity hangers-on. I shovel my spoon into a pint of vanilla ice cream.

"Of course he does." Raina slides a bowl across the counter and subtly urges me not to eat right from the container.

"So you're not surprised?"

Jeremy chuckles and opens the fridge to grab a beer.

"Raina predicted this would happen exactly."

"I'm good at reading the tea leaves. Lawyers learn to tell when people are saying one thing but meaning another."

I drop a spoonful of ice cream into my mouth and let it dissolve.

"Also, I slept with Theo."

"Holy shit," Jeremy says.

"Wow," Raina exclaims.

"I know," I sigh. "It's not great."

"It's great!" Raina says.

"Holy shit," Jeremy repeats. Raina shoots him a look, and he raises his eyebrows and swigs his beer.

"He hates me now," I say.

"He doesn't hate you now."

"I don't know what to do. I'm so tired. I can't turn my brain off. I don't know how to decide."

"Don't decide," Jeremy says. "Just see what happens."

Raina slaps his shoulder, and he yaps.

"What? Guys do that all the time."

"I've spent my whole life waiting to see what happens, what the universe has in store," I say, and Raina nods because she knows. "I don't want to wait but I don't know how to choose either."

She scoops out more ice cream and refills my bowl.

"Okay, so lose the husband," Jeremy shrugs.

Raina spits her own ice cream back into her bowl.

"What? I never liked him that much. If now's not the time to come clean, when is?" he says.

Raina laughs until tears form in her eyes. When she regains her breath, she says, "Oh my God, you are such an idiot."

And I say: "Me?"

And Jeremy smiles, "No, me."

"Don't get me wrong." Raina looks at me. "He's *my* idiot."

"And Shawn?" I ask.

"Oh, sweetie. All men are idiots." She reaches up and cups Jeremy's cheek. "You just have to decide what sort of idiocy you can live with."

"That's how we're still married." Jeremy kisses the top of her head.

Later, when he's gone off to watch ESPN, Raina turns to me and rolls her eyes and whispers: "No joke."

Bookmarked Favorites
Facebook/login
1 friend request: Theodore Brackton
Accept
Ignore
Deny
I hover my mouse for only a sliver of a

second, before I can give it too much weight, before I can think otherwise.

And then I click:

Accept.

35

DARING YOURSELF TO A BETTER LIFE!
By Vanessa Pines and Willa Chandler
  The Last Chapter:
  The Theory of Opposites
  Seattle looks different this time around. Like I can literally see everything more clearly. The water is bluer, the skies are clearer, and though I think about Theo at every turn — his houseboat, the hidden passageway on campus, the fifty-yard line — I also try not to think of him too much. Or at least not in the way that I did when Vanessa dragged me out here just two short months ago. Back then, all I could do was wonder "what if?" Now, I realize, armed with everything I have learned and all that I have become, I only have to answer "what now."
  Dare You! puts us all up at the same quaint hotel near the Pike Place Market. Vanessa has texted the cute guy from Safeco Field and slipped out of the hotel with a

quick wave and goodbye. So Nicky and I strolled the hilly cobblestone streets that night, the air pungent with fresh fish, the evening full of possibility.

"What do you think they're gonna do to us?" he said, as we relaxed on a bench and watched the boats coast by.

"I don't know," I said, "but how bad can it be?"

"You obviously haven't watched in a while," he replied.

Our call time was a death-inducing 5 a.m. — I'm not even sure if Vanessa slept. Tandy, our segment producer who wears cargo pants, leather boots and a camouflage shirt, and who has biceps the size of my thighs, picked us up and whisked us into a van with blacked-out windows and said, "It's not that we're trying to scare you, but you can't have any idea what's next. The game starts now."

And Nicky's eyes got wide, and he said: "Fuck yeah!"

I still had reservations about Nicky coming. I tried to dissuade him all week, but Amanda had already given her consent, and I could see her point, too. Nicky had been through more than any kid should have been through: why not let him savor something for a moment, why not let him try? Vanessa had assured me that our task

406

wouldn't be life-threatening, and there was also the hard-to-dismiss notion that for the first time since puberty had taken its grip, Nicky seemed honest-to-God happy. Not happy because he was, like, finding his Judaism or irritating his elders. Just . . . happy. Like twelve-year-olds should be. Most twelve-year-olds want a Wii or an Xbox. Nicky and his fate or destiny or just really shitty timing were too complicated for that.

Tandy put us in the black-ops van, and within thirty minutes, I vomited all over the front seat, which the cameraman did a really tight close-up of. I'm sure you've all seen it by now. Sorry about that.

After a few hours, the van parked, and we found ourselves at the foot of a mountain, the very same mountain — Mount Rainier — where Vanessa shocked my system with this whole thing to begin with, when she started everything. Two cameramen jumped out alongside us, and Tandy handed me a map, iodine pills, a first aid kit, a headlamp and GORP.

"You cannot be serious," I said to Vanessa. "This is my one thing."

"You have a few things," she said. "I had to pick."

"I jumped off a goddamn bridge for you."

"I thought you jumped off the bridge for

yourself."

I turned to Tandy. "I specifically told you that I hate mountain climbing. In my questionnaire — I stated that I hate mountains."

"What do you think this is, a day spa?" she asked. "Thirty-six hours. Solo. That's it. That's your dare."

"I can't be alone for thirty-six hours on a mountain!" I swiveled to Vanessa, who placed her hands on her hips and shrugged.

"You can't be alone for thirty-six hours because you told us that you hate being alone," Tandy said. (She wasn't dumb.) "The map has places where we've hidden food. If you hike well enough and accurately enough, you'll be fine. And well-fed. And it's not technically a solo since your cameraman will be with you. And after twenty-four hours, your path will intersect with Nicky's, so you get the second day together."

Nicky bobbed his head. "Sounds cool. Am I gonna get to meet Slack Jones?"

I didn't bob my head. I said: "No way."

Vanessa said: "I dare you."

And I said: "That's so lame."

And she said: "No, that's the point."

And I shouted: "This is total fricking BS! This isn't what I signed up for!"

But Nicky said: "Come on, Aunt Willa. This will be fun."

And because I felt that odd new sensation that seemed akin to a maternal tug — and because I didn't want to be the loser who disappointed him, I huffed out a melodramatic huff and said, "Fine." The opposite of what I thought it would be. This would be anything but fine!

"I hate your theory of opposites," I said to Vanessa, as she stepped into the van before it steered away.

"Don't hate the playa, hate the game," she said, slamming the door. As if that made any sense, as if that had anything to do with anything.

Nicky and I hugged, and he consulted his map and started off to the left, hiking up and up and up, the cameraman on his tail, getting smaller and smaller until he disappeared around a ridge, and then it was just me. (And Rick, my cameraman, the very same one who had emailed me the bungee photo. But he wasn't allowed to talk to me unless I was faced with a medical emergency, so it was mostly just me.)

Thirty-six hours solo. On a mountain. It figured.

Since I didn't have any choice in the matter, I put one foot in front of the other, and I started walking. My map indicated that my first food stop was about three miles away, which didn't seem so bad. It was hotter than expected, but I wiped the beads off my brow and kept going. I had all sorts of positive self-talk and theories to steady me, to steel me, so I focused on the ground beneath my feet, and I thought about my guts and not too much else. Not Theo, not my dad, not Shawn.

And looking back, it was easy to see how the producers set their trap — how they lull their constants into a false sense of security — the vipers or bears or lethal berries never look too dangerous until you get closer, and that's when the trouble starts. When everything is near enough to kill you. That first mile up the mountain was cake.

Then I came upon the rock wall descent. I turned to Rick and said:

"Are you kidding me?" But he wasn't allowed to answer. I saw his lens focus in on a close-up of my huge and open pores that were emitting an angry army of sweat, so I turned around quickly and said, "Fuck it," and read the instructions to the harness, and then secured said harness to a boulder and jumped over the side. I'd done it before, after all. I could see now how Vanessa had prepared me, training me like a soldier, raising me like a child who would finally be ready to go out there and face the world.

I may have jumped off the Brooklyn Bridge, but I'd never scaled the side of a mountain. I bounced and bounced and bounced against the scorching hot rock, limbs splayed every which way, profanities shouted every other way. My elbow started bleeding, and a gruesome cut opened up on my left cheek. About halfway there, I looked down and realized exactly what I was doing: dangling 100 feet in the air off a cliff with no literal net, with the sun crushing down on my shoulders and GORP as my only sustenance, and that is when I started to panic. The all-too-familiar rebellion of bile arose in my throat, but I inhaled through my nose and out again through the same pathway, and I found my reserves.

So what? What now? What's next?

I steeled my shaking hands, and I eased down until my feet hit the dirt, and I rejoiced, "Hallelujah."

Rick was already waiting for me at the bottom, which I thought was a little fishy, but when I questioned him, he mimed a little zipper in front of his mouth, which I found super-irritating, but I continued on my way. Two miles or so later, I reached my first food drop, and I thought:

"I can do this. This is a joke! This isn't a dare!"

And I sat and enjoyed my Gatorade and my two granola bars and banana, and I let the sunshine soak into my cheeks, and for a moment, I felt content. I thought about Nicky and knew that he'd be killing it, that he probably had already reached his camp-site, and I deemed myself the most genius substitute mom in the world. How cool was I? Taking my nephew on to *Dare You!* I was the coolest. I was going to be the coolest mom in the history of the world.

When the sun starts setting on the moun-tains, the temperature drops perilously quickly. You don't think about things like this when you're a city girl, and your only experience with mountain climbing is one other outing on Mt. Rainier, a mistaken abandonment in the Alps at the age of eight, and cyber-stalking Cilla Zuckerberg's Chicks Who Dig Mountain Climbing page on Facebook.

I should start by saying that in hindsight, I had gotten overconfident. I lingered on my snack site too long. The sun felt good, and I felt good, and readers, as you well know by now, it's not often that I, Willa Chandler, just feel good, so I may have savored my Gatorade (*Dare You!* is spon-sored by Gatorade) a bit too long, not minding the time (we weren't allowed watches anyway), not caring too much.

I was here! I was on *Dare You!* I had guts!

I drank that Gatorade like it was champagne, and I thought about how I would tell my father what I had done. I climbed a mountain; the Alps hadn't scarred me for life! And then I tried not to think about him again, but that didn't prove easy either. The truth is that we are all, always, works in progress, so yes, I sat on the rock and I thought: *screw you, Dad! This is so much better than the fucking Alps!* But then I also thought: *I hope that he forgives me for doing this.* And I considered that for a long time, wondering why I needed him to absolve me or why his absolution still mattered.

And then I contemplated fate and timing and how if Vanessa hadn't dared me in the first place — way back in June — I'd be home with Shawn right now, not here on a mountain, with the taste of freedom on my tongue, with that freedom throbbing in my veins. And then I thought about the broken condom and how fate probably does mean something. Just likely not everything that my dad always said it did.

By the time I pushed myself up from my resting place, the sun had dipped below the crests of the surrounding mountains. I

413

consulted my map and saw a fork in the road. When I turned to ask Rick for guidance, he was packing up his gear, ready to head back to where we started.

"You're leaving me?"

"The mountain is rigged with cameras. You're covered."

"So now you talk to me?"

"Just following protocol. I'm here until sunset. Then I see you in the morning."

"You suck, Rick."

"It's just my job. I'd rather be filming for Spielberg if it makes you feel better."

And just like that he was gone, and I was alone.

A solo. With a fork in the road. Two options. One choice. Even I got the metaphor.

I stared at the map until the sun had nearly disappeared. How could I choose? I had no idea what lay ahead to my left, what lay ahead to my right. This was the moment where my dad's philosophies should have offered comfort: did it really matter, since both paths allegedly returned me to Nicky, to sustenance, to shelter and a warm shower? Perhaps not. But in that moment, it did matter. Left or right, right or wrong, Shawn or Theo, my old life or a new one? If we always take the path of least resistance, if we embrace inertia, if we never leap, if we never accept accountability for our choices, how can we find any triumph in our victories or any remorse in our losses?

And still, I couldn't choose. And I stared at the map and stared at the map, not really seeing anything, until I looked up suddenly, and it was black. Blackness on both sides of the fork. And a mountain enveloped in blackness is so very, very different from a mountain warmed by daylight. You have no depth perception, no sense of what is next, no view of what you're about to step into or on top of. My pulse accelerated in my neck, and I tried to exhale in the way that Ollie would want me to. I remembered my headlamp, which I switched to "on," and I reached for my phone on instinct, because I thought the screen could light my way. Of course, they'd taken my phone from me, like they'd taken everything else.

The headlamp was flimsy, at best, and offered only a foot or so of visibility. Within three steps, I overlooked a gopher hole and my ankle turned, the snap so loud it echoed down the canyon.

"Fuck!" (This is the first of many beeped-out portions you heard during the aired telecast. Sorry.)

I sank to the ground to assess the damage, the tendons in my foot already throbbing. I unspooled the ace bandage from my first aid kit and wrapped myself up the best I could, in the near dark, on a mountain, without a nurse. I hobbled upright but realized I still hadn't chosen: which way — right or left. Or down. I supposed that I could go down. It wouldn't be the first time I had quit on a mountain.

I quit!!! I yelled just a few short months back.

But before I could decide:

Something stirred in the bushes, and I definitely heard a yap. A whine. A yelp. Then branches cracking and leaves stirring and crunch, crunch, crunch. And I forgot about my ankle for the moment, and I only thought mountain lion or bobcat or bear or something that is definitely not human, and I started running. With my busted wheel but running all the same.

Left or right, left or right, left or right?

I didn't even think, I just ran. I gave into what my father's theories have taught me all along: that it didn't really matter, so just go. Just run. Just point yourself in a direction and leave everything else behind. Wherever you end up is meant to be.

The ruckus trailed me all the way up the path — the rustling of the bushes, the endless crunch, crunch, crunch, the smashing of twigs and leaves and dry brush. I wasn't in nearly as good shape as I should have been — better than before, sure, but not even close to where Ollie would have wanted me — and I was slowing. I could feel myself lagging, feel the creature behind me gaining. I thought of how I was going to die on this goddamn mountain, bloodied and flesh-eaten and totally unrecognizable because a mountain lion had chewed off my face.

I screamed, "I am going to die on this goddamn mountain! And my sister, Raina Chandler-Farley, is going to sue your asses off! I hope you hear that, Vanessa Pines! That I am giving Raina the right to ruin you!!"

And then I remembered all the many things I have ruined in my own life, and then my left foot sank into another goddamn gopher hole, and I tripped and landed on my face and split my right eye open.

And that's when, naturally, I threw up.

Then, for my next act, I started to cry. I wailed, and I moaned, and I shook my fists at the sky, and I screamed: "This was the worst idea in the whole fucking world! Do you hear that world? THE. WORST. IDEA. IN. THE. HISTORY. OF. YOUR. WHOLE. FUCKING. EXISTENCE!"

And when I finally stopped screaming, I noticed that the crunch, crunch, crunching had stopped too. But I felt something still watching me, something eyeing me, wondering if it couldn't just take me out, wondering if I might not make a nice dinner. I was pretty sure that it wasn't just the cameras that the crew had hidden along the way, so I wobbled to my feet, and I tiptoed (metaphorically) to the bushes, and I crouched down and used my headlamp as my eyes. (And I'm not going to lie: I felt like I was in the middle of the *Blair Witch Project,* and when you saw it back on TV, it looked, actually, like I was, right?) Slowly, then slower still, I crawled along the path, searching for whatever it was that hunted me.

And then I froze. Paralysis.

The headlamp beamed out and what beamed back at me were two eyes that were as dark as the landscape in front of me (but hungrier).

My shriek echoed down the canyons of the mountain, and then I leapt to my feet and kept running. The pain in my ankles was gone now, the blood from my eye irrelevant. What mattered was that everybody dies sometime, and right now, when I still had the chance to unruin my not-so-horrible life, I didn't feel quite like I was ready for my time to be up.

I ran until my left ankle snapped. It literally gave way completely. I tumbled onto the ground and felt my head hit the crusty mud and the cold air sweep over me, and then the pain mounted all down the left side of my body, and then, whether or not I intended — because, to give credit to my dad, some things we cannot control, even when we'd like to: I blacked out.

The sun woke me when it rose. The first light of morning on my face was too bright. The old vomit in my mouth was sour, and the blood had dried underneath and around my eye, which was also mostly swollen shut. I pressed myself up and dropped my head between my knees. I pried open my GORP and managed to swallow three yogurt-covered raisins.

So what? What's next? What now?

"Can someone please come get me?" I yelled. "Like, I know that you're out there. Don't I qualify for an airlift yet?"

But no one came. I was left, as I always feared I would be, to my own devices. Solo.

I crept to my knees, then to my feet, though my ankles shouted in agony. I consulted the map, and saw now what I hadn't seen last night, blinded by the dark-ness, blinded by my faulty notion that my choice didn't matter, that all roads led to Nicky. No. In fact, when I examined the map closely (which I was only able to with my good eye), I saw that the path — the one I'd chosen — was a dead end. There was a tiny line that ran perpendicular to my course. A crevasse. Or a rock wall. Either way. All of my progress from last night was for naught. This wasn't the road that could bring me home.

"Fuck you!" I screamed. "Seriously, Vanessa, I hate you!" I cried. "This wasn't part of the deal!" I raged. And finally, because it was simply my instinct, I threw my weight behind the most furious parts of my voice and shrieked: "I QUIT!!!!!"

But despite all of that, despite everything, my words just bounced around the land-scape below. The birds tweeted back, the trees sighed out, and the mountain lions (because I knew they were out there) kept sleeping.

The only way that I was getting home, readers, was with my guts, by rising and rewriting my master universe plan. By get-ting the hell up and moving forward. There literally wasn't any other way. My tears began again now, quick, hot, heavy. Washing some of the crusted blood away, stinging the open wounds that the blood left behind.

I matted my face with my dirty shirt, and I realized, just like Vanessa had urged me to since we were eighteen, and just like Ollie and I had discussed when I made shadow bunnies on the wall, and just like Theo had wordlessly pushed me into conviction — that "meant to be" could add up to a lot of things. There's always more than one path, and to think otherwise is what resigns you to fate.

When Vanessa and I embarked on this book, we did so to disprove my father, to prove that not everything happened for a reason, that control and choice and human spirit mattered. What ended up happening along our journey is that I no longer felt the need to disprove him of anything. My dad is a Ph.D., and he is lauded the world over. I will never be as revered as he is; I will never have the physics or the mathematical equations to demonstrate all the ways that he is wrong. But what I know is this: I know what happened up there on that mountain. I know what happened over the past few months of my life. And these are the lessons we hope you take away from this book, readers. Not that my dad must be wrong, but that there are so many other ways to be right. That night on the mountain finally gave me clarity, finally set me free: not to be William, but simply, to be me.

No one really can have any idea if it's luck or happenstance or timing or fate or the universe or just smart choices that grant you a good life, a happy one. All we can do is decide to own our choices no matter what, to honor them and ourselves as best we can. That whatever is within our control (and there is plenty that is not) is ours. Mine. Responsibility. Conviction. These are the lessons I've learned, that I took down with me from that mountain.

This sounds simple, and this might not even be a great revelation. And yet, for many of us, it comes down to this: that the best way not to be lost is to be your own map.

I inched my way forward that morning. Like that goddamn turtle I said I thought it might be nice to be for a day. Or a lifetime. I inched down the path, back to the fork, and then, inch by inch, down the right path. It took me eleven hours to make it to Nicky. On TV, when you see it, they show me in fast-forward, my movements accelerated, because it's too painful to show my suffering in real time.

But was it suffering, actually? Only in the moment. When I eased around the last turn on the map, and I saw Nicky sunning his cheeks in the late rays of the afternoon light, sleeping under the *Dare You!* banner, waiting for me with the faith that he knew that I would make it, it didn't feel like suffering at all.

It felt like guts.

It felt like choices matter.

It felt like even if I'd scrambled up the wrong path, that it wasn't like I couldn't scramble back down and find my way again.

"LIVE FREE OR DIE, NICKY!" I shouted.

And he startled awake, and then grinned the most delicious grin, and I weaved my way over like the wounded warrior that I sort of was, and he pulled me into a bear hug on the ground, and then we both laughed until we cried.

"I talked to my dad last night. On my solo," he said, when we both found time to breathe. "He told me it was okay to let go."

"Funny," I said back. "I kind of heard the same message."

Live free or die. I was finally ready. I finally got it.

I finally got what's next.

36

I sleep for what feels like a thousand hours after we're delivered back to the hotel. Medical has wrapped my ankle and stitched my eye, and other than some purple welts that won't subside for weeks — medals of honor, I suppose — I'm mostly okay. When I finally come to, I tug the shades back and wince from the sunshine and then allow my eyes to adjust, and then absorb the beauty of day, of the Seattle harbor, of its jewel tones, of all life's possibility. It's all there, right in front of me.

My stomach lurches, and I locate my toilet kit, scrambling for something to soothe that which still ails me.

I sift through the pouch, through the nail clippers, and lip balm and my deodorant, past a loose Xanax that I didn't realize I still had, a few Q-tips that need to be tossed. I find the test on the very bottom, which is exactly where I thought it belonged. I'd forgotten, until right now, this very moment, that I'd bought a second one that morning at Duane Reade, in case my nerves got the best of me, and I needed a second test for back-up.

What had they called EPT way back when, a lifetime ago on BabyCenter.com? *Essentially a Piece of Trash.* Of course the first test proved unreliable. But then I wonder if maybe that wasn't the universe talking too, though I'm smarter than that now: to put my trust in the universe. But if I'd seen the plus sign, the double-line, a few weeks back, I'd never have gone on *Dare You!* I'd never have really mustered the guts. I'd never have forged the road not taken.

I steady my breath, and I try to ignore my inner voice that is still whispering about doubts and maternal instincts and how I've done everything wrong. *No.* I gulp the air in, and I push it out, and take the hard turn left when I have always turned right. As simply as that, everything can be different.

And just as I have for eight other months, I sit on the toilet with my underwear around my ankles, and I wait.

It doesn't even take the two minutes. The second pink line is there as quickly as the first.

My father would call this fate, but I know

better now.

I am wise enough now to merely call this life.

I ask the Town Car to stop at my father's apartment on the way home from the airport. Nicky waits in the lobby while I take a swift trip upstairs. My dad answers the door in his bathrobe, with wild hair and skin that's too pale and pasty. He looks sad and spent and surprised that his doorbell has rung so unexpectedly.

"Oh. William," he says when he swings the door open. "I don't have time. I'm getting ready for Piers Morgan."

And I say: "This won't take long. I'm on my way home."

"Okay then. What is it?"

"I went on the show. I'm doing the book. You can choose to never speak to me again, but I hope that you will."

And he looks very, very angry, like an old man version of a Chucky doll or something, for just a brief moment, and then he waves a hand and relaxes his face and says: *Que sera, sera.*"

"*Que sera, sera?*"

"Whatever will be will be."

And I say: "You really believe that crap, don't you?"

And he says: "Everybody has to believe in something."

And I say, before walking away: "Everybody does."

We hold a viewing party at Raina's for my episode of *Dare You!* in early September. It's also a goodbye party for Ollie because he's headed to the clink for three months, which was part of his plea settlement. Though it isn't really the *clink,* or at least that's what Raina has assured us.

"It's basically like where Martha Stewart served her time, but for guys. Like, where the insider traders go. Think of it as a spa for morally ambiguous men," she told us when the judge issued his ruling. "I mean, look. There has to be accountability for what you did, Ollie. Even if you didn't mean to."

Ollie hovered his hands over his heart.

"I get it," he said. "And they agreed I can lead their yoga program. So it might be sort of cool. Future clients." Raina rolled her eyes, but Ollie dropped his palms to his waist and said, "I'm kidding. No one wants to end up like dad, so it's time to start being responsible." And then he squeezed my hand because he knew I'd get it, too.

My mom and Nancy fly up for the premiere, and Amanda and Nicky make their way in from Brooklyn. Nicky's invited three buddies along, and they keep slapping each other high fives and saying things like, "Holy shit, dude, I can't believe that you got to do this! You rock, bro!" And Amanda keeps checking her phone and saying, "Sorry. There's a crisis in Nigeria. I'm not trying to be rude." But Nicky doesn't seem to mind, probably because he's used to it, but also because, I like to think, he has me. (And he has Shawn, of course, too.)

Nancy sips Pellegrino, and my mom pours herself a Scotch.

"Maybe we should have invited your father."

"Come on, Mom," Raina says. "He put himself in this position. He wasn't exactly supportive of Willa."

So my mom sighs. "I know. I just feel bad for him these days. He doesn't seem to have anyone on his side."

"I think he might have a new girlfriend," Raina replies. "I saw something on Facebook."

I overhear them. "Dad's on Facebook now? Jesus."

And Ollie says: "I'm on his side. I've always been on his side. Though I don't really believe that we should take sides because then it gets into yin and yang, and there is no good middle ground."

And Raina says: "Oh, shut *up*, Ollie." And then she bugs her eyes at him but she's redone her Botox, so she can't look nearly as annoyed as she likely is, so she just huffs and retreats to Jeremy, who is manning the bar, and then to find Gloria to see if she's given all four kids their showers.

Vanessa whirls in and hugs me close. "Holy a-mahz-ing, I can't believe you did it. I cannot believe you had the balls to do *Dare You!*"

"We did it together."

"True." She kisses me on the cheek. "But you still did this on your own."

Just before 8 p.m., my own phone buzzes:

Text from: Shawn Golden
To: Willa Chandler-Golden

Good luck 2night. Bet ull be gr8t.

And I smile because he's still doing that annoying thing where he types "8" instead of using the extra few seconds to actually type the real letters, and I smile wider because I bet he's also still using too much mousse and is back to calling people "dude," even though he just wants to be the

429

old Shawn. But without me, he's had to figure out what that new old Shawn is.

Though I can't say any of this for certain because I haven't checked his Facebook profile since he headed back to Palo Alto two weeks ago — he moved there for good after I broke the news.

When I returned home from *Dare You!*, I asked Shawn out to dinner at Hop Lee (actually, I scheduled it on our *Together To-Do!* app, which I promptly deleted afterward), and I told him I was pregnant. And he got really excited until he did the math, and then he got a lot less excited. And I took a bite of an egg roll and explained that it wasn't the pregnancy that made me decide, decide that we shouldn't be Shilla. But that we should be Shawn. And Willa. Each on our own, each as our own. And that was why I was making this choice. Owning this choice. Learning to have guts and aim higher. Because with him, I would be eating eggs on Sunday forever. I'd never start running, even though what I always did was run from everything. He looked confused at that, and I clarified: "Like, running 5Ks. Or up mountains."

And he said: "Well, if you wanted to start running or didn't like eggs, you should have just told me. You didn't have to get pregnant."

"I'm pretty sure you know that's not the point."

"This never would have happened if I hadn't been such an idiot."

"Maybe not. But it's probably better that it did."

And I thought about that for a long time after he left. How life rose up and surprised the both of us. But it was more than that, too — it wasn't just life that rose up; that's how my dad would say it — but how we both rose up and changed our lives by exploring the forks in the road. Left or right? It can change everything. Nothing is meant to be, unless you're talking fairy tales, and I was never much of a princess.

I texted Theo from Seattle and asked him if we could meet when I was back. There were things to say. There were things that I owed him. He was in D.C. consulting on a top-secret project for the State Department, but he took the Acela back into town and met me at the hospital the morning after Shilla was no more. I told him I was doing post-show medical tests, and I'd like him along in case I decided to sue.

He held open the door at Mt. Sinai as I hobbled in, and he ran his palm over the stitches near my eye.

"Is it as bad as it looks?"

And I said: "No, nothing's really as it seems. I've actually never been better."

And he looked at me for a long time, waiting for me to explain more, and I looked at him back, knowing that if he knew me well, he would know that I was here, ready, brave, chock full of guts, and no other words could do it justice.

Finally, he said: "Okay."

And I said: "Now come on, we have an appointment."

And he said: "*You* have an appointment. I'm just here for advice. And counsel, in case you decide to sue."

"No. We have an appointment. There are three of us involved now."

"There . . . are . . . three of us? What? I don't . . . The three of us have an appointment?"

"Sometimes, the first test fails." I smiled.

"What?"

"But the second time around, the second chance, that's the one you never doubt."

"What?"

I placed his hand on my belly and rested my own palm over his heart.

And I said: "You really don't know everything in the world, now do you?"

And he said: "Is this what I think? Oh my God, is this actually what I think?"

And I said: "Y.E.S."

DARING YOURSELF TO A BETTER LIFE!
By Vanessa Pines and Willa Chandler

Acknowledgments

There are so many people to thank for this book, but we have to start with our readers. It's hard to believe that *DYTABL* has now gone back to press twenty times! While we made headlines for bumping Dr. Richard Chandler's (my dad's) own book out of the number one spot on the *New York Times* bestseller list, what has truly been the most gratifying is hearing from you, our fans, who have also become our friends, our family. We have received over 400,000 posts on our Facebook page (Facebook.com/daring yourself), and your tweets and quotes and daily thoughts bring us joy every single day. Yep, that's really us replying, really us "liking" your own dares that you are kind enough to share.

Also, thanks to you and your outpouring of support, we have been lucky enough to partner with *Dare You!* and establish a fund that sends 9/11 children (and other children who have lost parents) on solo wilderness hikes, and because of this, we aren't just changing our own lives, but others' lives, too.

But this is a section for thank-yous, so in no particular order, here goes:

Thank you to Richard Chandler, who recently friended me on Facebook. I accepted his request. Que sera sera, you know?

Thank you to Kylie Chandler-Brackton, who was born after twenty hours of excruciating labor (in which I abandoned any belief in God), and then started sleeping through the night at eight weeks (in which I started believing again) and is sometimes so close to heaven, that she almost convinces both Vanessa and me of serendipity.

Thank you to Raina Chandler-Farley, who is guts personified, and also, to her husband, Jeremy, who has proven to be a surprisingly excellent occasional emergency babysitter. (Who knew?)

Thank you to Ollie, who challenged me to discover conviction but who also taught me about inner peace. It turns out I was doing the whole breathing thing wrong.

Thank you to Theodore Brackton, for finding me on Facebook and changing everything.

Thank you to my mother, who told me that changing everything isn't the end of the world.

Thank you to Nicky, who waited for me on a deserted mountain because he knew that I wouldn't quit.

Guts.

Live free or die.

What's next?

We're ready.

ACKNOWLEDGMENTS

The general rule is that the more books you write, the shorter your acknowledgments should be. (Cool factor and all of that.) But I have a lot of people to be thankful for, people who encouraged me to write this book and to hold steady in my path and to, at the risk of repeating myself, follow my own map. I'm so fortunate to have been touched by their kindness and advice and counsel and just general goodness. So I'm ignoring convention.

Here goes:

Elisabeth Weed: how lucky am I to have you as my partner in crime? Eight years later, I still love you as much as when I said I do.

Laura Dave: you remain ever so wise and wonderful.

Allie Larkin and Claire Cook: what an ambitious, supportive trio we have made. Thanks, ladies.

Ann-Marie Nieves, Jon Cassir, Jessica Jones, Jenny Meyer, Jennifer Garner, Juliana Janes Joudi, Liz Pearsons: it's an embarrassment of riches to work with you all.

Robin Beerbower, Liz Egan, Kimberly Hitchens, Jess Riley, Michelle Visser, you guys as well. You went out of your way for me for no reason other than your immense generosity. Leslie Wells, thank you for such insightful editorial advice. Jennifer O'Connor, thank you for the brilliant cover for the original publisher's edition of this book.

Unconditional and devoted thanks to my mom, who proofread this manuscript with a red pen and unrelenting eye more times than even a mother (well, really anyone) should have had to. And to my dad, who read an early draft and called me to announce that I'd "written *The Catcher in the Rye* of my generation." What more could a daughter ask for?

My kids and husband, who are always my Point North, and also my sun and moon and stars.

And you guys: the readers. There was a time not too long ago when I, much like Willa, sat on my figurative mountain and thought I should quit. You all sustained me; you all reminded me why I love what I do; you all encouraged me — whether you realized it or not — to take a left when it might have been wiser to take a right. I'm grateful; I'm indebted; I'm so very fortunate. Who knows if we make our own luck or if everything is truly meant-to-be. But no matter what, I'm damn appreciative of where the universe has landed me. Thanks to all, for all, for everything.

The employees of Thorndike Press hope you have enjoyed this Large Print book. All our Thorndike, Wheeler, and Kennebec Large Print titles are designed for easy reading, and all our books are made to last. Other Thorndike Press Large Print books are available at your library, through selected bookstores, or directly from us.

For information about titles, please call:
(800) 223-1244

or visit our Web site at:
http://gale.cengage.com/thorndike

To share your comments, please write:
Publisher
Thorndike Press
10 Water St., Suite 310
Waterville, ME 04901